Deep Vellum | Dalkey Archive Press
3000 Commerce Street Dallas, Texas 75226
www.dalkeyarchive.com

First Dalkey Archive Press Edition, 1990. Fourth printing, 2024.
First Dalkey Archive Essentials Edition, 2024 All rights reserved.

Support for this publication has been provided in part by grants from the
National Endowment for the Arts, the Texas Commission on the Arts, the City
of Dallas Office of Arts and Culture, the Communities Foundation of Texas, and
the Addy Foundation.

Paperback ISBN: 9781628974980
Ebook ISBN: 9781628975239
Library of Congress Cataloging-in-Publication Data:
Names: Barnes, Djuna. 1892-1982, author.

Classification:
LCC PS3503.A614R9 1990
DDC 813/.52 90002769
LC record available at https://lccn.loc.gov/90002769
Cover design by Justin Childress
Interior design by Douglas Suttle
Printed in Canada

Praise for Djuna Barnes

"So it is that *Nightwood* takes its readers into the circle of fury and smashes them to the canvas. It's brutal, ugly and cruel—but no more so than the world it describes. It's also tremendous."

—*The Guardian*

"Few authors have achieved so much celebrity with one novel as the elegant, exotic Djuna Barnes, without whom no account of Greenwich Village in the teens, or the Left Bank in the 1920's, is complete."

—*New York Times*

". . . [T]he wonder of *Nightwood* is not only stylistic. It lies in the range and depth of feeling the words convey. There is irony here and humor, too, but in the end, the novel is a hymn to the dispossessed, the misbegotten and those who love too much."

—Siri Hustvedt

"Her body of work, including *The Book of Repulsive Women*, *Ryder*, and *The Ladies Almanack*, spans aestheticism, Dada, and high modernism. Her books are deep, often challenging, and crucial."

—*The Paris Review*

"Barnes's sentences, like Burton's, like Joyce's, are rhythmically precise rivers of language, rollickingly pointless litanies sweeping the reader along on a tide of lexical self-infatuation."

—*MAKE Literary Magazine*

Other books by Djuna Barnes

The Book of Repulsive Women (1915)

A Book (1923)

Ladies Almanack (1928)

A Night among the Horses (1929)

Nightwood (1936)

The Antiphon (1958)

Spillway (1962)

Creatures in an Alphabet (1982)

POSTHUMOUS PUBLICATIONS

Smoke and Other Early Stories (1982)

Interviews (1985)

New York (1989)

Poe's Mother: Selected Drawings (1995)

At the Roots of the Stars: The Short Plays (1995)

Collected Stories (1996)

Collected Poems: With Notes Toward the Memoirs (2005)

Vivid and Repulsive as the Truth: The Early Works of Djuna Barnes (2016)

The Lydia Steptoe Stories (2019)

Biography of Julie von Bartmann (2020)

Djuna Barnes

RYDER

with illustrations by the author
and an afterword by Paul West

DALKEY ARCHIVE PRESS
Dallas, TX / Rochester, NY

To
T.W.

Contents

Foreword

This book, owing to censorship, which has a vogue in America as indiscriminate as all such enforcements of law must be, has been expurgated. Where such measures have been thought necessary, asterisks have been employed, thus making it matter for no speculation where sense, continuity, and beauty have been damaged.

That the public may, in our time, see at least a part of the face of creation (which it is not allowed to view as a whole) it has been thought the better part of valour, by both author and publisher, to make this departure, showing plainly where the war, so blindly waged on the written word, has left its mark.

Hithertofore the public has been offered literature only after it was no longer literature. Or so murdered and so discreetly bound in linens that those regarding it have seldom, if ever, been aware, or discovered, that that which they took for an original was indeed a reconstruction.

In the case of Ryder they are permitted to see the havoc of this nicety, and what its effects are on the work of imagination.

DJUNA BARNES

Paris, August 8, 1927

A Note on the Text and Illustrations

The text is taken from the first edition, published by Horace Liveright in 1928. It is an expurgated text, but the only one available: the original manuscript was destroyed during the Second World War, and Barnes declined the opportunity to restore the censored passages for St. Martin's 1979 reprint.

Several of Barnes's original illustrations were also censored, but happily these survive. To the nine drawings that illustrated the first edition, St. Martin's added two more—those heading chapters 12 and 15. This new edition adds all the other drawings originally intended for *Ryder* (pp. 16, 80, 145, 214), including an unfinished one (p. 49), that are now in the Djuna Barnes Collection at the University of Maryland. All the illustrations, with the exception of those for chapters 12 and 15, were photographed from the original drawings in the Barnes Collection and made available with the assistance of Blanche T. Ebeling-Koning, Curator of Rare Books and Literary Manuscripts, Special Collections, University of Maryland at College Park Libraries.

Ryder

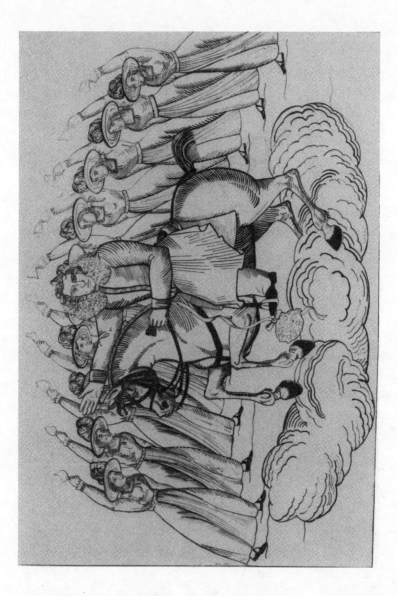

Chapter 1

Jesus Mundane

BY WAY OF INTRODUCTION

Go not with fanatics who see beyond thee and thine, and beyond the coming and the going of thee and thine, and yet beyond the ending thereof,—thy life and the lives that thou begettest, and the lives that shall spring from them, world without end,—for such need thee not, nor see thee, nor know thy lamenting, so confounded are they with thy damnation and the damnation of thy offspring, and the multiple damnation of those multitudes that shall be of thy race begotten, unto the number of fishes in thin waters, and unto the number of fishes in great waters. Alike are they distracted with thy salvation and the salvation of thy people. Go thou, then, to lesser men, who have for all things unfinished and uncertain, a great capacity, for these shall not repulse thee, thy physical body and thy temporal agony, thy weeping and thy laughing and thy lamenting. Thy rendezvous is not with the Last Station, but with small comforts, like to apples in the hand, and small cups quenching, and words that go neither here nor there, but traffic with the outer ear, and gossip at the gates of thy insufficient agony.

When thou goest to thy knees, overrate not their bending. It is not for thee to know how little thou hast, neither is it of great trouble to thee that thou art ignorant of the length and the breadth of thy faith; whether it goes a great way or a little way toward heaven, as a new tree goes but a little way toward heaven.

Reach not beyond the image. For these idols and these lambrequins and these fluted candles, with their seven burnings and their seven times seven droppings, and the altar, and the chancel, and the nave, and the aisles, are not for thee in the spirit, but for thee only in the outward manifestation; nor are the Beasts for thee, with the eyes back and the eyes front, nor for thee the bleeding of the heart, with its fire and its ice. Neither shalt thou have gossip with martyrs and saints and cherubim, nor with their lilies and their lambs and their upgoings. For some is the image, and for some the Thing, and for others the Thing that even the Thing knows naught of; and for one only the meaning of That beyond That.

Bargain not in unknown figures. Let thy lips choose no prayer that is not on the lips of thy congregation, for though it is not given to all men to pray alike, nor blame alike, nor suffer alike, it is not shown thee to know the difference in these matters. Therefore when thou dost ask for the mercy of God, do thou ask it as thy neighbour seems to ask it. And when thou art pitiful, be pitiful like thy sister and thy brother.

Yet think not, when thy stays creak and thy latchets loosen and thy hands go forth in grief, that they are as the man who weeps beside thee, without altering of his breathing, or loosening of his belly strap; for it is given some to come out of their skins, and for others to dwindle therein, and thou art not the one to wonder on such matters.

When thy heart loosens to hear the Miracles, and of the

dead arisen and the damned that were and are not, and yet are, when thy heart tightens to the direction and the way to Holy Places, that have been found and lost again forever, think not that it is a tithe of the loosening and the tightening that was among the bowels of Him who gave them birth and who gave them death in the selfsame dream. For thou knowest nothing of the mighty rains of Heaven that come down of Him and that return to Him, that even thou might be included and yet made nothing, for thou wast only one within the way.

When thou goest into the field and markest thy goat's eye, think not that thou knowest why it lies like meek fluid in the head, or why thy kine have an unknown regard from under their eyelids, nor why the hawk flies among its feathers, and the fishes have a hard smile within their mouths, and go forward always. These also are within the way, but all things are not equal about His feet.

Think not, when thou risest in the dawn and goest among the green things, and the coloured fruit, and the hard wood, making thyself and thy people a safety against the time of snow, that thou couldst advise the fig, or question the wheat, or bargain with the tree; for thou bindest them and slayest them against the Judgment. Canst thou know what the Judgment had been, had the corn given forth barley or the barley put forth figs? Art thou not part and parcel of thy pastures? Thank thy melons for what thou art, and blame thy figs for thy failures, and gather in thy differences, and go to thy mourning as one a little gathered from the earth, and as one going a little toward the earth, and of the earth judged.

For thy life is a going and a coming, and a coming and a going, that thy harvest knows better than thy people.

And when, of times, thou art in no wise concerned with thy religion, and art not touched by the Nativity, nor confounded beneath the Star, nor made still by the dust that goes down from God, then go thou to thyself, and pluck thyself against the day when thou wilt need thy past days for a sign and a seasoning, for thou art thyme unto the Lord, or rag-weed, or sweet incense, or ordure, but that which thou art, that in the end must thou bring as a sign against thy body.

Go now, and lift up thy cries from about me, for I have done with thee awhile and thy ways, and thy ways' ways, and the things that thou hangest about the places of the soul. And speak not of Me, for thou knowest not of what thou speakest, nor knowest thou of thy need, nor knowest what thou hast given or taken, thou knowest not where thou beganst to ravel and where I caught thee up on my needle. Nay, thou knowest not the extent of thy wound, nor the matter I have with it, neither knowest thou how far thy soul comes toward me, nor yet how far I lean outward to catch it by the hand.

Knowest thou if thou hast troubled me, or how thou hast inconvenienced me for thy sake? Or if thou hast pleased me in any way, or hast not? Thou knowest not where the station is that I go to meet thee in. If I have travelled a long way, or if thy soul hath been a bubble rising, and my coming a long while.

These things are as the back of thy head to thee. Thou hast not seen them.

Chapter 2
Those Twain—Sophia's Parents!

The right reckless Jonathan Buxton Ryder, sitting in his chair by the open window (as he had sat for thirty years, off and on, his head in relief against a background of lace curtain depicting barley branch and corn sheaf), eased himself in his trap-door trousers with pride, as he beheld the leafy verdure of the maple-sown highway, for he in his youth had planted the same (is there a man in Connecticut who will not claim as much?), and thought of his then new wife, now lying under a canopied bed with her fourteenth.

She had been a rare beauty then—Cynthia—with parted close-bound hair, coming down a long flight of paternal steps, her sisters behind her, singing, "I lament o'er graves of hopes and pleasures gone" (she then but sixteen!), in a thin Quaker voice, untroubled with passion, a passion flower in her hair, creaking in whalebone and much satin, looking to see what he, Jonathan, book-dealer, would do, and seeing what he would do, and accepting it. The day when, in gibus and swallowtail, and with square Newgate fringed jaw, he had led her all trembling up to the altar, to do with her afterward as a Puritan saw fit; and the organ pealing out splendidly, the place filled with innocent women, all downcast of eye and mothers of twenty, saying: "Tish, tish, tish! Look at the bride, now a Ryder forever! And isn't she a darling in her simple laces? With the blush rose of girlhood just shading into the apprehension, so delightful and yet so painful, which preys upon that tender state in which she now stands—that hair's breadth between 'What is it?' and 'Is it this indeed?'"

Ah, yes, she had been a lovely creature then, tall and strong and comely, with bewitching ways,—and the carriage waiting, the flowers smelling to heaven, and the white satin slipper tossed merrily (by some rake, be it observed however, had the party but known) into her lap as she rode at a smart pace down the main street to end the matter in a well-appointed, quilted four-poster, an ear-pillow with a corner knot of baby blue ribbons atop, for her only, making the whole thing a forethought most amazing.

Then the hour when, leaving her to disrobe as becomes a virgin, he, Jonathan, had walked out into the corridor, looking with pride upon the twelve oval framed engravings of his forefathers hung down to the very door, as much as to say, "I shall not be found wanting!" and she, in all probability, coming upon her linens with more and more trembling and sweet terror until, in night-cap and ruffled, four-flounced nightshift with a square yoke, she laid her down to the unspoken in man. How he peeped in a full half-hour later, and found her soundly sleeping, rosy cheek on insertioned sleeve, and how, with much compunction and no little drawing back, he did divest himself of his flowered vest, with an eye up and toward her, and how, much later, he did come into his courage and did touch her with his arm upon her side, inquiring tenderly how she found sleep now that she was a married woman. And she awoke with a cry and said, "Oh!"—and there we draw the curtain, until she said "Oh!" again, in like manner, all in due time, near unto nine months, the one "Oh!" being the mother to the other.

Now with her fourteenth, madness had crept upon her, for the bearing of fourteen is no small matter, and she called her daughter, Sophia (eldest in that long line), to her where she lay, and she said:

"Sophia, how many children have I?" And Sophia said: "Thirteen, and me."

Cynthia, perhaps because she was a little wandering and no doubt but that she thought it a wise gift to a child, said:

"Your father is a hairy atheist, but a penitent for all that; all nature lovers are, especially these. Remember."

She groped among the blankets. The room was dark, only the canopied bed stood out (whereon were stamped birds of a gusty wing), a terrible suffering centre without extremities.

Sophia swept forward, stopped. "Mother!"

Her mother looked upon her, noted her swelling bosom, put a hand thereon. "You have a child. One breast shall be for my son, and one breast shall be for thy son."

(Truth impels me to say that Sophia had indeed a son, but it was three days bastard, got of John Peel, the tutor, before he mended the matter.)

Sophia took up the new-born all in its long clothes, and put it to the sister breast, for she remembered her mother when she was beginning that she had finished.

Chapter 3

Sophia and the Five Fine Chamber-pots

Aye, Sophia Grieve Ryder came of a great and a humorous stock. By "great" is meant hardy, hardy in life and hardy in death—the early Puritan. The type in men who wore their breeches to a whisper by their indomitable will to roister. The type in women who gave no parole to a single stitch in that whole, magnificent fabric, the wardrobe. Women who, by deep breathing at inevitable births, suppled the bodice; women who, by ample groaning over the necessary deaths, stretched the gorget, women who, by sighing to the very root of the matter in love scenes, distended every inch, every ruffle, every pleat, every tab and every band that went to fashioning that astutely piled ramification, the garden dress, and who, in giving up the ghost, rammed in firmly the bark of the soul at the port of No-Returning.

By "humorous" is meant ability to round out the inevitable ever-recurring meanness of life, to push the ridiculous into the very arms of the sublime. Sophia, born robust, leavened at the maternal bosom, and became magnificent. She noted early which uncherished fury in her palsied maiden aunt had intervaled that shaking, she knew to an hour when her father's heart (which was swung on a longer tether than the hearts of gentlemen are supposed to sport) listed to the right, which meant that to-day it was Abigail, and when to the left, which betokened it as safe at home. Sophia had in her the stuff of a great reformer or a noisy bailiff. In that house of thin partitions and sounding existence, she had hatched on every side and, coming forth, noted with approbation the moment when sympathy in the father for the new-born, newly come, took him at four in the morning in dangling nightshirt, to the "Flowing Bowl" (or night vase), for as she later wrote to her friend, Tollop, of the *Gazette*, "It did please me to see in my father consternation and its accompaniment."

In after life it proved a step in the mastering of her métier. When Sophia came of age and set up house for herself (as her humorous stock would have done before her), she rendered tribute to this memory by making something both rounded and excellent to enshrine it, for she ordered, and saw executed, five fine chamber-pots of a lustrous finish with one line each upon their bellies' surface (just under the lip, lettered in flourished gold, and garnished with devices in bows and cupids) of the axiom:

> "Needs there are many,
> Comforts are few,
> Do what you will
> 'Tis no more than I do."

And in this manner killed two birds with one stone (for of what else is humour made?) in laying the foundations not only of relief but of observation, for between the time of a lover's leaving for the express purpose of, as he said, "laving

his hands," and his return, she learned to know what mind he
had for observation, what taste for poetry, and what faggot lit
to mirth, for the countenance upon the entrance was, unless
the person were utterly void of observation, a thing to see, and
gave up, no doubt, more than half the lining of his nature.

The fifth of these bowls was dedicated to her own use, and
was for her eye, and for no other (showing, as will presently be
noted, that Sophia was, beneath everything, a good Christian),
yet one night in the first year of her second marriage—for husbands have that privilege by the unwritten law—Alex, coming
upon her suddenly, and possibly for no good, startled her into
a premature rising and commotion of ruffle, and saw what
she had indeed been brooding upon, the single word "Amen,"
and when breaking into hearty laughter (for though he was a
foreigner still he had ripened wonderfully), she answered him
somewhat tartly: "He marketh the sparrow's fall!"

As nothing is eternal saving destruction, and as amazement
often strikes from a hand that which but a moment previously
has been firmly clutched, these jolly vessels vanished one by
one. So that what had been in 1877 five lively fellows, were,
ten years later, but three, reading, ranged in order:

> "Needs there are many,"
> "Do what you will,"
> "Amen."

And then one day, Julie came confessing, "Alas, alas! there goes
'Do what you will.' " "Needs there are many" and "Amen"
then stood alone, brother to sister, for another ten months,
whereupon Kate (of whom more anon), being too heavy, there
were "no needs," and only an "Amen" to fall back upon. Sophia
looked upon this catastrophe with something of fear. "When
that goes what shall we do? Amen is the end of all good things,

and I've never heard that anything comes after," she said: "It's undoubtedly ominous!"

In nineteen hundred this great line of humorists had culminated in Sophia Ryder's salon. That this salon, a wandering thing, had always formed in Sophia's bedroom, does not throw any shadow on the true excellence of these gatherings, or the things there discussed, flavoured though they undoubtedly were by the knowledge that under the silken cover there were sheets. Is there not under the coat of a bishop a shirt?

Sophia contrived to have what she wanted without in any way altering the looks, the behaviour or the manner of those who helped her to it, or even suffering the displeasure of hearing herself addressed, either at home or on the street, by their wives other than as "Sophia-all-Soul," "Dearest of the Dear," or "Wonder of Wonders," for she held women as she got them, in every walk of life, by the simple magic of the word "mother." If, when talking to this great man or that, she observed his wife draw in her enthusiasm by so much as a circumscribed gesture, this one she immediately approached in her flowing Liberty silks, her turbaned head held slightly back, and with true and masterful intonation said: "Call me mother!"

What woman could refuse her? The older they were, the more appeased, the younger, the more eager. It was a charming and a legitimate device, the device of a woman who knew that a mother might be condemned, but never quite cast out.

Those who gathered about her found a most bizarre setting, for though a Puritan, Sophia was by no means satisfied by the flowers of her own climate. Before she was forty she had plucked well abroad. Where she had travelled, she had observed. She wore English silks, French drawers, German corsets and Swedish slippers—a Cuckoo who sat on a nest of alien eggs.

Her walls were covered with multitudinous and multifarious

crayons, lithographs and engravings. There smiled forth the women she admired: George Eliot, Brontë, Elizabeth Stanton, Ouida, the great Catherine, Beatrice Cenci, Lotta Crabtree, and the great whore of the spirit, the procuress of the dead, the madame of the Bawdy-house-of-the-Shades, the miracle worker—"Caddy-Catch-Can."

There were the men she admired for this and for that,— Proudy, the railroad magnate (who had passed her on every line running west of the Hudson), Burgoyne, Pepys, Savonarola, a massive head of a Samoan chief who had presented her with ten heathen teeth, and, flanking this, a pencil sketch of the Divine Dante, to say nothing of those later celebrities who may have found themselves on her walls because of the beauty of their prose, Stedman, Browning, Wilde and Thompson.

There were prints of all she abhorred, the rack, the filling of the belly, known as the Extreme Agony, the electric chair, the woman-who-died-of-fright, the woman-who-could-no-longer-endure-it, the man-with-the-knife-in-his-heart, the man-who-left-the-letter-behind, the fox that ran and the hare that was hunted. Yet even these were doomed to change, for coming in slowly, reaching further and further down the wall, like the obliterating and relentless wave, came photographs of the handsome Swede who was later to win her trust.

From this increase of Alex, her court became aware of the condition of her heart, and when the last picture in the room was covered by one more of the bandit with the bandolined moustaches and the passionate wet eye, they left her for a little season to put her house in order.

Indeed, Sophia's walls, like the telltale rings of the oak, gave up her conditions, as anyone might have discovered and they had taken a bucket of water to it, for she never removed, she covered over.

At forty these pictures were an inch deep, at sixty, a good two inches from the wall; the originals were, as she herself was, nothing erased but much submerged. "This is the secret of the amusing woman," she said to her son Wendell, who was to become in the end her only courtier, the last of the ears open to her fading wit. For poverty finally bedraggled her salon, nibbled at the grandeur and, sitting like a bird of prey above her solitary splendour, shed his droppings upon her felicity, her memories, and her spirit, with implacable mutation.

Even Alex had gone, he, who had for so long held sway, slowly ebbed, and in his stead rose that last tide, clippings from newspapers. For in the end this was her court,—false prophet, false general, the pretty girl untimely raped, some woman aptly killed, some captain who claimed discovery of the North Pole, some Jack who had climbed a steeple top; all in a conglomerate juxtaposition, and under all, smiling in forlorn inevitability, Beatrice Cenci, Shakespeare and the Divine Dante.

The end of this woman was as amazing as her beginning. Flowering superbly amid her glamorous setting, quick of wit, pinked by obscenity, she in the end put her little feet, once the pride of more than herself, upon a hassock in their rusty juliets, her strong capable hands (trophies of her past manoeu-vrings) in her lap, the silk of which had once been Amelia's wedding-dress, the throat encircled with the barbaric offerings of her grandchildren, fancy stones tied with string, bits of carved bone fashioned by the idling fingers of Wendell. Her strong grey hair down her back, she sat at a table fashioned of crates by her son, pigeon-holed for nothing less than the birds,—though they had winged away long since,—dipping a pen, made from a shingle and a hen feather, into ink contrived of soot, she wrote in elegant script those nobly phrased, those superbly conceived letters of beggary that had for the last ten years kept her family from ruin.

She never mutilated her power by that lack of secrecy which has, at different times, through the weakness of some priest, threatened to undermine a religion, that has made faith tremble in the balance between restoration and restitution; she held her peace with a fortitude second to no Pope. By not so much as the shadow of an ill-gotten ten-cent piece did the family guess, until long after her death, that she had been a mendicant of the most persistent temerity, that she had lied and wept and played the sweet old woman to the partial undoing of every rich man in the country, and of one of the Presidents of the States.

When someone, none too wisely, questioned her on this matter, she smiled and said: "I am writing," and she was writing. Into those hundreds of begging letters went all of Sophia Grieve Ryder, her cunning, her humour, her deceit, her humbleness, and always, with unerring faithfulness to her original discovery of the way to the heart of man, they were signed "Mother."

In the early dawn of winter days she dressed herself by the light of a kerosene lamp, standing before the dying fire, making ready for the pilgrimage to the city that was the usual culmination of discreet letters. She went to sweep up her gains. Dressing in irreproachable linen, wrapping her pauper's cloak about her, that threadbare green-grey cloak of thirty summers past, that garment that she was wise enough to add to the appeal in "mother," that spoke even louder of her need than her words, this over her bent shoulders, and an ancient, rusty hat, redecorated and redecorated with pink ribbons and black lace, banded deep with beads strung by Julie, thus she went forth, clinging to a sagging purse, to an umbrella faintly darned. Sophia at seventy!

Sometimes her son, out of ignorance, knowing not how his knock would impale her on her own means to an end, would come to her door and she, starting, would say "Busy," nor rise to open, her pen hastily lifted from the page; and then would bend back again to form "My dear, dear, do not fail me now, my son's eyes cry vengeance upon me for that he suffers in that mould of too great measure of genius in which I cast him" . . . etc., etc., though, in hearing that knock that had so stricken her, she knew him to be fat and forty, and in health enjoyed.

To Julie she turned her best love and, doffing her *connaissance* like a true gallant, would take her up on her knee, lying to her of this and of this, calm in the wisdom that realism is no food for a child. She told of her youth, of the way it was with her as a girl, as it had not been, for when Julie should come to womanhood, the portrait would stand real enough in its true colours, and in those that she gave it, for Sophia knew, and suffered the knowledge with a brave heart, that some day when she was but dust, what she had been in truth would come upon Julie, and she said to herself, "What I tell her in lie will stand there too, and the truth the prettier for it," and so it was.

For Sophia held it a mistaken idea that a lie discovered wipes out its purpose in the discovery. "Know the truth as she may," she said to herself, "the thing I've seemed will balance the account." And balance it it did, for in after life Julie held her grandmother's lies as the best of a capacious soul.

Sophia was born gross, witty, gentle, enduring. Upon this fabric she had leaned for the courage to renounce herself, that she might in herself be equal for that struggle, self-imposed—a passionate and precarious love of family. A family in need had brought her to this pass, and a family in need it must remain to be kept at heel; and for their blind devotion, she had a locked mouth, and a stubborn heart, crying where they heard not, "Pity the poor," and "God bless you, my sweet lady," and "The Lord keep you, my fine gentleman!" Beggar at the gates, to be queen at home.

And obeisance she did exact; she loved, but she would be obeyed. She was the law. She gave herself to be devoured, but in the devouring they must acclaim her, saying, "This is the body of Sophia, and she is greater than we!" Devour her they did, and said, "This is the body of Sophia, and she is greater than we"; all but Julie, who loved her most. It was Julie who gave this queen her mortal hurt, for that she loved her best. Sophia offering her heart for food, Julie spewed it out on a time, and said, "I taste a lie!" And Sophia hearing, cried in agony, but Julie went apart.

Chapter 4

Wendell Is Born

Wendell Ryder, second son of Sophia Grieve Ryder (she gave him no father's name but stayed by her own for two reasons, one engraved upon a razor blade, and the other that she had learned to dislike John Peel), was born in the winter of the year 1865, Sophia then a wife of five years.

In the cradle he looked much as he would look in the grave, a hawk nose, a long lip that upon the nipple seemed too purposeful, and a body like a girl's.

Wendell begins to remember what happened as early as two years of age. He remembers that he played with matches, that incident to this habit he set the barn afire, which in turn communicated its ardour to the house and left nothing standing but a gutter-pipe, a marble-topped table, and such of her things as Sophia could cast from the window, among which was an ivory-handled curling iron, a Sèvres jar, which instantly flew into a thousand pieces, a blue house-gown, and a farthingale.

Wendell remembers that at five, he looked under a wee bit of a ruffled petticoat, and there found two little legs in no wise as simple as his own; that he was called John, and that later he spoke up for an unfatherly given name, and was handed a history of England to choose from. He chose Rufus, and held to it for three summers, when he developed a colossal passion for Black Gilbert. So many and so varied were these appellations that a great number of them slipped his memory entirely by the time he had reached fifteen. Nevertheless, he recalls plainly that when he fared forth into the world a man, between the moment of his trial and his complete coming of age, he was called Wolfgang, but that he lied, not to disturb the lady who brought him to the pitch, for she abhorred names German, saying that it was simply the other way about of Wendell, which name he kept to, more or less, throughout his career.

He remembers vividly the three weeks spent as a drug-clerk to Burroughs & Welcome, at the munificent sum of ten shillings and threepence per week; how he longed for and could by no means procure an extra large English pudding with whacking diamond-shaped gobbets of suet shot through; where, to a block, his mouth watered as he pressed the glass front of a certain ale-house, displaying in its window boiled mutton and plates of tripe and tongue; and how, on one Saturday, it had not watered in vain, for he had gone in, and sitting upon one of the stools, had ordered half-a-pint with a sliver of beef to the side, and being, with this expenditure, quickened of blood, became stricken with the difficulties surrounding the making of a living.

At the end of the three weeks, his shadow was exceeding lean. On the coming of Saturday he was sacked. (His companions in clerking saying that it was due to his delivery of prussic acid to a weaning lady in Chiswick, in place of bismuth.) Never again, oh—never, never again to battle as a self-supporting unit! To this vow he clung throughout life with a persistency and fervour worthy of a better cause, indeed, thirty shillings and ninepence was exact and all that was ever counted out to him for service rendered.

He remembers that his mother's second marriage, to Alex Alexson, was the cause of this effort toward independence, as but one encounter had filled each with a long and separate loathing. Sophia was a fond and doting wife; she had by this means endeavoured to remove each from the path of the other, with the success already noted.

He remembers his mother's soirées (she had just returned from a tour in the States with Elizabeth Stanton). Why should he forget? Was it not at one of these that he had been called, by no less a person than Lady Mary Glynn, "Prophet in the wilderness," and had not Archbishop Benson deigned to hold word with him, in regard to our Saviour, the same evening, as he tapped his varnished boot upon the rug? Had not Oscar Wilde himself, with his then not-to-be-denied right hand, lifted his, Wendell's, auburn forelock, murmuring, "Beautiful, beautiful!" He had indeed. Moreover, had not Lady Bridesleep, sighing softly, chucked him beneath the chin?

Yet more often, standing like a lonely heron on the topmost stair of the noble marble staircase, he would listen and observe the ways of the "menagerie." It was on this stair one night that he heard Alex whisper to Mary Anderson, "Call me Bubbles," and a moment later the voice of his mother rallying Willie Wilde for "leaving a chocolate drop in the exact centre of my pansy vase, for . . ." she added delightfully, "do you not realize, my dear, that I have a retriever's heart, and all things that come to me, I take to Alex?" And Willie's fervent "Pig of my dreams!" which was, no doubt, a sort of compliment intended, as he pressed her palm with his lesser-Wildean hand.

He remembers that he went away then to the upper music-room and there, his short legs upon the pedals, his hair thrown

back, hummed from between long lips to himself and that portion of London that he could see from the casement, a snatch
from the "Beggar's Opera," leaving off just at the moment
when Oscar said, as he had often said before, "Ah, Sophia,
bien chaussée, bien gantée!"

He remembers that he was well into the difficulties of the
funeral march, when an itinerant playboy, one of those beggars who get their living by ambling about London on stilts
some six feet long, looked in at the window, smiling, bowing,
whispering, "Rain, my lad, in the offing."

He remembers quite distinctly that he answered: "As to
that, we'll see good days and bad, for such is the lot of man,
but for you, who stand a good six feet out of God's weather,
what difference can it make?"

"All the difference in the world," said the stiltsman, "for I
am that much nearer God's wrath, and what's nearer to hand
is never spared."

"Vanity is everywhere, and the world and his wife are with
you, high or low."

"The world and his wife," answered the stiltsman, leaning
his elbows on the sill, "pass between my legs, but Messalina
could have said as much, and if her fare and mine is no more
than an onion, an onion is but an onion still, no matter where
you eat it, up here or down below." He went on: "You may
have noticed, my good lad, that whenever an army goes forth
to battle, or a great man dies, when there is some ungovernable manifestation of nature whatsoever, be it mind, mineral
or what-not, to that manifestation there is always erected an
arch on the road leading into, or out of town, yea, one can aver
that no deed whatever, an it outstrip a man's own estimate of
man, but that an arch springs up over it, as its natural heritage,
and methinks Messalina was a wise wench when she erected

herself (though it may have been an arch most prone) to the
wonders of upstanding man. In like manner I, poor Tom, do
erect myself to myself, as it is not likely that by other than my
own achievements I shall reach that pinnacle of renown."

"True," said Wendell.

Said the stiltsmaster, "Everything is true that is honoured."

Wendell ceased playing. "I fled you down the arches of the
years," he murmured.

"There you are," quoth the stiltsmaster, leaving him leaning at the window, and taking a firm hold of the shafts of his
profession, "it is the arch that stands for the achievements of
man."

Chapter 5

Rape and Repining!

Lock windows, bolt doors!
Fie! Whores!

What ho! Spring again! Rape again, and the Cock not yet at his Crowing! Fie, alack! 'Tis Rape, yea, Rape it is, and the Hay-shock left a-leaning! Ah, dilly, dilly, dilly, hath Tittencote brought forth a Girl once again, no longer what she should be, but forever and forever of To-morrow and yet another day!

'Sblood's Death! Is it right, m'Lords? Ravished, and the Cream not risen in the Pantry! Ravished, and the Weather Fork not turned twice upon its Vane! Ravished, and no Star pricked upon its point! Can Hounds track her down to Original Approval: the Law frame her Maidenly again; the not-oft-occurring-particular-Popish dispensation reset her Virginal? Can Conclaves and Hosts, Mob and Rabble, Stone her back into that sweet and lost condition? Nay, nor one Nun going down before the down going Candle, pray her Neat.

A Girl is gone! A Girl is lost! A simple Rustic Maiden but Yesterday swung upon the Pasture Gate, with Knowledge nowhere, yet is now, to-day, no better than her Mother, and

her Mother's Mother before her! Soiled! Despoiled! Handled!
Mauled! Rumpled! Rummaged! Ransacked! No purer than
Fish in Sea, no sweeter than Bird on Wing, no better than
Beasts of Earth!

Hark! Doth the Eland crying in the Forests of the Night
so tweak at your Heart's Blood, good Husbandmen? Hast
heard Panther Howl, or Lynx or Deer, or Fox or Owl, of such
Deflowering? Doth any crouching, ambushed Flesh, in leash
of Fur, turn moaning on Clenched Paw for loss of Filament or
Film? Bewailing with Grim Hackled Jowl, its Season's knowledge? Hath any Stag slunk down against the Wind, loosing
such a Difference? Nay, but read me aright, 'tis another Matter
this! A Girl hath come to Mourning, in Spring again. Fare
forth then, wind loud the Horn, and call a Spade a Spade! 'Tis
Ripe Time for it, when Unripe Woman falls to Ripening! Set the
Black glove by the White glove, who shall say our Judge wears
not the one or the other come this time Nine Months? Oh, for
a digression in that exact duration! Come Seven, come Eleven,
were she a Wanton still? Damned she is, and set a-counting, her
Days are numbered, and her Nights are timed. She shall not put
her Foot outside of it! A Wife in Bed only, and all in Merrie
England, and in the Month of May! Drab of Tittencote!
Thatched Tittencote, the Stocks tidy under the Butter Cross!

Alas! Alack! Woe is me! Rape has stalked abroad and found
one capable of alteration . . . 'twas ever thus! Hath the Leg
drawn on the Tight Boot! La, what a Wicked Wakeful Waking
for a Lass! Turn then backward, O Time, in thy flight! Doth
Rape sit hot among the Wheat? Springs it up in the Corn?
The Unlawful, Carnal Knowledge of a Woman (before she
was teachable) has been gained, the Lad, in the full Legal sense
(being but fourteen) incapable, but for all that, a Satisfaction
and a Regret.

Girl, hast fornicated and become Wanton before thy Time? What Presage had you of it? Woke you early to the Madman's Bell, and his cry of "Six o'clock, and all Good People to the Brook!"? Or was your Back from the Cradle seeking for the Soft Grass, and your Neck for the Warm Arm? Who told you, Hussy, to go ramping at the Bit, and laying about you for Trouble? What thing taken from your Father's Table turned you Belly up? What Word in your Mother's Mouth set your Ears outward? Bawd! Slattern! Slut! Who gave you Rope to turn on? Slain you are of Slumber, and your Family mown down before that Sword of Sorrow. Thy Brother weeps amid his Diapers, and thy Father behind his Beard! No longer has thy Mother Pride in the Century-old *pro ocreis Reginæ*; for the Annual Rent paid to the Queen, to keep her in Leggings, cannot make Tittencote smack of Tittencote, and you gone slipping down to Hell!

Great things by Little are thus brought to Dust. Fair Rome sees Men come buttoning up her Appian Way, and an Ass brays over Babylon. Strong Nations rise and come to Flower under the Hee of one Emperor, and are brought low by the Haw of the next. And here, in the Heart of excellent small things, a County over which no Blood has been shed, save once in a Slip of History, a Girl has brought the very Rafters and Pinnacles of her House about her Ears, her one Nocturnal Tear bringing down many in the Morning.

Yet: Is it not a Woman's quickest way of laying herself open to Legend? For now some say she has whelped Sad Melancholy, and that she do run about in the Night from Hedge to Hedge, and has a Look as if the One who brought her to Great Grief had been Dead a Thousand years, for such Thick Sorrow is given off by her, sitting and standing; her Soul springing from vein to vein, a Hound sensing a thing not common to it, while at the Waist a Solemn Silence hangs.

But of all this, what can be said to better purpose than that she is Raped, yea, Horrid Raped! Oh, Beastly Stale! All the World knows no thing so Mad, so Daft, so Poisonous, so Balmy Glut of all Ill Luck! Doth not the Shudder of it crack the Paint of Historic Beds?

Ear to the Ground, my Gossips! Hear you not a Sound of it, though you touch Dirt a thousand miles from Home? This way, good Wives! Muzzles to Windward! Is there not a Stench of the matter in every Breeze, blow it East, West, North or South? Have on, Milling, Trampling, Wrangling Multitudes! The Hare is running, and you are well behind! She whisks over the Common and you cannot get scent of her! Darted she Left or Right? Who is the most Infallible Pointer among you? Milady or her Slattern? 'Tis one and the same, White Meat or Dark, would you let the Quarry off? Lift up your Hundred Feet, and let down your Hundred, have you not, at your Beck and Call, twice your Numerical Hate, with which to make a catch of her and an Example? Now, now! She falls at yonder Ditch, and, like a Deer, turns face on, weeping for clemency. Now, have at her!

And how was it, my Pretty Love?—Box her Ears, the Dirty Wanton!—and was it coming over the Stile, or was it this side of the Fence or the other? How went he about it? Did he lie to you, Frowsy Smelt? Said he that you had Sweet Chops and a Winter Eye? And you, how fared you at that Moment? Were you easily bedabbled, or came you reluctant to the Filthing? Backward looking, or leaping at the Bait? Leaping it was, I warrant me, and I'll give my Neighbour here my second Best Rolling Pin, an I'm not in the Right of it! Or were you, Little Cabbage, in a State of Coma, wherein a Man may step, the Beggar, and find you all he would, though nowhere Yourself! 'Tis a Pox of a Pity that a Woman's Wits may be as scattered as

Chaff, yet her Chastity well enough in one Place to bring her to Damnation! Out then! What will your Mother say to this? And what will you do from now on for a Life?

Thou art less than a Farthing, and may be spent at one Ale House. Or have you a Philosophy ready risen for the Deed, as some Panders have, the instant they step upon the Stoop of Ill Fame, so that there be those in the Market Place who think their Wits are better for the vending of their Wares, thanks to his Vain and Empty Prating, and Loose Rein in High Places. These several and such do shake the very Matrix of the Truth, and spawn a Thousand Lies, which flood down upon us like a Rain of Stars, but though most Gaudy Showy, are no man's Verity. Oh, Fie upon you! What have you done, but make some Pimpish Fellow a Braggart and a Nuisance in all the Streets that run a Blind Alley! And shall the child, Girl or Boy, stand in after Years a little at the Pump, and say aught that shall contradict the Wry Proportion of its Begetting? 'Tis such who Poison Wells, and make the Hackle rise on every Pubic Inch, and do split the very Bells by which we tell the Time!

Adder in the Grass, Ibex on the Peak, Fish in the Wet, Bird in the Air, know something of it, but do they write Books, or talk at Bedsides, or whisper in Galleries, or make the Laws? Still, Girl, such shall judge you, perchance even more rigorously than we.

To the Oblong Eye of the Deer, is not your Condition lengthened? By the Owl, is there not purchased a Dreadful Rotundity? To the Shallow Eye of the Fish, you are but a little staled, but to the Bossy Eye of the Ox, you may ride as High and Damned as Jezebel. And what of the Multitudinous Insects, and the Infinitesimal Conclusions of the Ether? To the Myriad Pupil of the Fly, what can it but manifold your Grievance? Consider these yet others, infirm of condition, who have Spots on the Iris, or suffer Jaundice or Bloody Issue, would they not impute their malady to you, saying that Death settles on your Cheek, Decay rides your Flesh? And what of your own Eyes as you saw not the Tops of your Boots, but the Sole? Is it not, therefore, imperative that, while in the World, you consider the World's Eye, and of how many Facets your Crime consists, according to the thing it walks before?

Have not all Philosophies of Avoidance been Penned for you? Do not Mathematics, take them where you will, prove there is always a Deviation that brings down a Marvellously Different Total, an you had wished? Has not Science proved that no Bodkin takes the Riband but at will, and the Thread makes no Conquest of the Needle, and the Needle has not a leaning to the Thread?

Have not Logicians, from Seneca to Plato, settled it, that no Proposition may come to a Head an there be Wit for evading? Shall not a Council of Women, such as we, make clear to you in a Sitting that had you a Vocabulary of Movement the Case had been a Riddle still and not a Certainty?

Must we send our Girls to School that they may learn how to say "No!" with Fitting Intonation, both for Dish of Porridge and for Dish of Love?

There is a "No" with a "Yes" wrapped up in it, and there is a "No" with "No" enough in the Weave, and we have been sorry amiss that our Girls have not learned of it. Learn now and it is too late, learn Yesterday, and To-morrow had been a Different dawning. Thus the Bobbin fats with Knotted Thread, and when it comes to sewing, what Garment shall be stitched of it, that shall not rip in Open Places and shame the Leg? It is the Unpleasant Nature of Man's Mind (being what it is, in these days) that he does not, like the Ancients, need to magnify Your Deed to make it most Stinking, Large and Awful!

Or put it thus:

Have you not taken that which Better Women have refused, and in so doing, been most unmannerly? Is it well to grab Sweets that an Hundred Guests, at the same Gathering, have left untouched, and thus greedily to limn their Savour? You have but one Life, yet in one Night you have changed the Complexion of All Nights, thus pilfering from the Community, which has honoured you as True Coin, only to discover you Counterfeit, thereby changing a Known Sum into a Sum needing Recount. Have you not, therefore, made the whole of Society a Dupe, and shall we not, for that, have you in the Just Distaste we evince to the Forger? You Mint with your false Metal, Metal as false, so that from now on, we must watch our Change, lest there be Lead in it, or such Alloy as might make us sadly out at Pocket. You have corrupted the Fabric of our Council by this one Brief Act! Made of Society an Unknown Quantity, and this we are not built to bear, for this a Man will fury all his Days, and none shall commerce with you, without first turning you over to see where the Die stamps Treason!

Or put it thus:

You have stolen Time, such Time as lies thick about Tittencote. Time made stout by Good Wives stitching, and washing, baking, and praying. Firm with Household Duties well done, within the narrow excellence of Wedlock, paced to Monogamy, fortified with Temperance, made Durable with Patience. You have bent Time with the Tooth of Lust, torn the Hem of Righteousness, and the Wind may enter and the Cyclone follow!

Or thus:

Man is born to die, and we, with Fortitude, have made the Farthest Outposts of Death a Lawful Goal, but you, in this Wanton Act, have advanced that Mark; and your Child shall, on the Day it first takes Breath, set before the World the Farthest Point yet gained in this Misfortune. And at that Hour when the Child cries its first Cry, will Tittencote reach a point more distant in Sorrow than any as yet prepared for. As if Death were not Terrible enough, this on which all Eyes must direct themselves, is a Divided and a Bastard Death and, like a False Monument, must destroy, rather than dignify, that which it was set to commemorate.

Think you what this must inevitably do to corrupt a Whole Body? It is wretched enough that Man must continually pace himself to his End, taking Measure of his First Hour by folding it over until it touches his Last, like a Linen Draper, that he may not be too much caught up and despoiled of his Yard, by creeping, unwarned, upon its Selvage; that the List may not run upon him when he is naked, that his Whole Life may not shrivel into naught, because of the concussion of this, his Last Moment.

How much more miserable then is that Man who contemplates with what Fortitude he may, the spectacle of an outpost that flies an Uncertain Ensign?

Or so:

Whose Child do you harvest? Whose First-Born springs from your Lap? Is he not your Neighbour's Son, had you clung fast to the Laws of your Country? Is he not made Fatherless by too fast Fathering? Is this not turning the Just Proportion of Generations backward? Does he not ride before his Mother, seeking his Mother? What Nation has the Son first and the Mother second? What Tree springs up before the Orchard, saying, "Orchard, Orchard, here is the Tree!" What Infant gives Birth to its Parent, what Child crawls out of the Cradle, that its Mother may have where to lay her Head?

Who plants the Staff, Crook down? Who suckles the Wind for a Mother? Who combs the Wind for a Parent?

Who sets the Child backward upon the Beast of Time? Who makes of his Son no Kin but the Tomb, no Generation but the Dead, nay, bequeaths him no Dead and no Living, no Future and no Past? He must move forward seeking, and backward lamenting. He is whirled about in an Uncertainty, and his People shall inherit him for a Birthright, and his Father and his Mother shall say, "We resemble that Hereafter, which was before, and is not."

Or better:

Thou art Witless Whey, and should be Scourged! Flayed! Whipped! Stocked! Cried against! Howled over, and spent quickly, that you get from out our Country and over the Border and into some Neighbouring Land, there to lie, until some Blithering, Scabby Potsherd mends a Stewpan with you, or lays you between Hot Iron and Hot Iron, and so melts you down, to make a Cap for his Heel. So shaken loose, so cut-pursed that the Uncertainty is out of you, so set you back as Current Coin. So lay about you, so scratch, slap, pinch, pull, that you turn to Honest Flesh. Thus, to come to the very Pip and Core of Truth, through Good Woman's reasoning—though to that Faculty no Credence has been given by Philosopher or Scribe adown the very ageless ages—to make of a Point no Point at all on which to haggle, that indeed no Wits be spent on you, no Candle burned to a Wick in Attics and Dens by Grizzled Beard and Shiny Pate; throw Lots for you between us, to determine to which of us you shall fall; there trust to that Pity which passeth Human Understanding—which God forbid we should have hereabouts—and so make of you what we will, now that you have filched what you would!

And I myself ask no Better Portion than that you fall to me, for then should all Eyes behold the Bone of Truth, the Marrow of Justice! For I'd have all Destruction in you well destroyed before the Striking of another Midnight Bell!

Or thus:

It is Spring again, O Little One, the Waters melt, and the Earth divides, and the Leaves put forth, and the Heart sings dilly, dilly, dilly! It is Girls' Weather, and Boys' Luck!

Chapter 6

Portrait of Amelia's Beginning

In the small British country seat of Tittencote (described in the last chapter) in the year 1869, John Johannes de Grier lay dying. A long horse-whip, his last partner in this world's work, lay out beside his bed. It had lain there twenty-four hours, for the day before he came to die he had chased his favourite daughter, Amelia, then seven, about the yard with it, because she, poor unwitting, had thrown the clothes-basket into the hencoop, thereby setting loose upon the air feathers of all sizes.

John Johannes was of French descent; in the time of the Huguenots his blood, as it was in his fathers, crossed over into England. By trade, John Johannes was a builder, by heart a cabinet-maker.

He greased his riding-boots every morning with super-superb yellow tallow, rubbed his horses down, and went flying over every hedge on the way to church, chasing the hag-ridden end of a rabbit. His wife said that he always came to the Lord, not as other men, but hanging on to the butt-end of a hare. Be that as it may, he liked the fields better than the prie-dieu, his furniture better than his wife (which is, after all, not as bad as it sounds, for furniture can be most proud and beautiful, and has at times a flowing felicity of limb not vouchsafed woman), and Amelia the best of all. This affection was not meanly come at, for he had to weigh in the balance eleven others.

Amelia de Grier was dark and thin; she fastened herself into her dresses with that single emotion with which one draws on the slip of a sunshade. At seven, as is the ruling of nature, she had no breasts; at seventeen she was no better; two little nipples held lonely sway over that territory. She was a good girl, she feared Irishmen, as she was told, particularly if they sported an auburn poll; she had read little or nothing; she was amazed at the quantity of rum her relatives would down, and she had a marked partiality for the canker in the family tree. Tramping about in the woods she turned up the leaves for moss and bugs with a high pleasure. She was "death on dishes," as her dear Wendell said later, when he had cause to know, and she hated the house and all the work in it.

Her mother, who was a thing of beauty with her slow voluminousness and her tight head, like the head of death that had known no corruption, sat long with her hands folded over that silken garrison that had housed the troops of the de Griers. She seldom spoke; when she did it was by way of warning:

"You have an aunt, her name is Nelly, she is like a doll in a holy place, because," she said, "she has been brought low with suffering and honour and disgrace, and has been reinstated, and this is a secret," she went on, looking out of the window and away from her daughter, "and you must tell it never. Well, but the Duke of C—— got her with child, and, of course, as is the way of great gentlemen, he, in the course of his prayers (somewhat neglected of late), came to the conclusion that this deed could not go with them, so he married sweet Nell to a handsome fellow, one of the Royal Guards, all six feet in his feathers, and a bucket of blood in every vein.

"So she and her guard, most truly guarding, go riding together under the trees, the leaning willow trees, she riding up front, in a green habit of scolloped velvet and of a lovely perse at the revers, and a boy's hat on one side of her head. The day is fair, the sun shines; it warms the backs of the hands and the shoulder point, and the outer leg. The flowers in the bushes are so strong, so red, so fit, that they might have been embroidered in the hedges. The sky it swept, and one pern, wheeling and wheeling in the heavens as if all parts of that day were equal. The moles in the field came forth to see what could so trouble the stillness of the earth, and the moles of the earth sensed a silhouette against that day, touching and terrible, for she rode high and straight. Her rounded bosom, held in stiffly by whalebone and fifty cut buttons, was no man's, but from there down a rotundity took liberty with the velvet. And because this Guard loved her, it was more than he could bear, and with long, even strokes he whipped her as she rode, with his riding crop, and she never turned her head, for can one man whip out the dog in another? That was your aunt, and you may not speak of her."

Amelia said, "Why?"

"Because it is a disgrace," her mother answered, looking out of the window into the fair English country.

Presently, passing to leave the room, she came up to Amelia too close, as one comes up to an object in the dark; it was her way of secrecy: "Never let a man touch you, never show anything, keep your legs in your own life, and when you grow to be a woman, keep that a secret even from yourself." She shuddered. "Never, never, have children. And God forgive me!"

"Forgive . . . ?"

"For making you mortal; if you live you will be a fool. It takes a strong woman to die before she has been a fool. No one has the imagination; I did not, you will not." She went out of the room uncrying, holding her hands darkly in the folds of that skirt that took the widest possible liberty in the room.

In 1886, Amelia de Grier was twenty-four and in London for the first time. She turned her head from side to side, as was the way with her, looking at St. Paul's, the Thames and the Tower. Her brother had come up with her, and her eldest sister Ann, for their mother had died leaving equally among them the de Grier estate. There were now eleven in all, for little brother Joseph had dropped off shortly after a Sunday dinner involving a slightly high leg of pork, and he and the pork went to God in the speediest possible manner. Amelia and Ann set up a very neat apartment in Shepherd's Bush, with a wall about it, and gooseberry bushes.

Now Amelia gave way to her nature, which was sentimental and longing, and took up violin and singing at the Conservatory of Music. Had she not had her picture taken for a career? A tight-fitting velvet, with buttons all down the front, and her lovely hair hanging to her waist, a wave to every hand's span, a tobine mantle nicely left to find its drift upon the bench beside her, with a massy tod in back, just showing above her shoulder—art of the photographer—to say nothing of the look in her brown eyes of rapture for all notes gone hence into the belly of time. Her little hand laid upward upon the pile of her lap, in that exact interval of finger that proved her a mighty worker at the toccata, and calloused at the tips, to give weight to her boast, "I put my whole family down upon the G string, and see what it has done!" For if she did not become a virtuoso it was no fault of her strategy. As for her brother, come up to London with her, he had taken her to the Cathedral, and there, watching the man working at the bellows, that the

master organist might close his eyes and yet roll out a great
anthem, why, she would not be content until she had laid eyes
on the organist in very deed, and that she did, whereupon he
became most careless of God, for the nonce, and would have
gone listing in the winds of love, seeing which her brother,
young John, thinking he had left her in exceeding good hands,
clipped back to his horses and his hounds and his languish-
ing lady of high degree, to whom he was houndmaster, and
never so much as put pen to paper Amelia-wards until a full
six months later, when he came to great need of her, for the
pox had come down out of a nice ruffled apple-green shift,
claiming him for lodging.

Amelia explained it well later to Sophia (for she became
aware of that lady's existence upon the other side of her wall,
when her son Wendell sat thereupon, in green twill, reinforced
as to seat, and dangling with white rats, for be it said Amelia
laid hands upon him that afternoon, and sent him sprawling
upon her inner court) as "the innocence of the lad, him never
having set eyes on a woman in all his life, other than to observe
that they were a bit heavy in the beam, and now see what it has
done," which was a favourite remark with her, as we have said.

Sophia's retort was characteristic of that lady's warm heart;
she said, "Call me mother," and from that day forward, Amelia
held her close to her bosom as the very flower of woman, and
'twas thus that Amelia, making over her legacy, that was to have
put her in the way of a few grace notes and a technic upon the
violin that began with a loose wrist and was to have ended with
a tremolo and a public performance, 'twas thus, I say, Amelia
gave into Sophia Ryder's hands (much against her sister's
advice, for brother John was in constant need of bandages),
that little property, and thenceforth became an inmate of that
house, sitting at Sophia's knee listening with rapt attention

to all that she might say. And how quick Sophia had been in making her daughter, and all that seemed to go with it, was recorded in after years, for one could tell to a quaver when Amelia left the Conservatory of Music (just hard upon eight months). She could play upon the violin Schumann's "Spring Song" but not the great rhapsodies, she could sing "Buttercup" but not "The King of Thule." Her little accomplishments were, therefore, as exactly timed in their immaturity as a child of like months, and it was a great pity to see the way she turned from the piano in after life with that puzzled look in her brown eyes that told of nipping in the bud.

Yet at that knee she learned much that was unexpected. She learned that Sophia had met the King of Sweden and had by him been given a bloodstone ring, in the shape of a heart; she learned that Sophia's second marriage was with a renegade, a strapping Swede (a priest had been his "coming of age") with black mustachios ('twas he who had looked kindly upon Amelia as she passed on her way to school). She learned that Aaron, the youngest of Sophia's three boys, had died in his sixth month; the other, Gaybert, was a surgeon, and that Wendell was just recovering from the too meatless diet of vegetables, and was by this proven, in her mind, an artist. She learned that great statesmen, great doctors (who must have, for the moment, relinquished imperial pulses) and as many generals as you could horse on a dozen steeds, had shot fireworks to her; she learned that Sophia moved among the Pre-Raphaelites as accustomed as a glint of steel, and she learned that in a Swedish trunk with seven locks, and three bands of iron, lay many a note from the renowned, that would have caused a great lamenting and wailing among women who were wives.

Amelia discovered that Sophia, under her increasing flesh, kept memories of what that flesh now covered, sweet breasts hidden by time, shoulders impertinently swamped, legs that walked in their old way beneath inglorious pounds, and a foot that yet played small.

Sophia said, "You have read very little."

"Very little," said Amelia.

"Therefore," said Sophia, "you know not what is in a foot. Running and tapping, lying and standing, the foot has been much overlooked. Large feet and small feet have played a great part in the history of man. On tip-toes went Peeping Tom. Would he be a by-word now, had he walked flat, and saved not the shanks of his boots?

"Swiftly Salome whirled upon her toes. Would Johannan be dead of his head's need, had she remained rooted to the ground? Does not the past sound with feet flying to doom? Would Napoleon have been great an he had shuffled in his fate, or gone about mincing? And when a woman becomes a great name, is it for the sound of her feet, or for the innate ability that she has for keeping them clear of the floor? How many a humble man owes his advancement to the great foot thrust in at the closing door, and how many women owe their advancement to the fact that their soles are clean of dust?

"I have gone to meet many destinies in little shoes," she added, "but none so harrowing as on that occasion when, going for a Latin lesson, I returned a mother."

"And how was that?" inquired Amelia.

"Thus," she answered, for she was a brave woman, clean shoe or dirty shoe. "When I had a fancy to discover a transitive verb: 'I lie—he lies—they lie—' thus," she said, laughing heartily, "was my youngest conceived, and now you know everything."

In this manner, making a period, she did her most cruelly out of the story of Beethoven, which anon. . . .

Chapter 7

Sophia Tells Wendell How
He Was Conceived

This is the dream that had been told by Sophia Grieve Ryder
to her son, Wendell, when he reached the years of discretion.

"You know well enough how thoroughly I hated your father.
Would it be conceivable then, that I, of some mettlesome quality, should give him access to that place that so heartily com-
plained upon the first intrusion? Thy brother is, in all truth,
evidence of that tardy rejection. Let us say no more. But is ever
a cat (and I more like that breed than the dog) brought back to
her vomit an she be a beast with a temper whatsoever? I think
not. Therefore, having laid me down to sleep, composing my
mind for a good night's lodging with some neat-mannered
dream or other, I did no sooner close my eyes than, behold!
I was in the temple of music and saw one coming toward me
in a long robe, his hands behind him. His large head was set
about with lank grey hair, and I knew him to be Beethoven,
for the likeness of him was on every pillar in that temple. Now
the doughty part of it is (due to the circumstance of dreams
being what they are, boiling up from, and returning to, some
miraculous source) that he came toward me, melted into me

on my human side, and came out upon my marvellous, without so much as a 'by your leave,' or 'if it please you, madame,' or a pass at the weather, and in nine months, by the Christian calendar, I was delivered of you."

"God's jerkin!" cried Wendell, "am I to understand that thou hast cohabited with a mirage and brought forth a son?"

"No other," said his mother, "though properly speaking it was no cohabitation, it was an infusion, for I tell thee he did not so much as pass the time of day with me, or ask me how I did, or inquire of my health, but passed through me, boots and all, and came out on the other side, without unclasping his hands, and continued for all I know," she added, "walking away into the region of Limbo without turning his head. But that I got thee nine months later is no myth."

"I shall inscribe this," quoth her son, "upon my razor."

Chapter 8

Pro and Con, or the Sisters Louise

Early in 1887, two young lady pianists (sisters) with hook noses and fingers dedicated to nothing less than an octave, were sitting over their duet in a room with double windows at which hung two lengths of sufficient lace, their backs to a goodly collection of Fielding and Smollett, Daudet and Mallarmé, facing two heavy marble busts of Chopin, which stood on either corner of the upright. As they played they discussed the uses of adversity.

"I think," said Louise, taking a trill, which was followed by a flight of her sister's fingers in the bass, "that never man before so thoroughly enjoyed his parts, so trusted to them, and so managed them that"— she took a *diminuendo* with her sister at this point—"others trust in like measure."

"So nicely put, so simply and yet so direct, sister," her companion answered, "that I could not find it in my nature to contradict your—shall we call it your opus, were there not within my mind a floating doubt as to the ultimate importance, shall I say, satisfaction, of man to the mass, when—" she concluded, doing her utmost with a heavy bar, "the mass is female and the man is Wendell. Can you," she added, chasing her sister's fingers up into the very closest treble, "conceive that nature in one man can be perpetual?"

Her sister turned the page, passing her hand over a minor chord. "Hardly perpetual," she conceded, "but perhaps recur-ringly satisfactory."

"He maintains," said her sister, putting the now completed duet down upon a pile of Brahms, "that no woman, however fanciful, however given to speculation and to trial, to coquetry and to gorging, can be happy without his peculiar kind of collusion."

"He paints a rosy picture," retorted her companion, "of polygamy for—" she stressed, "the *man*—"

"Let us hear how it runs," quoth her sister, taking up some fine needlework, a bulrush and a Moses, and a Hagar, symbol-ically crying in the wilderness in white, three-ply floss tears.

"Does it not run something like .this?" began her sister, closing her eyes for a prolonged *piano*: "There was Tessie, aged forty, all pure and lean and waxing haughty; with her was one Mazie, a girl of twenty, once nurse, once mother, once mourner, once happy, once unhappy, nor once wife. There was Bell a chit, and Bebe a doll, and Hester a rogue, and Caddie, a farm-er's daughter."

"It reads," murmured her sister, stitching a bright red navel in the just right spot, "like a school for scandal—"

"Hushed, my dear, with obscurity. What—" corrected her companion in the womb, "could be more proper? However," she continued sacrificially, "let us on. Observe the trees, thick-rooted, fair-fronded, some shadowed, some gleaming, and here observe the undulating ground, bursting with pea-pod, bean-pod and chicory, melon plant and gourd plant and rutabaga; here the eyes of the potatoes looking forth, and there the deep-banked fires of many a mound of manure, a perfect prostrate

tapestry of fecundity, my dear. Observe above you, far as eye can see, the wild hawk and the pigeon, the sparrow and the robin, and the one wheeling hearse of the skies, the crow, and between heaven and earth, these six, sewing, washing, swelling—"

"And," climaxed her sister, "loving?"

"May I soliloquize?" said her companion, tentatively.

"Plunge, my dear," she was answered.

"Laughing, I might say screaming, the six rushed out of the house, pinching and pushing their fertile fingers into ribs and buttocks, snatching at their companions' individual herbage and soft spots. Rioting, they flew down the grove of trees, their merry jests sending the pigeons high in the air in a flurry of hardy wings. Panting, they flung themselves in threes beside the murmuring fountains, on the lush greensward, hair dishevelled, clothes awry, hot and with leaping heart and pelvis, and fell over upon each other, laughing and limp. But hold! Was there not a blunder made in the Restoration? Did not Antony overlook something in Cleopatra? Is there not a Judas at every board, a weak plank in every liaison?

"So here rose up a figure in each brain, accordingly mounted to that fancy's ability, of Wendell setting forth from the earth with stupendous great wings, outstripping the cornfields and the mountains, and rising up into the clouds, like an enormous and beloved insect, with strong hands upward and arched feet downward, and thundering male parts hung like a terrible anvil, whereon one beats out the resurrection and the death.

"Then slowly, as cats move, the muscles in the arms, the tendons in the legs, the strength of each craftily enlisted, they turned each to the other, with springing jaws. Writhing, biting, tearing, scratching, screaming, crying, over and over they rolled, in blood and tears. Over the greensward through the parsley, through the roses and the gillyflower, through the barley and the bramble, and down, down into the valley's bottomless depth, now she on top, now she, now she under, now she, and into the ravine at last, where between tall rank grasses the rubbish blooms."

"Do they return?" her sister asked languidly.

"Does Hell spew out its damned? It does."

"I wonder," she said, and then, "Shall we put it to the test, pierce the veil and encompass a return?"

"My dear," she was answered, "stir up the fire for tea, and remember that Hell is not for ladies."

"I understand," replied her sister.

"Nor . . ." said her companion.

"My dear, I picture it down to its *finest* detail. . . ."

"In that case," her sister agreed, "let us not run it into the ground."

Chapter 9

Tears, Idle Tears!

In which Amelia prepares to leave London and her sister for Wendell and America.

––––––––

"Ah, my God!" sighed Amelia's sister Ann, "our poor brother Edmund has the pox, my Jack has turned scoundrel, and you are leaving for America, that outlandish country! What will become of us all! I never could see what in those Ryders so eats on your fancy. Sophia is no better than she should be, Wendell is nothing to lift the skirts to, though it's a mercy Alex is waning."

"I'll write to you once a week," said Amelia, down on her knees before the new steamer trunk, "and I'll tell you all about the Indians and such things that I am like enough to run into, and I'll send you some of their feathers for quills, if they are not a myth, though it's my opinion," she added, folding up the last of a dozen, "that they are probably like all heathen—more flesh than down."

"Oh, my God!" said her sister once again, "what will

become of us all this time thirty years? You'll be as black as an Ethiop, I as pale as any spinster, my Jack in jail, no doubt, and poor Edmund out of his head like enough, for the pox do mount, 'tis said, unless you keep it in control, and what has Edmund, outside or in, that would keep anything from flying straight up to his head at a moment's notice!"

"I'm a wicked girl to leave you, and that's the truth!" said Amelia, wiping away a tear, "but love is once and marriage hardly ever, and time fleeting. What am I to do?"

"What all women do at least once in their lives," said her sister, turning her head away, "that which can noway be altered."

"You do frighten me!" said Amelia and, laying her arms upon her trunk, put her head into them and burst into tears.

"I'm a wicked girl, and that's the truth!" cried Ann, and came flying to kneel beside. "There, there, my poor dear, you can be sure of nothing but death and rent-day, and it never rains but it pours, and it were better never to have been born, but you will be happy for all that, and everything will turn for the best, and it's better late than never, and a rolling stone gathers no moss, and she who sings before breakfast weeps before night; so wipe away your tears, my darling. Oh, my God," she added, herself in unrestrained grief, "what will become of us all? Why, how know you but that Wendell will have his way of you on the stormy sea, for no one can be sure of anything on board a ship, it pitches and plunges to that extent, and everything is upside down most of the time, and what chance has a woman to keep what belongs to her, when everything else is where it shouldn't be? I would that you would marry this side of the sea, I should feel that safer; but an American marriage you will have, and what can I do?"

"Oh, dear, oh, dear!" cried Amelia, "don't say such things. I've never seen the inside of a ship in my life, but surely there's a captain aboard, and officers enough to see to it, no matter what the sea may be planning, that there be a place for everything and everything in its place."

"Oh, my God!" said her sister, wiping her tears away with a self-sewn cambric, "a place for everything and everything in its place! 'Tis what has ruined the lives of all women since the first came up out of a man with his rib sticking in her side! A place for everything on land is quite a different thing from everything in its place at sea! I've never laid eye on the inside of a ship myself, but this I can say, what with all that slewing about, in cabin and in hold, if I were you, I'd have my lines well within hand, for once married, the ship might pitch and roll, or sink, for that matter, and whatever you came to, you would come to as befits the law. There's but one way that a woman can have the law well around her when she is all which-ways, and that's in having her which-ways mingled with it. Marriage, my dear, is the better part of valour."

"My Wendell," said Amelia, now on the return from apprehension, which is courage indeed, "is a proper man, and he will see that no shame is brought upon me, for he loves me from his heart, he do say, and what then have I to fear?"

"I, myself," retorted her sister, now on the return from pity, which is pride, "have heard that young man voice strange sentiments for one who intends to stay well within bond. Have I not, with these very ears, heard him say, time and time again, that one woman was never enough for a man?"

"That," said Amelia, "is a theory which he holds for the race in general, but surely not for persons in particular."

"Where the race in general enters a man's head," retorted her sister hotly, "there, in the end, you'll find many persons in particular. Why, even a man who loves monogamy as the very apple of his eye, and whose tastes all lean toward but the one woman, and that his wife, has cried, more times than you could count, 'What bed is this? Indeed, I thought it was my very own!' for," she added, "they all seem to be able to remember, to a knob and a castor, every other article of the family furniture but the bed. Howbeit, this they seem to think exceeding familiar wherever they meet it, and do rush upon it with an 'Ah, my dear-little-well-known-much-beloved-familiar-resting-place, how came you here?' As if," she sniffed, "all beds were like those in the Bible, and walk of themselves, and likely to be found in Woking when only that morning they were arose from in Putney!"

"What is this you say!" exclaimed Amelia. "Is there indeed any such mishap likely? Then I shall get me a bed that no man could mistake!"

"It will have to be a monster!" observed her sister.

"Indeed, I'll get me such a bed that no husband could misplace," cried Amelia, intent in taking the trouble out of matrimony. "I'll paint it a bright red, tie it up in sashes, drape it about with lace, and in the very centre of the coverlet, I'll stitch, in bright scarlet twist, the reminder, 'Here I be!' That will do the trick, think you not?" she said, clasping her arms about her sister, and laughing to think what a woman she was for setting the world straight.

"'Twill do little or no good," replied her sister, "for where a man lies, there is the one and peculiar spot that he can never identify with any satisfactory regularity!"

"He shall stand to the business then!" cried Amelia.

"It might be as well," said her sister, "but somehow, even standing, I have little faith in the fellow. Not that I think him much worse than another. My very own Jack is, alas, no better than he should be, but I had foresight to jilt him, so no matter where he meets my bed abroad, he shall never have the half of it at home. And I think, were you a wise girl, you would end this trouble you are laying up for yourself in like manner, and settle down with me and our poor Edmund, who is man-near-enough for a woman who likes them about, without having to worry where they keep their memories."

"Shall I," said Amelia, chin on hand, "have my wedding-dress all of a rosebud, or side-draped with chenille and net?"

"Oh, my God!" said her sister for the fifth time that noon, "what will become of us all? I see that I shall have the sense of the family all the days of my life, and you that which shall exercise it, and as for thy Wendell, he will be the sore bone of contention, mark my words, for the lad has a look to me of someone's else husband."

"That he has not!" cried Amelia, starting to her feet. "'Twas what attracted me to him from the first, he has a look, back and front, of mine own!"

"So much the worse, then," said her sister, "for I see you are deep in the slough of love. Jack had the look to me, back and front, but I mended my ways, knowing him for what he is, so that his front looks like nothing I would, and his back but the lid to it, so he may go back forward or forward, as he reminds me of nothing so much as himself, and that," she added, "is the only way to take a man."

"As to the money," said Amelia, hesitatingly, "I know we will be pinched at first, for Wendell is too ill of health to get for himself, and his mother is but poorly, and my little is all."

"And a scandal it is!" exclaimed her sister, now bursting with indignation. "From the very first day you put foot in that house, did they not begin to pluck the very feathers from your breast to line their nest with? They did, indeed, and now what can you be sure of? When want flies in at the door, love flies out at the window, and all in America too!" she said, coming back to her choicest torture, "in a land swarming with pitfalls, and wild men, and murder! Oh, indeed," she said, bursting once more into tears, "I do expect, by the very first packet that arrives after you land, a parcel with your ear within, or a slice of your scalp, for they will think nothing of murdering and eating you!" Her voice rose into a wail of agony. "It's one of their customs, and if you will go into a country where the custom is to eat babies and women, why, you'll have to submit, and I . . ." she said, "shall receive your ear by post, and there's no doubt about it, and what shall I do?"

"God knows," said Amelia. "Think, dearest Ann, what in the world can be done with an ear? It's the most dreadful predicament to be thrust into!"

"Are you making mock of my terrors and fears?" demanded her sister, for in truth Amelia was smiling.

"Why, then, I am a little," said Amelia, "for I've heard a deal of America from Wendell and Sophia—they were born there, you must remember—and if the custom in that country were the eating of babies and men as well as women, how is it that Wendell and his mother have lived to tell the tale?"

"Through some miscarriage of justice, no doubt," said her sister. "Someone always escapes, but that is no reason for walking into the very jaws of death; it's like tempting the devil!"

"God forbid!" exclaimed Amelia, "I hope I'm as good Church of England as they come."

"Speaking of churches," returned her sister, "what faith has your Wendell? None that I ever heard on."

Amelia was downcast for a moment. "I do believe," said she, "that he is a free-thinker. But what does that hurt? If one is free to think, they might hit on a most amazing good church. Our very own, perhaps," she said brightly.

"Did you ever know a dog," said her sister, "who was free

to choose him a home, who would not nose out a dung-heap? For free-thinking dog or free-thinking man," she said, "never seem to come by anything with their thinking but the refuse of other people's!"

"My Wendell," said Amelia, "might be as free as the wind, but never, I am sure, would he come to such a vile place as you have chosen for him. And how a girl as nice as yourself can think of such a thing is more than I understand," she added.

"It's only with restrictions, I've found," said her sister, "that one thinks at all! When one is free-thinking like your Wendell, nothing comes of it but fate and the devil!"

"How you do ride on!" said Amelia crossly. "You'll be sorry for it when you are aunt to three or more strapping nieces and nephews."

"Oh, the poor things!" said her sister, weeping anew, "what is to become of them with their very tongues hanging out for hunger, and their bowels as thin as tissue, for lack of nourishment, and I unable to help them!"

"I shall have milk more than a plenty," said Amelia haughtily. "How can you stand there and cast aspersions on the build of your only sister!"

"Oh, my dear!" cried Ann, "I am not casting anything on your build, and well I know that you would flow like a mill-race an you were able. But where is milk to come from when you yourself will be a shadow from privation, so that your very child, when within you, will look like a cocoon on a stalk!"

"I'll not bear it!" cried Amelia. "Am I to stand here on our last night together, and hear myself called a stalk, and my unborn child no more than an insect! Why, it goes past all endurance! I should think you would be ashamed of yourself to talk to me so!" And she burst into tears.

"I mean no such thing," said her sister, wiping her own

eyes, "and well you know it. 'Tis because I love you so dearly that my bowels turn to water in thinking of what is to become of you alone with that man, to say nothing of his mother. I'll allow that Sophia has a very smart tongue, and would pass for more than educated, and has an appearance far from revolting, yet there's something about her," she said, "that in spite of her small stature, do make me think of Gulliver!"

Now did Amelia see her opening. "She is a woman in a million," she assured her sister, "a woman of such wit as I never lent ear to. She can tell you more things that you could not believe in ten minutes than you would bargain for."

"I don't doubt it!" said her sister.

"'Twas only yesterday," added Amelia, "that she was telling me what was in a foot."

"And what is there," said her sister, "but, in a few rare instances, the wisdom to run?"

"Why, destiny is in a foot," said Amelia, "and by the foot-fall, she did affirm, you can tell the whole of a character, light or loud, soft or strong, on tip-toes or well on the flat."

"In that case," said her sister, "what of her own?"

Amelia blushed, and thereupon told Ann, with much mis-giving, the story, saying: "'Tis how Wendell came upon the scene."

When she had made an end, she looked up and perceived that her sister was dried of tears, and sitting straight, her hands in her lap. "My God!" she said, for the sixth time that noon,— but it was God with a difference.

"What in the world is the matter?" exclaimed Amelia in fright.

"Matter?" repeated her sister, her eyes darting fire. "Matter! You sit there and ask me what is the matter! Are you dead to all virtue? Deaf to all customs? Lost to all propriety? What is this tale but the shameless confession that your Wendell—no, I forbear to call him so longer—that that man is a bastard!"

"How so?" cried Amelia, as shocked as Ann would have her.

"How so?" said Ann. "Does she not as good as put it to you that she got him running about on an intransitive verb; and was ever a child not a bastard who did not get to the making by single means? Why, I never heard anything like it in my life, and I do think it such a scandal, indeed, that I blush, though my own sister tells it me. And now," she added, "if you have a second thought but to jilt that person, you are no sister of mine!"

"But the teacher was her husband!" said Amelia. Her sister paused in her pacing of the room, up and back. "Is that the truth?" she demanded, fixing Amelia with a doubting eye.

"And why not?" said Amelia.

Her sister came to a stop, somewhat calmed but by no means ready to give over.

"Well," she remarked, "it may help the case in some slight degree, but if there were one way in the world to unravel husband and wife right back to the two separate conditions in which they stood at the altar, I never heard a better. It's enough to make the child an idiot for life!"

"Why?" asked Amelia, thoroughly puzzled.

"I will not voice it!" said her sister, "but if you cannot see why, shifting the poor creature at such a rate, then I shall not be the one to tell you."

"But you carry on so!" said Amelia. "I cannot open my mouth but you fly into some devilment or other. What is there about me, and my leaving for America, and there marrying my betrothed, that should set you in such a twitter?"

"Do people go to Timbuctoo every day in the calendar?" demanded her sister, indignantly. "Is there not reason enough that I should have the horrors and hair standing out all over me? Is not my only sister about to walk into the bottomless pit, leaving me forever? Oh, I know it's forever!" she said, and promptly broke down.

"Indeed, and indeed it is not!" said Amelia, in her arms in a moment. "We have never got on together, dearest, because each has a way of looking at things that in no way fits the looking of the other, but when we are apart I shall long for you in good earnest, and be thinking of you much of the time, and writing often, and some day, when we can afford it, we will come back to see you, and perhaps . . ." she added, hiding her face, "I shall have something to show you, though now you see nothing but trouble."

"What can you have to show me but more trouble, a little shorter than yourself?" said her sister, sobbing, "and what will become of me? Edmund has near gone through what little we have, and I have jilted my Jack, and never, never want to see another, and what shall I do, unless I go out to service!"

"Oh, shame!" cried Amelia. "Service is not for you, my bonny! Why, look at you, are you not the pride of Tittencote, and did not the Duke come to falling from his carriage the day he caught sight of you by the corner of his eye? And isn't that enough to make a girl hold up her head for a lifetime? For it's not every girl," she added, "who can be said to have lifted royalty off its bottom, and that's the truth. And," she continued, "if you are not the very image of dear Queen Alexandra, then I never saw a double. And how can you talk of service?"

"I am but the likeness of her," said her sister calmly, and with dreadful resignation, "and, like the copy in the supplement, can be put to service. Did we not see Edmund lighting the fire with her but yesterday? And what then that I should light fires too, yes, and sweep and dust and become a slavey, and bent and haggard and old and toothless and grey and wandering, before my time!" she added, her tears flowing in such good earnest that Amelia put her own handkerchief into her hand, saying in an effort to comfort her, "But remember, sister dear, that you are the handsomest, best-looking, most up-standing, finest-mannered girl in the whole of England! And have not ever so many people said as much? And had you not ten offers before you were twenty?"

"But one and all of them," said her sister, "were somewhere corrupt, as you well know, for have I not jilted three, and I but twenty-nine this moment?"

"'Tis because you are too fearful," said Amelia, sitting down at her feet, "and no sooner see a touch of green but do think the whole man a little game. Why, your Jack is none so bad, but races a bit and gambles when he has nothing better to do, but think what a nice boy he is at other times, and how well you like his walk."

"I never, never, never," said her sister, "will wed a man I cannot look up to, and as there are none such, into service it is. And what sort am I best fitten for, think you?" she added more cheerfully, for the idea was not so unpleasant as she had imagined. "I myself think that as companion I would shine."

"Indeed, it is the very thing!" exclaimed Amelia, struck at once with the idea, probably because it was the one accomplishment her sister had not. "I can see you this minute, sitting and reading some proper novel to a nice old lady in a lace bonnet."

"It might be borne," said her sister, "though she would be certain to fall downstairs at full length, at least every six weeks, and that," she cried, on picturing it, "would set my nerves on edge, but old ladies always do, for nature must worry a woman in some manner or other, and if it's not the one thing then 'tis the other, so I must make up my mind to a deal of picking up and dusting and setting straight, for I can see I shall have no say about it."

"Perhaps," said Amelia, lighter at heart for the turn it was taking, "she will be a pretty thing, all organdy and laughter, and fitted with song."

"Just like the silly fool," said her sister. "I'll have nothing whatsoever to do with a young miss, they are worse than the old ones. What I should like," she said dreamily, "would be some proper parson in a sweet old parsonage, who did a deal at sermons, and likes his tea on time."

"Why, then, that will be the way of it," said Amelia, "a parson it is, and why not, there are many."

"Perhaps there are," said her sister, preparing for bed. "I like to think there are men in the world who dote not on the flesh, but do turn their minds to hell and damnation."

When they were well within the blankets and the lights out, Ann began to cry afresh: "Oh, my God!" she said for the last time, "what will become of us all? To-morrow you will be on the sea, and as you go to Paris first, the agony will only be the longer, for that is a country," she said through her handkerchief, "where civilization has worn everything down to the instincts, and they were never wholesome in the French!"

"Nay, truly?" said Amelia.

"And I shall never, never, never see you again," said her sister.

"Yes, but indeed you will," said Amelia. "'Tis but a little way, once over, and a lesser back again, and days to come about the doing of it."

"Never," said her sister in the dark, "did I think when we were children together, that we would be women apart!" And she wept so bitterly now, that Amelia got up and went into bed with her, holding her in her arms, crying, too, for she knew not what.

"And you'll be murdered in your bed, and I shall get your ear in a package, and oh," wept Ann, "what shall I do with it? It is all because of those rubber boots," she said into Amelia's shoulder, "and mother not wearing them out in the rain, and coming to her death of it, that this has happened, or we might yet be in Tittencote doing our hair to please ourselves, and coming to be old without dreadful alternatives. Oh, never, never, never," she cried, "shall I see you again, and what shall I do with it? Oh, what shall I do with it!"

Chapter 10

The Occupations of Wendell

Now ye of all good virtue, bring your sewing, For
herein sleeps a dog beyond your knowing.
And all ye Burghers rowdy, drink and spit.
For this be wholë cloth of Wendell's wit.

THE TALE

Dan Wendell[1] was, forsooth, a man of spice,
Where others thought but once, he thought him twice
Of thingës that he occupations call,
In nightës time, and eke in timës small,
When Ámelie[2] was bedded on her side,
And Katë-Carless[3] in her dreamës tried
Her hand at japes[4] for swerving of that tool
Known in that place as "Wonder," and y-rool

---

[1] Philosopher—in this case Wendell Ryder.

[2] His wife.

[3] His mistress.

[4] Tricks, jokes.

Or "Turning of the Back," on commerce rife
Yclept "The offering of Hendy[5] to the wife"
For Dan Wendell weenëd[6] each caress
Would number him gay children as in chess.
He thought, "Another castle, horse or pawn
Will, God wot, in nine months be born!"

Or if, in kill of prowess, he ran hard,
He breachëd tighter for a better card
To stack a deck of daughters and of sons,
Aces and spades, y-hearts and diamonds.
Yet nold I falsen,[7] if then at the back
He lost a deal, at front he squared the pack.
Nowise he was content till fifty-two
Were shapen each to go as cardës do.
And where they liggë[8] named he every one
Blake[9] for each daughter, and y-red for son
And as the harës bright sprung on the crown,
Eke[10] then to shape his fancy, cut them down
To take their place throughout the lefë[11] games;
And though they borë not these very names
Upon their polls,[12] there sprungë hearts or spades
Or diamonds small, or clubs, so that y-braids
Like Autumn leavës to the ground y-fall
Not one of them had length of shode[13] at all.

---

5 Handsome.
6 Thought.
7 I will not lie.
8 Lay.
9 Black.
10 Also.
11 Dear.
12 Heads.
13 Hair

For in the end he set his heart, I guess,
Upon the more, and soon renouncëd chess
Saying: "If Ámelie and Katë wisely draw,
And be not dread of motherhood before,
I'll have my game, and joker too, despite.
And be these twainë not enough, the night
Is large with wenches, for the matter wood."[14]
Thus he for safety wenchëd where he could,
And in the dealing missëd not a trick
But cut and dealt his gledes[15] unto the prick,
That eke in time, if time drew eke in team—
Thirty or more abreast, his parchêd dream,
Would one day be well watered by their wombs
Though all, alas, in time unto the tombs
The game must go. Yet many a yearës round—
As Alice went in Wonderland astound,—
Play on the earthës checkerboard a pace,
Till death y-kiken[16] long into their face.
And in the wrath of sleep, put forth her claw
And draw them in, to play not anymore.

Betimes this game on coldë hours fell,
Then Wendell worked his other wits as well;
How thingës of small consequence to make,
How bread from bran he mightë roll and bake,
That child and cattle fodder from one bin,
For kine, he held, were kith, and infants kin.
And other ways he'd twist to save a coin;
While spendeth he most lavish of his loin
Most saving was of gold and silver bright,

---

[14] Mad.
[15] Hot coals.
[16] Look.

So that he had full wit to make at night
And yet to save by day. Thus he did preach:
"Store every sacking strong, for shirt and breech,
For hams come diapered as babes y-clout,
Yes, what y-ham wears in, y-babe wears out"
Natheless[17] of foreign thrifts he was averse
Thrift of y-Franks who savë by the erse;[18]
Thrift of Greek, and Trojan countenánce,
Saith he, "Such Gauls wore never virile pants,
For at the parting of the ways of every pair—
Which runës thence in legs, is never fear,
For in the lap of every man of salt
There speaks no voice which plaineth[19] loudly "Halt!"
Nor in the petticoat of worth, a sentinel
But crieth loudly: "Stand ye one and all!"
That nature be not cheat also, he tried
To make the mount of pleasure to the ride.
For this he shope,[20] with craft, an oxen bone
That with pleasure might his Katë groan
For he had read that savages y-bare
A crown of thornës on their here-and-there.
So, much abacken taken was he, when
His Katë, ruffled, rose up like a hen,
Y-clack for painë, and for sad surprise.
Y-water of reproach gliss[21] from her eyes
And groaned she, lamenting long and sore,
For where he would again, she would no more,
But got her hence, with scornë none awane,

---

[17] Nevertheless.
[18] Arse.
[19] Complains.
[20] Shaped.
[21] Slid.

Saying: "It shower never ever but it rain
In this y-great despond you feign[22] call nest,
Wherein, algate,[23] no peahen getten rest,
But brent[24] must be, with hookës and bright fire,
For hounding down the game of her desire."

    *   *   *   *   *   *
    *   *   *   *   *   *
    *   *   *   *   *   *
    *   *   *   *   *   *

Now be the moment come when you shall hear
How Wendell stuck his fancy through the ear;
And how he thought his dames to prick and pierce
With pinnës long, and cork and courage fierce,
That in their lobës might a jewel hang,
A hoopen round, a knob, or wolfës fang,
For making of them comerly,[25] and how
He did the samë office for his cow.
Sweet Dolly Sodam, little calf of doubt
With newë waxen horns, more in than out,
And twin *Gamorra*, littered at a throw,
And sister heifers, *Versus Con* and *Pro*,
And, most in special, that fresh dam and good,
Proud *Jenny Cocklehorn*, down-drop of *Prude*
Whose sire was none other than King York,
But how, with neither bodkin nor with cork
He pressed into her nosén hoop of iron,

---

[22] Pretend.

[23] Nevertheless.

[24] Burned.

[25] Comely.

That grazing in the greves,[26] a bullë spyin'
Would feel his heartés blood y-stint[27] for hope
And go a ramping long upon his rope,
To see so fine a setting for a ring.
Preenéd she for pride, and now she sing
With mooës soft, for gladness of her snout,
Whereat her lifen flittered in and out,
Full gladly that for this it was bedight[28]
With worldly omamentë round and bright.
When every cow was brodered,[29] every wrist
And ear of slut ajangle, then he list[30]
Of his own soul, and said: "I be a melt,
If every blood there be not in me, Celt
And Slav and Scot, and Tartar, and eke Dutch
For at my every turn, and every touch,
I do within me see another man;
Sometimes a rich, sometimes a poorë wight,[31]
Sometimes a castle have, sometimes the night
Alone do shine upon me, helter-skelter
Beamës for shingles woven in a shelter,
And doorë knobës three, upon the grass
To mark the way of rooms, wherein to pass,
And rest in peace. At other times am I
A king in robes, a swineherd with a sty,
A pickpocket, a beggar and a priest,
And often driving largë from the East
A caravan of mirrors and of spice,

---

[26] Groves.
[27] Cease.
[28] Adorned.
[29] Embroidered.
[30] Listened.
[31] Fellow.

To make of me both towen times and twice.
At other times there creeps on tipë-toes
The anxious blood of children," and, God knows,
Thinking thus, he named himself aloud:
"Jack Willingboots and Merry Dick McCloud,
Justin-all's-Well, and, Lord Percy, gent,
Plain Tom Swift," and eke for devilment
Advertised in the "Cattle Call"
As Tommy-Tapper, trouble's seneschal[32]
Adviser, father, brother, friend in ruth;[33]
The one and only vat of seething truth
Wherein the garment of repentance, flung
Returnës twice as light and neatly hung,
That man might sport again that filthy coat
That sin had tightened long about the throat,
Redipped unto the sense as sweet as rose
A newë soul within the oldë clothes.
And how his ádvice clean, and counsel clear
Sting from the heart, blake[34] sorrow from the tear
And how, through him, man mightë yet be blessed
A dollar down, another when the rest
Was to the liking. If that soul still went
His way full siking,[35] and no way content
With this correction, then that dollar dance
Swift through the mail, and back into the pants
From whence it came a-skipping, and the clerk
Could prove the case, or in the second jerk
Have what he lost, and that of Tapper too.
What moren can an honest villain do

---

[32] Steward.

[33] Pity, compassion.

[34] Black.

[35] Sighing.

And he in business? Goodë business make
Less give, I guess, than other men can take.

And when this passed, he to his books y-stored
For he would live both heren and abroad,
In China now, in Persia now, and now
No place at all that common knightës trow;
In Íreland, in Greenëland and Wales,
A travellér in mind of hills and dales
He had heard tell of. Often sitting still
He fancied that he sweated up a hill
And breathëd loud, for in the thought 'twas steep,
His leggës twitchëd like a dog in sleep.
And when he was bespoke of wife or Kate
To lay a hod of coal within the grate
He waved his kerchief quickly, and perspire,
Crying: "Nay, nay, my loves! observe, I climben higher,
Full woefully fatigued! My leggës shake,
For many a longë day I no jot slake
The thirst of this pursuance. So below
Ask of me nothing, but yourselvës go
And dress the victuals, for I shall return
A famished corsë, and my gorge aburn
For draughtës of sweet cider or new beer.
So fly about, my dovës, to make cheer!"
And when this passed, he to his neighbours took
Well underpeight,[36] his lustës,[37] in a book
That ran a deal to wenching and to wives.
How a man y-thirst, and how he thrives
On polygámy much; and then astound

---

[36] Tucked under.
[37] Pleasures.

With serving witty reasons for his ground.
"For," said he, "alas, alike, alack!
No woman lien always on her back,
And when she standeth up (and ye be wed)
There is no doubt, much nothing in the bed!
Ah! What a horrid sight are double sheets
When on the one the other one but meets!
So every man in truth, unless he lie,
Would have his beddë stuffed like a pie
With wenches sweet between the towen crusts,
For 'sdeath, there must be parry where be thrusts!
No *bon vivant* can bide a beddë thin
For lack of little partridges within!"

Soon every farmer thought Dan Wendell dighne[38]
To look into their souls, and through their eyen
Into the heartës loft, where there be store
The lumber of their days; such furniture
Too heavy for their lostë youth to move
Too mantled with forgotten dusts of love.
Yet gave him leave to enter when he would
And hold converse with things there under hood
Of nodding darkness old, with needle bent
On sewing up the soulës garëment
In silence ever. And to Wendell turned
Like mazëd[39] children on a furnace burned.
He brought their wivës from their birthës through,
Milked their cows, eke brayed[40] their corn, and drew
Bean from the nose, pea from the ear, and oft

---

[38] Worthy.
[39] Amazed.
[40] Beat small.

Clombed[41] with the speculum aloft
To sweep the cobwebs from the bridal grot,
For many a thing therein a man forgot.
Took their dying calvës on his arm,
And stricken beastës all unto his barme.[42]

Now while Dan Wendell thus his cunning girt,
Six damen halt in wonder at his shirt,
Amazëd were these laundresses how fair
Its flip-flap was, for to each suddy mind
Came thought how, with great carelessness behind
And great frivolity in front, a shirt is pied[43]
As for it many a tub of water sighed,
And how this was, they know not to this day,
Yet will I tell: it was his neat "nose-gay"
In other words, a sponge of fibers soft
Which well before, and well behind he oft
Hither and thither about his bum y-swoped,
To this exceeding niceness had he groped
Out of a still small voice which said: "No pains
Can be too cunning where dame nature reigns."
So well he rode his sponge, his shirt was light
And cleanly well, and flappen ever white,
Nor would he travel one mile out of town
But to his pommel hung this "nose-gay" down,
And as he went no lady but her laughed
To see how well provided was he aft,
And Hisodalgus, that great horsë still
Piaffëd[44] lightly that no drop should spill

---

[41] Climbed.
[42] Breast.
[43] Piebald.
[44] Trotted slowly.

Of thilke[45] chalice delicate bestride
And for no thing afoot would turn aside.

Eft[46] Wendell pondered, and he say him "Sooth!
What is this swims like dregs within the truth
That animal and man be set apart?
I hear not muchë difference in the heart
That beatës soft and constant under hide,
And this same hammer ticking in my side!
For many a springës eve among the fern
I've seen the lovë-light in sheepen burn;
And many an even in the bosky[47] greve[48]
Have seen the flame of love on weasels feed
And brin[49] the eyes of lynxes through the night
Now flowing long and soft, now short and bright,
And harës too, and all the birds that fly
Have oft a something longing in the eye
And I have seen up in the skyen blue
The sparks of lovë falling down like dew;
There on a twig the nightling them upflung,
And in the mist this flower of passion hung
A'blooming softly, till it melt and fade
To fall upon a nestling in the glade.
And seen his claws for love how grippen are
That he unto that bird might give a ba[50]
And turn and twist with joy of her begot,
What then have we that all y-beasts have not?"

---

[45] That.
[46] Soon, shortly afterward.
[47] Bushy.
[48] Glade.
[49] Burn.
[50] Kiss.

Now long he of this question gan to reck[51]
How his cock-hens might eat two grains a peck,
Or how his speckled wyandotts be mate
To lay a time not onë egg but eight
And while acluck in prowess, lay eight more
That like a fountain might the eggës pour,
Y-lich[52] and lusty,[53] thinking thus, he fand[54]
His children flocking on him every hand,
For he had murmured long in allegory
And they would hear of him a simple story.

Wendell Telleth of Pennyfinder the Bull

"Whilom,"[55] said Wendell to his begettes three,
"There throve a Bull as great as any tree
Who was besainted in the town he ran.
Loved was he, by every child and man.
Pennyfinder of Pearls-Hoof y-named,
Deep in y-dos[56] and in y-ribbës famed
For noble strength in bonës and eke hoof
And for the prowess that he oft gave proof.
He came a-gaiting[57] through the town abumble,
His cuddë of sweet pippens made y-rumble,
His leggës lifted, *benedicité!*
For his safe going, save us all and three!

---

[51] Reckon, think of.
[52] Alike.
[53] Pleasing.
[54] Found.
[55] Once, formerly.
[56] Back.
[57] Walking.

When he raised his lippen for to roar
Many a dame came running to her door,
All flour and bren[58] bedabbed, to give him greet
As he went slowly lowing through the street.
Lite[59] children all y-clapped to see him come
His hertë beat out loudly like a drum.

*   *   *   *   *   *   *

And when he oped[60] his largë eyen twain
'Tis said the people crossed themselvës well
As those who fear the brightë pangs of hell;
And when he turned himselfen round to sterve[61]
The wholë town began to weep and rave.
And infants from the windows fell in grief,
And all the treën shedden every leaf,

---

[58] Bran.
[59] Little.
[60] Opened.
[61] Die.

And all the fishen in the running brooks
(That were not starkly hanging on y-hooks)
Clombed[62] on the rockës for to wax of breath
So harrowing to nature was his death.
And all the birdies in the air made jig,
And trembeléd most grisly on the twig;
And all y-doggies rose up on their erse[63]
To think that all sweet beauty wane and pass!
And all the churchë bells began to ring,
Though none had raised a hand to cause the thing.
And all the dread long day none sat to meat
For that the bullës cloven hoofs were neat[64]
And only a sprig of grass between them clipt[65]
As down upon the cobbelés there dript
His redden blood; and eke his heart beats faint
Betokened heaven with the deed acquaint.
And when his body was y-served for sup,
Why then, God wot, no soul but ate it up!
Thus man y-grieves and aye forgets it too,
For such the Lord has willëd him to do.
For though the eyen pour, the buckets dip
From out a well replenished by the lip,—
All the ducts were stricken with the drouth
If sorrow's locks were long upon the mouth!
So with this rigmarole I will have done.
Not any soul is but the like, and some!"

Now when he had made finish, at his feet
He cast his eyen long for sorrow sweet

---

[62] Climbed.
[63] Arse.
[64] Clean.
[65] Fastened.

"But for,"[66] he said, "life was not shope[67] for all
To go alike, but some are large and tall
And on their bonës much of honour wend
The wordë fulsome, and the kiss of friend
Do glut their livers, their pylorus[68] swell
For of the banquet doth the turdë tell,
And rown[69] in the belly's dark alway
And secrets of the supper all bewray,[70]
For man hath at both endes got a door
But animals go silent all before
And speak but little gossip undertail,
And eke in full assembly none prevail
To tell the other what upon them eaten
And deep in silence their still heartës freten."[71]
So while his beasts about him browse and graze,
He set a plan a-crawling up the maze
Of his mind's wit, a wizardry to seek
That every beaste in kindë mightë speak.
Now Hisodalgus was his very dear,
And to him first would whisper in the ear.
Thus while his kine upon their cuddies chew,
He put his arm about his neck and drew,
So that they were as close as towen sticks
And eke the heart of each as soft as flix,[72]
And told him thus most kindly of that source
So very greatly comforting to horse,

---

[66] Because.

[67] Shaped.

[68] Opening from stomach into duodenum.

[69] Whisper.

[70] Betray.

[71] Devour.

[72] Beavers' down.

How his dam was queen of all brood mares,
For nothing so the very soul outflares
And brings to speech, as flattery of breed,
And where he offer honour to his steed
Or cow, or fish, or bird upon the wing,
And all their different praises should y-sing,
He would them have by moonfall ramping proud,
That by the break of day they speaken loud,
And up their hovës liften in the air
And clop them all together in a prayer
To think they have a brother right at hand
And if their joy of life be proudly fanned
Would flock about him sickerly[73] in herd
As flocked to Saintë Francis every bird.
So thus he spoke unto these beastës all;
Y-litë[74] linnet with the feathered caul[75]
And eke y-duckës and ye geese attend
Their gentle heads upon their neckës bend;
And up the hackle rose on every cock,
And straight the haren sprung on every hock
Of sire and dam, to hear good Wendell tell
From out what noose their greatë glory fell.
As taking Hisodalgus 'round the halse[76]
He said, "My loves, I speak you nothing false,
You all were wellë born, as prove your names,
Bespeaking each the foal and get of dames,
Touliou of Gunther, and ye queen
Maria Bounce, ye get of Daisy Green.
All of you most elegantly dropped:

---

[73] Certaiuly.

[74] Little.

[75] Hood of feathers, crown.

[76] Neck.

The noble stream of blood was never stopped,
But all full rife it ran in time of rut
To hook ye well in promise to y-gut
Internal of that beast ye callë dear,
And löved well, as forth you sticked an ear
And brayed acceptance of the deed in all,
As downward fell your newë hovës small,
To scamp[77] upon the green and whinnied soft,
In loving-kindness to your mother oft
Who, in that deed, at last a way had found
To set her heart agraze upon the ground.
Now I would have each one of you to mull
This cud of thought, that right into each skull
A flowing brook of speech be haply hung
To rill in wordës all adown your tongue,
So that you take not only to the bit
But both to wisdom and alike to wit,
That nevermore your throat y-corve[78] is none
For man be fright[79] to pick the rack of bone
That to him spoken has, and to this end
I would that each and all of you should spend
An hour a day of invocatïon
Unto that God that blast you never one
And would have each of you to choose an herb
Best suited to the thought that thoughts disturb;
That in this wise there rise up to acquaint
The Jesus sweet your plightë in a plaint
That like the Jimpson weed,—that hardy plant,—
It batten on the skies and therein rant
And so bespeak you, that unto your nod

---

[77] Scamper, run.

[78] Slashed, cut.

[79] Afraid.

He'll take the matter rashly[80] to your God,
And in such wise will make of you, I pray,
A greater matter than a moo and bray.
And now, whereon you naught but death bestride,
May Glory leap the stirrup for the ride,
And give you greatë cheer as friend, and eke
A seat at table and a comrade's cheek
To lean upon in trouble, and your neck
In times of joy with wildë flowers deck,
And with you hold long argument, God wot,
That you and he together lifen trot
A neck-to-neck, and flee the dusty rack
Of destiny that rideth at thy back,
And in the tombë lie, while deathë dree[81]   ,
Saying, 'Hunter hunting huntsmen, here we be!'"
Now, when Dan Wendell pausëd and made close
Not any beast or fowl but up them rose
And turned on him their eyen soft and sweet,
And Hisodalgus lifted up his feet
And placed them on his shoulders light and strong
And looked into his eyen deep and long.
And this be nonë false nor read me wry,
He lookëd long into that mortal eye,
But what he meant, or if he understood
I would not tell ye children if I could,
For it is best such matters to leave plain.
Or capel[82] be afright to do again
That miracle. So now I will make close
By saying, on mine honour he arose!

---

[80] Hurriedly.

[81] Endure.

[82] Horse.

Chapter 11

However, for the Reader's Benefit

When Amelia embarked from France on her way to the States, Wendell beside and his mother, she came to her fears in earnest. Every half-hour she would ring for the steward. She was not an hour out before she said that nothing could so distress her as her stomach, and where had it been this long time that she had never noticed it before, and that she had never seen the waves so high, and how was it that they had not washed away the half of England; and that never rolled anything as that boat did that did not turn over completely; and when the captain had been to quiet her for the hundredth time, she cried: "Ah, captain," and clung to her sheets, for she had given up trying to stand from the moment that she had found herself, unexpectedly, in the arms of Wendell, and both in the arms of the chief purser, and all three up against a pillar, in the far end of the dining-salon.

"You will not sink," said the captain, "and why are you so frightened? The waves are nothing. I think, indeed, this bodes fair to be one of our best and smoothest passages."

"Oh, my God!" exclaimed Amelia, "have you lived through worse things than this! I see that my poor dear sister was only too in the right. I'll never cross such a tempest again, for it bites me asunder with the most lamentable terrors, and my dear Sophia is not herself, for at most times she is most gay and witty, and but look at her now! As for my husband to be, he is dead, I am sure, or he would have been in here inquiring. Do you go, now," she begged the captain, tears coursing down her cheeks, "and see if, in number nine, there is not a corpse rolling about, for he was never strong, and why should he live through a thing like this indeed, when a dish of fried bananas do set him vomiting!"

The captain reported, however, that number nine was doing famously and was eating a bunch of grapes as placid as could be, though, he said, a little green about the chops.

"Oh, the hard-hearted creature!" cried Amelia, "is he up and about and never so much as asks to know how I do? Oh, how right was my sister, indeed. On what have I embarked?"

The captain assured her that though Wendell was eating grapes, he was lying on the flat of his back, and did not look able to walk.

"Does he keep them down?" she inquired plaintively.

"Now and again," said the captain.

Amelia wept.

Chapter 12

Amelia Hears from Her Sister in re Hisodalgus, That Fine Horse

What you tell me, dear sister, of your Wendell does most amaze me. Now who ever heard that it was comely or fitting to put the kitchen-range into a haywagon, and surround it with what was well enough as a tent, merely to go riding for the mails, and so, in outlandish manner, keep himself from the justice of the frost?

In England we do not such things, and never yet had I my ear tortured by Hisodalgus for the calling of a horse.

Oh, my dear sister! I am fearful that with such a thinking man, with so many strange convolutions to his brain, that you fare but poorly of nights! What must your neighbours think on it? How insecure the suckling babe in those parts where the mother must, for curiosity, be flying to the window to see such nightmares pass! How can a child flourish on such scrambling nourishment? Nor can it be that the poor animal (I forbear to name him), be he ever so low of spirit, and spavined to boot, and handsomely jaded, takes it lightly, but must he not be forever uneasy and nervous and most frequently at a wetting? Now it does come to my mind that the poor creature, according to your account of the eighteenth instant, has already lost the freedom of his own prowess of nature to that extent that it can neither this nor the other matter, but your Wendell do dismount to pat and cozen him.

What state of affairs is this, my dear sister? For when an animal can no longer ease his mind at his far end there's something wrong in the way of the world. Would you make an heretic of him and have him ease it at the fore? Such-like it was, or I am much mistaken, which aroused the attention at Gomorrah. Demoralization may eat well into a man and the sun set and rise, but when it puts tooth to the nature of the beast, then were it best to leave that land. The Royal Guards, 'tis said, can be got at a pound the hour at either end— (thirty shillings with their boots on)—but they are men, not horses, and may be excused for their confusion. But that a woman, and she my sister, should put up with such malproportion, and so inverse her mind, is more than can bear thinking on; for when women do not know one end from the other, what can you expect of a man?

And speaking of women, dear sister, was there ever a woman made a good convert? Tell me your mind on this, for I would know your opinion. Mine is most terribly set on it that they are but poor at anything but that which they laid hands on in the cradle. And no matter how they do turn from their natures, it is with perfect intuition of where that nature is left, and with a backward looking. Not so is it with a man, for his nature is never of a certainty with him, because of his notions of chemistry and such logic, and when he leaves it, it is with a conviction (born of this philosophy) that he is stalking it. No such muddle can be in a woman, and I'll tell you the why of my conclusion: My last lady, whereto I'll go no more a-dusting and sweeping, turned from Catholic to Protestant overnight,

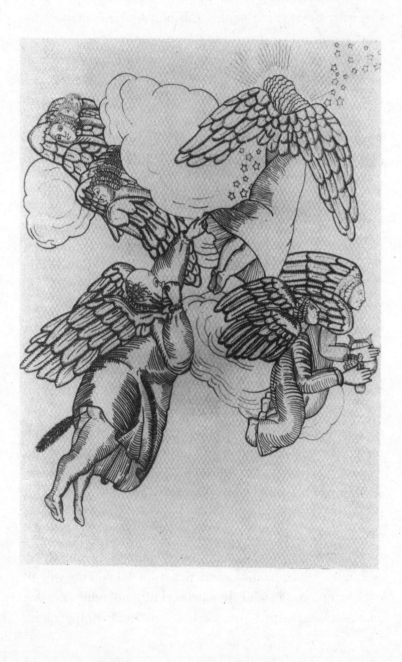

for that she had bedded with dissension in the shape of a pair of heathen breeches, and I heard of the matter as she sat upon the commode. Now, imagine a new-blown Protestant sitting upon a sempiternal pot managing aught from her converted bottoms that would give pleasure or relief to those parts that had been Catholic all the days of their life! Nay, but she must sit upright to achieve a trifle of heathenage, and would turn upon it with a killing gaze and a nocturnal farthing dip, to see if it were of the same mind. Now I know, as I sit here writing to you, my dear sister, that she would stalk herself back to bed most well divided, for change your mind from this to that, the pot doth remain faithful to its first leanings. And she might sleep in her truckle bed as converted a Protestant as another, but she would be Church of Rome to the last smell. So there's no wit in a woman thinking one thing and doing another.

Yet still more am I amazed at others about in our good London, for that they have become so frothing furious on matters of no account, which they hold as advancement. Our friendly Mrs. Chubble, who used to be most happy to sew a fine seam, now strides about the conservatory of Manor House, knocking over the plants, her hair on end, her bust extended, farting like a bull with trumped-up fury against the restrictions of home, and she, who never laid her hand to a thing, what with a host of servants and money to her chin, and ten men dangling attendance on her every want! It puzzles me most wretchedly. These people no longer believe in truth and have taken a winging to the side of destruction; nor are heaven and hell what they were, nor is there proper fear and reverence for death, but they must add or take away from the manner and custom of going. For an illustration of this, then but listen to what Horace Chubble said himself of the matter not later than last Shrovetide. He, being in fettle from much Strasbourg

pate and fine port and larded to the remark by the playful
words of the vicar, said: "When I die, my good friend, I shall
have a beautiful new pair of wings and a cambric nightgown,
and with a goose-quill in my bottom, I'll brush round heaven
looking under the angels' garments for duplicity."

Now, why the goose-quill, dear sister? It was not necessary
in our fathers' time. What new need that I have not heard of
can make it of advantage now?

I think, an I had talent, I could write an ode or a philippic
of kinds on "Why hair turns grey and we are brought in sorrow
to the grave," for somehow we have lost the instinct for the
good and narrow way, and go prancing about in a quandary
hearing things among the bushes that are not meet for us.
Those bent on heaven and those bent on hell have got fearfully
confused as to direction, so they do stumble into each other
on the way, learning things not fitting to their separate goals.
Therefore imagine, dear sister, where we will all land in the
end,—somewhere in mid-air, no doubt, for that we are fit for
neither place, and a dreadful sight is that space between two
stools, where Mr. Chubble can be heard remarking on goose-
quills to my lady—who at the very moment might be in the
act of saying her beads—and the two planned for a different
destination all the days of their lives.

I doubt not but that in the end they will go mad of that
uncertainty, for the one has robbed the other of hell-fire—
which presumably may have been dear to him—while he on
his part has snatched away her dream of felicity—which may
have been a life-work with her.

As I employ myself long hours on the vanity of all things,
dear sister, I sometimes come to the ravelling end of myself,
and must chew the stitch until there is no stitch for chewing,
so but write me of thy Wendell and what he has taken into

his head to do these last few weeks. It makes a tough meal for my ponderings, and lasts me many days. So if you write me but often of that man, I shall not tear my brain to bits upon itself, but shall have stout gobbets to fling it an it get ravening.

Thy Most Devoted Sister.

Chapter 13

Midwives' Lament,
or the Horrid Outcome of Wendell's
First Infidelity

And died so—in pitched child bed, ere the North
Gave up its snowy custom, and came down
To waters in the heavy watered sea,
There turned to roaring on the sands of her
Who died as women die, unequally
Impaled upon a death that crawls within;
For men die otherwise, of man unsheathed
But women on a sword they scabbard to.
And so this girl, untimely to the point,
Pricked herself upon her son and passed
Like any Roman bleeding on the blade—

Chapter 14

Sophia's Last Will and Testament

Last will and testament of Sophia Grieve Ryder Alexson, penned upon semi-pink butcher's paper of raggled cut; the Swedish scissors with the filigree butt, representing heron, feet and claws, the points thereof the bill, very unpleasant to the thumb when thrust therein and pressed upon, to gain the proper purchase necessary, being employed for that purpose. Dated March the ninth, 1897.

In the event of my demise, sudden or timely, I, Sophia Grieve Alexson, née Ryder, wish to be interred and laid within,—after the appropriate interval has expired, for the coming on, passing by, and leaving off, of my friends in their sorrows, serious and less picksome,—in a deep, slightly shelving, well-dug section of "Dear Reason" Cemetery.

The coffin to be of polished box, with a convex lid (explained later) six feet six long, three feet wide, and of a depth of five, with hinged section in upper portion of slightly convex lid, inset with a heavy chamfered plate glass, a scroll thereunder of silver craft, the initials of myself and my husband, Alex Rudolph Alexson, therein bitten. About, upon and around the coffin, a fretwork, chiselled deep, representing calyx, stamen and pistil, and neatly disarranged closed books, with a frieze at head and foot, portraying the convolvulus at hazard with the hawk.

The tomb-piece to be lasting but simple to withstand the lichen and inroads of time and climate, with the inscription: "Here lies Sophia Grieve Ryder Alexson and Alex Rudolph Alexson, in death as in life, but a little parted."

A weeping Greek or Athenian surmounting all, leaning on a lachrymal urn, draped in the folds of a double-skirted cloak of grief.

The laying out of our separate and collective bodies (for who shall hint that we die not upon the same hour?) thus: My right hand (with the heart-shaped bloodstone ring on the index finger, gift of the King) to be placed upon him, the said index finger to be depressed inward, and slightly touching, as the evening star rests upon the finger of the dawn. My left hand (with the worn, thin gold band of bondage encircled) to be placed palm in and about that part of him which **********, as the evening star rests upon the finger of the dawn. The left wing of my nostril set toward the right wing of his nostril, that our breaths, never passing, may have but the one road. Our feet made straight (though alas! not foot to foot, as his six feet four and my five feet one preclude such a possibility—need I assure my executors that this is not our inclination, but nature's, the irremediable misfortune that intervals them with a difference).

Alex, breast to my breast (mouth, nose, etc., disposed of *a priori*, as must be evident to the hardest sceptic of the most ferociously cavilling mind, that no otherwise could it be, without contortion and miscarriage of nature), his right hand (the ring finger thereof encircled with a dragon in fine silver and set with emeralds in mouth and tail), to be placed upon the half of the side that sees not, the index finger (or finger as may be particularly specified and requested, according to the mandates of his most exceeding nice taste—and feasibility) touching * * * as the evening star rests upon the finger of the dawn, his left hand to be placed, palm in **********, as the evening star rests upon the finger of the dawn (as per request).

Between the heart of him and me, the photograph of myself and of himself to be placed. That photograph representing Alex as a Moorish noble, swept about with a double-lined talma of Isabella velvet face, holding a distaff (mine own), a bit of slub depending. I in basque with shoulder-knots of lace and brazil braid, side face, with a swail pin in single mastery over my ear-locks and abundant youthful mane.

On and about our persons, rings, ear-rings, bracelets, neck-laces, coral as well as amber (they'll look never so well on another), the briar-mouthpiece to his horn, the Swiss move-ment watch (inset with rubies), and such of our private effects as seem unlikely for the quick (I have made it a fine point to collect only such, for what should be so personal as personal-ity?). The tear-jug from Smyrna (though methinks 'tis no little touched with pinchbeck), the collapsible drinking-cup from Pisa, representing the Leaning Tower (whereon I did piss me in time of travelled need), the crystal seal, the pearl-handled knife, the pear-shaped paperweight, the oblong-shaped paper-weight, with the falls thereunder, the platinum paperweight with the Virgin and Child therein intaglio, slightly indented and eroded by the prying blade of said knife, in an endeavour to discover how much was of platinum and how much base lead. The Swedish apron, the Moroccan slippers, the cashmere pelisse, with warp of silk and woof of wool, the *pince-nez* with the gold chain and bow of enamelled silver, presented to me on my natal day by my granddaughter Julie; the brooch with the Scotch agate greyhound head, the horse-head cuff-links, shoe and whip surrounded, the carved bone beads, the beads of painted wood, precious testimony of the love and veneration of my grandson, Timothy, made by his own childish hand, and presented with the same, in the flood of his youthful heart. The ring of bone given me by the hand of my second son, Wendell, first intended, and carved with painstaking lust, that the utmost aboriginal satisfaction, due the women of his house, might be rendered; the red and black worsted bag knit by Amelia in her hours of travail, and the ladle-shaped silver tea-spoons (my mother's) valued for the teeth marks therein placed by the biting mouth of my first-born, Aaron.

Should any portion, or the whole, of the congregation be moved to song, let him or her or them render such portions as they can recall, or supply, of "Allan Percy" or the "Soldier's Lament" (my most favourite), adding, for a *coup de mort*, "Shall I Have Any Stars in My Crown?" For though I believe in the Life Hereafter, and the World Everlasting, it is indeed grave cause for speculation, for in two that live no longer, there is a going away that we know naught of.

In after-life, Sophia looked upon this document with amazement.

Chapter 15

Who Was the Girl?

Who was the girl seen by Amelia long ago, as she leaned from her window combing her hair, now this side, now that, the girl with the mole on her lip?

Kate-Careless.

And who was the boy with the steam-engine, piston and rods, playing in the gutter directly opposite the house in Shepherd's Bush?

Arthur Edwin Dupont, Kate-Careless's younger brother, younger by two years.

And who indeed was this Kate but she who played the street-organ for her mother, the buxom contralto from Cork, the eagle-nosed Señorita from Cork, she who heaved beneath "Non e vero" in the streets of London, all on a summer's day. For a great voice was in her, beating against her heart and her lungs, a windy brute terror, tearing and strumming the nerves and the arteries of her body like some monster plucking a prison of harp strings and singing, divinely and terribly, against her kidneys, so that she could not take her rightful place on the operatic stage, but must stand athwart the gutters, singing and ***** like a stupendous hound dog, and her child sitting beside playing tra la la, la la!

The same child, Kate, who played the part of a drummer in the Haymarket, come Thursdays and Saturdays; come Tuesdays and Wednesdays, a consumptive in the "Bells of London," and wearing on these two and several occasions a drummer's pink tights, slightly soiled and mended at heel, trunks of shot silk, in pale blue, and a thirteenth- century troubadour's cap with a pink ostrich feather buckled in front and sweeping around from left to right, where it hung down over the lobe of her closely-set pearl-tinted ear. Yet again: a long, tattered and rent grey garment, secured at the throat and wrists with pale bands of the same, girdled with the ravelling of the same, and accompanied by folded hands and stressed, mathematically arranged groups of coughs.

It was queried, was she a virgin? But the matter was not known, though be it said that the dresser had her opinions, and was quoted in the recess of many a girl's memory as having said, on one wet and gloomy day, that there was not one unshaken matrix in the company.

No one rose to deny it with clenched hands and with quivering haunches. Kate herself was creaming her neck, and may or may not have heard it, for the odour of sophistication was hard upon the Haymarket, and some have said it descended not a little way into the street.

Her home life was between her mother and her father. (Her father was a Pre-Raphaelite painter of the sea.) At times it seemed that the two were not united in lawful wedlock.

Does it seem to follow that Kate-Careless was a bastard? It would seem to follow, and yet who can tell how craftily a child makes legitimacy prey upon her condition?

She was not truly clannish and loving of her family, in that she left this struggle between good and foul to her sister, who

polished boards in a mahogany shop of antique furniture; for Kate ran away, consequent upon the closing of the said timeworn dramas that so long had claimed her histrionic art, with a painter of landscapes whose peculiarity was thatched cottages in and around Richmond, done in yellow water-colour, with an over-layer of sepia, with high lights on gutter-pipe and window-pane.

Has it ever been verified that she was married to him then or later? What matter it, for she left her sister the whole of her uncertain background.

Who enters in and pries where such a mating takes up its lying and its rising in a house-boat in Lake Erie?

Pleasant it was for her, for she entertained, and pleasant it was for him, for he drank. But for them it was not pleasant.

He drank from a leaking bung. This is the ware she set before her guests—who inquired but lightly for him—service from High Holborn of a white glazed background and thereon roses in tiny confusion. A chocolate-pot, tall standing, and six cups and saucers thereto, a bread platter and twelve great dinner dishes, three tureens with melancholy lips and braided handles, eleven soup plates (the twelfth fell overboard for that the chinchilla grew too hot in her pursuit of milk therefrom), a gravy boat and jelly dish painted with craft, and a delft fruit bowl with hectagon sides manoeuvring to a round centre, where gleamed a pansy. To say nothing whatsoever of the fish platter and the game plate, nicely depicting death in kinds.

By night she went boating with her choice into Lake Erie, and there argued suicide. Whether it was that she grew weary of catching him from among his breeches and about the collar, and crying on the number of things that she would see no more, or he should drown, or whether death had lost its perspective, is not known, but early in 1897 she gave up boating

and came to live with Sophia Grieve Ryder, then residing in
Storm-king-on-Hudson.

Here indeed lived Sophia Grieve Ryder with her second
son, Wendell, and his wife of ten summers, Amelia de Grier,
in a small log cabin of two rooms, one above the other, in the
pine woods of the hill directly north of the large and palatial
mansion of Sophia's first born, Gaybert, who was a doctor, and
who lived with a German woman, illicitly.

Lived Sophia Grieve Ryder, lamenting her second best husband, who had been turned from on that day when he was
found striving with the back fence, and a wench between him
and it.

Oh, sorrow that troubles her, troubling others! Lament, ye
many waters, lament, ye mountains and trees, and the grass
thereunder and the roots unseen! Lament, ye fishes of the sea
and birds of the air, and cattle ever going over, and mole ever
going under! Lament, ye dark cisterns and wells of well water,
and gutters to the rain, and pitchers at the spring! Lament,
all lachrymose things, milk of the breast and waters of the
mouth, and waters of the eye, and all waters that hang in
skins and all that lie in skins, and all that falls downward from
heaven in skins, and all that cometh up out of the earth with
a little moisture, in many shapes and in many ways! Lament,
ye women, coming and going to and from man, for Sophia
Grieve Ryder, struck down amid the little flounces of her drawers, with the stroke of uttermost lamenting that her true love
has departed hence and forever. Lament for Sophia Grieve
Ryder, all ye sisters who have, and who have not,—knowing
the consternation thereof, and the loneliness thereof, of things
that were known and are known no longer, in their peculiar
pleasant way of that knowing. For Sophia Grieve Ryder has
shut her garments, and her doors against her necessity, and lays

herself upon her bed, and weeps sorely for the sounds, and the odours, and the warmths that have gone elsewhere, with their known and exact quantity. Lament for the high window that is not looked from, and for the darkness wherein, unseen, Sophia Grieve Ryder lies, knowing, in that obscurity, the shapes of all things. The paperweight with the falls thereunder, and the seal of crystal with her name inbitten, and the penknife that was by him given, and the morning-glory camisole, and the nasturtium slip, and the little slippers that know her feet not. Lament, all ye of this earth who have wanted and have got, and have wanted and have not got, and have known likings and have lost likings, and have cast away, as the snake casteth its skin, the shuck of the heart and the echo of its words of love forever!

Lament for Sophia Grieve Ryder, who sits like an army that has no victory and no defeat, and no dead and no living! Lament for Sophia Grieve Ryder who has strong life yet a little, and many days that shall eat from her marrow the pleasant decay of her trouble, and who shall go forth yet again with her shadow unshortened!

Chapter 16

The Coming of Kate-Careless,
a Rude Chapter

In due course of time, we say, Sophia, as was her wont, seeing Kate's distress in the matter of her house-boat and her husband who could not shut his mouth except upon a spigot, asked her also to call her "Mother," and in calling her mother—which she did with excellent swiftness—what but a step was it to entering that little log cabin in the hills of Storm-king, known to the Ryders, Amelia, Wendell and the two children as home, and there to stay.

The Ryder cabin was fifteen feet high and twenty-nine feet wide, and was of hewn pine and had steps three to its stoop. From there the house was all at one look, for it was but a single room with a loft and a ladder that let down for the climbing.

Now the furnishings were this way. Two beds downstairs and two beds upstairs, and a large stove and table and four chairs. There was a broom and there were dishes, and on the wall one picture of Beethoven and one of Schumann, and the ladder that went up in the midst was of hewn cedar, by Wendell cut, on that day when he had gone with his axe into the forest, that he might know his loft.

Into this doorway came none but Amelia at eventide when she had charred the day out below in Wendell's brother's mansion (for at this time Sophia was stricken of a farewell to her Alex, and could not move to support for grief). Amelia had taken up the task of providing for the family, for could it be put to Wendell who never, since the days of his drugging, had been as a man should be in the pit of his stomach? Thus into this doorway came Amelia at night, Wendell at all hours, Sophia when she was not weeping, and Julie and Timothy when the broken china—which they excavated from the ruined backyard—had wearied them with subtle speculation. And one day, in at this door came Kate-Careless.

She wore a herring-bone bodice of dragon's-blood cashmere. At the throat, high up under the ears, a knotted satin bow. Her head was a waving paradise of feathers, among which winked the cunning eyes of a jet buckle. About her waist, coming down in a magnificently achieved V, a belt of mohair, buckled with the hat's twin. Her skirt, tucked and stitched to the full of the hip, fell from there in flounces to the prunella of her boots. Kate, at this period, was beginning that certain but imperceptible drifting toward stoutness that foretold a swelling chin, a bulging hip and, in due time, a bouncing belly. She came smiling.

"And this is Kate, my new daughter," said Sophia, and "this is Kate indeed," said Amelia, remembering her well, as she wielded the besom, and "this is Kate," said Julie and Timothy, not remembering at all. "And where is your father?" inquired Sophia, and came in, Kate following, breathing, smiling.

"That you may know your destiny!" said Wendell, and they all looked up, Julie looked up, and Timothy looked up, and Sophia looked up, and Amelia looked up, and Kate looked up, and beheld Wendell standing as he was born, one foot on

one side and the other foot on the other side of the trap door
of the loft which was three feet by three feet, and the ladder
drawn up, and he leaned a little over, and laughed, and the
eyes of Timothy came down, and the eyes of Julie came down,
and the eyes of Sophia came down, and the eyes of Kate came
down, but the eyes of Amelia did not come down.

"My God!" she said, and her eyes came down.

And he stood away and disappeared, and Kate sat down,
the feathers in her hat shaking, laughing and crying, saying:
"You have it very comfortable here."

Chapter 17

What Kate Was Not

Might Kate-Careless not have been Kate-Why-Not, living, perchance, in the very heart of the city in a sumptuous apartment, such a *tour de force* as accumulates about a woman only an she is curiously ill-fitting and irritating to her surroundings, as coral forms about a dangerous coast?

Would Kate-Why-Not have been long and oval and slumbrous, moving with a decorous indiscretion through her kitten-littered domain, coming in contact with every object in the place, as a beast comes in contact with everything on the way to death, to seat herself at the hand-painted spinet, and there to thumb out, "I like a silly girl, thinking it no harm," or some tune as racking to the flawless virgin instrument?

Would not this Kate have admired herself in every mirror as she went, stumbling and magnificent, toward every cuckoldry that put itself in her path, and having come a cropper on the littlest man, have whelped a strapping child, and have been thereby in need of the tailor's bodkin and needle, and when well sewn, have smiled away the evening through which walked in desolation her true husband, dubbed as he went his dizzy course adown the boulevards, "Master Seven-Stitches," by every clerk and butcher's apprentice? Or drowsed behind plum and apricot, while he drifted, never-to-be-the-same, through the long cold aisles of the Greeks in the museum, standing now and again in a daze, his eyes fixed upon some prehistoric and pristine pelvis, until his very fixity of absorption gave him back his reason, and he moved hastily on, before he was observed?

Might Kate-Careless have been Kate-Why-Not and yet have been Kate, dying as she lived, a pot of wanton roses by her side, watching with eyes that put no definitions on nature the amorous turtles in the garden walks, or calling in a goalless voice to her mating doves, or singing, "I like a silly girl, thinking it no harm—"?

Indeed she might!

Might Kate-Careless not have been Kate-the-Doll, symbol of virginity, the nation's ideal? With a head too large for the body, and close-matted aureole of curls, adored and honoured and revered as only angels are revered, honoured and adored for their unity of pale locks?

Do not all men, in evening trousers and in brick-laying jeans, worship at the font of the golden and the pointless?

Would Kate-the-Doll have raised her eyes in one socketless sweep, simpering beautifully at all empty things, and have been by them replenished, as is the strict law?

Given an empty beaker, would she not have quaffed and have become drunken; given a flowerless stalk, would she not have dipped her little nose thereto and have breathed "A rose! A rose!" in ecstatic syllables, thereby throwing all men from earth's end to earth's end to their knees with something of religion and painful lust, religion's breakwater? Given a corpse for lover, as empty of its man as the veriest bisque, would she not have clasped it to her bosom and have cried: "This is love!"? And would she not, in lying down, have given up the ghostless ghost with wide eyes, lashed and open, and have been buried and mourned and loved and acclaimed and honoured and worshipped and set up in every heart's niche, sweating corruption no louder than a toy?

She might indeed.

Might she not have been Kate-the-Whirlwind, the wench who committed nature on its own scale, preserving the past in the fumes of a voluminous depth, that nothing might remain surface, but have a terrible thickness also, herself suffering increase of herself, until she burst every gusset and placket, pouring forth abundance, and no tiny blood?

Might Kate-the-Whirlwind be pictured in love-bed, taking to her loins not man but braces of the breed, bearing not a child but littering children, drinking no cup of wine but the vintage of the year, and in dying saying, "We die!"?

Indeed and indeed!

Might Kate not have been Kate-the-Kick-Up, the merry wife, the laggart abed, the strumpet of care, tumbling to sleep head over heels, flinging her pants off with a heigh-ho, the cat and the fiddle, plundering like a thief, wet to the hips in waggishness, a bacchante without a breech strap and a "Here, my jolly gentlemen, drink, for naked you came and naked you go, and it's nip and tuck when you'll pass this road again!" Her house a pantry, with vigour's watermark bespattered, her heart racking her breast, her blood coursing visibly in her veins, leaving a high tide, her bowels like machinery thundering, her house booming from her within, and in dying, hear you not her shout to those within her house, "Wind the horn, my merry huntsmen, and chase me down to death, for I'm a long leg ahead of you!"?

Might Kate not have been Kate still?

She might, she might!

Might she not have been Kate-Cast-Pot? Pouring out of an upper mullioned window of that hostlery now known no longer by its rightful cognomen of "Ye Charmers All," but as "God-Bless-Our-Home," the brimming vessel's contents upon the periwigged pate of some good father of the law but that moment thinking deeply on the case lately brought to his attention, of a bawd who had snitched sixpence of excessively jugged hare, which she levitated from the stalls of some fine caterer between four and its quarter, and whether justice called for the utter extradition of said bawd, who was by birth half Welsh and half of Ireland's briny soil, for she was bom supine upon the boundary (she said, having little exact knowledge of matters pertaining to possibilities) of the two countries, thus giving her, she testified, the only uncertainty of her otherwise down-right life, viz., to wit, whether or no her middle was good No-man's Land, or All Souls', and held to the latter with a tenacity becoming, etc., for, said she, when in doubt, give the gentlemen the benefit, and upon the perry-coloured contents trickling down into the very roots of his wig, and thence into the grain of his bow-knot (now become a watered silk), did with poignant nervousness decide that all strumpets, wet or dry, should be soothly sent to hell, for what they did was no better than what they did not, hurling imprecations as he raised his eyes aloft, in an endeavour to fathom, with his mal-treated judicial intuition, which of the said windows was that from which the fair Roselda had tossed that she had deprived herself of to bestow on him (is not this the greatest virtue?). Seeing nothing, however, but a pure maid reading from a great morocco tome (from which dangled markers of red and green), he did decide that it could not have come from one so devout and of so scholarly a turn, though it was Kate-Cast-Pot indeed, capping the jest by seasoning the act with learning which, 'tis said, raises a joke into the realm of tragic humour so venerated by the Greeks, thus proving her no mean candidate for a fish of another water in her next incarnation, which as a matter of fact befell her within the six months, for she died shortly, five gall-stones paving her to the deed, and by some backsliding of nature she turned up as a *marchande de poisson* (was the sea created first, or the fish, or the fish vender?) with an odour *tout le temps* of deep-sea matters and changes, digging among the tide-fickle sands, for the bearded Sea-dog, the while she dreamed, as good as another, of a château (for this incarnation found her a daughter of France, much to her sorrow, as in that particular epoch it was not democratic) where beneath Louis the Fourteenth lustres she could, in her mind's eye at least, clap a curse over on hoi polloi as good as another's. She watched the lustres' iridescent glitter reflected by the aid of a million mirrors from famed Venice, with eyes, ah, so different, from those of the cultured, who used to gather beneath them for a sweet quadrille or stately waltz, and being but what she was, of a hodiernal cast, she was nowise of that impersonal nicety of the better upper classes, who see nothing but what is to be seen, and therefore would never confuse the said points of light, cast off by the said lustres, with fish scales, as she did, for being of a vulgar mind, where their glint ceased she, in her imagination, carried it on ad infinitum, so that the fishy mica, and the glory of Venice, in icy precision, worked their way down into the butt of the tail in flawless intervals, ending only where she came to, upon perceiving her own hand grasping the miracle. Nevertheless were they not doss and dung, one and the same in the bowels of eternity? And so thinking, she set up a fish-stall within the confines of the ballroom, whereon she exposed the one to the rivalry of the other. And when one of her kind called with one of his kind, and all of them the same sort, she offered a mackerel, tail up, at tea, and so continued no better than she was for a good long lifetime, dreaming as best she could of that which was better, only to turn up once again as Kate-the-Swoon, or the Victorian-at-Heart, who by some determination in her former period, due to the number of conceptions she had laid herself open to, overcame the custom of childbed, but paid for it heavily nevertheless, for there was one nook within which had not listened to reason. She therefore conceived, one shallow day in fall, in the *tubus Fallopii*, and no phlebotomy nor continually applied febrifuge doing any good, came to her death, for to such refinement had her organs balanced (in accordance with the whole tone of her neighbours, who in that day were narrow to the point of prudery), that they were mere knick-knacks, and what could a child do, who had it in him to weigh nine pounds, and room for less than the full growth of a thumb, but burst the retort, and dying unborn take with him that which had so hemmed him about? Thus ended Kate-the-Swoon, until she was glimpsed once more, and for the last time, so corrected that twins might have developed unacquainted each with the other, had she not been of too brief a stay, for this time she was Kate-Careful, but a moment lent by the Lord, seen but once in a garden close snip-snipping in hempen gloves, etc., at the wanton brambles.

Might Kate-Careless not have been this Kate also?

Ah, never, never, never!

Chapter 18

Yet for Vindication of Wendell

Out of the troubled heart shall spring
A birdë loud on tautë wing
Of loneliness made swift and clean
To caw the wintry march between
Man and his difference, there bind
The bleeding wound upon the mind,
For somë lives are empty groves
Wheredown the genius pond'ring moves,
Nor any game were lost or won
Were not there blanks to count upon.
So thus it was Dan Wendell sought
The outcast queen bereft of court,
The fishë wife with wrentë hook,
The burning bride with icy look,
The trull, the slut, the wench, the bawd,
And every woman without cord
To draw or lead her by, and eke
Was to them all what all wives seek,
The certain move that Godës hand
Had left undreamt of when he planned

The die that cast dame Cleopart,
The asp's immortal counterpart;
The move that made Elainë's boat
Forever down the heart to float;
The play that made of Helen's face
Of its own time an endless place,
And castë Leda to the swans,
And in some eerie, forged the bonds
That hold unseen the nunës wrist
So, link on link, their prayers tryst
With hidden sighs, unspoke, unspent,—
Like dreamë dogs upon a scent
Go panting down the spirit's heel.
And thusë God, perchance for weal
Of women's lives lost in the fray,
Shoped Wendell for their ends to play;
For nothing's lost that may be found
In sea, or air, or underground.

Chapter 19

Amelia and Kate Taken to Bed

Towards five in the afternoon Amelia wept that she was again to be a mother. Her feet in a pail of hot water, she said to her daughter, Julie, "The birds are singing and caring nothing of the matter, and I shall die this time, and there's no doubt about it, my darling. Don't cry, for you were not a girl when I was a girl, and what can you know? Once I was safe enough and I could not let well enough alone, but must get myself in the way of doom and damnation by being natural. So take warning by my size and don't let a man touch you, for their touching never ends, and screaming oneself into a mother is no pleasure at all."

In the music-room Kate was in labour also. "The scavenger," said Amelia, ceasing her crying for a moment. "It was as I thought, when your father left me, nine months back to a day, he did not go to get firewood!"

In the upper field, Pat, the labourer, leaned on his spade, looking down the rows of the planting, and out into the pastures where the cows lay, a little cow within. Over the fields and through the fine air he heard the voices of two women screaming their children in, and through it the childish treble of Julie, crying, "Wendell! Wendell!" as she lay on her bed of playful maternity, aged ten, holding to her breast a rag doll thrown from the door to the immediate left by the strong paternal arm of Timothy, who was God and the Father.

Wendell walked the floor with his mother on his arm. "What is all this crying for?" he said suddenly, stopping and looking at her. "Why all this tumult?"

"You should know," she said, and took the turn with him from the fireplace to the door.

Up in the furrowed field, Pat said, "Hark ye, what is that noise?"

"Singing," said Timothy, "the heavenly choir."

"It's a damned literal and unsettling song," said Pat, and spat into his hands, gripping the mattock's heft, "and it seems to me that I, mother and father of ten, have heard it before."

"Is there to be a doctor?" Sophia asked, and Wendell shook his head. "I am sufficient," he answered. "Go to your mother," he said, and Julie went trembling.

The curtains were straight at the windows. In the corner a white commode glistened. On the bed Amelia, with her hair about her.

"This time I shall die," she said, and Julie, holding her head back, began to cry obliquely, and her mother turned her face both sides and wept.

Amelia arose, stumbling and gripping. "The Eastern women," she said, "sit to it." She searched, turning round and round with her terror at her waist. Julie's hands were on the rim, and she leaned her head against her mother's haunch, kneeling and sobbing, but in an instant Amelia was away. "I'll lie down again," and she lay down.

Timothy passed the window, whispering through the casement, and Julie said: "Run, run, run for Dr. O'Connor." And Timothy turned and ran down the road in the dark.

"Mary, Elizabeth, Helen," said Amelia to herself in the bed, "John, Henry, David? I always liked David, it's a sweet name, and I always liked Helen . . ."

Julie was afraid because it was named. She stood holding her dress.

Doctor O'Connor came on doctor's feet. "Where are the scissors?" he said. "And I'll need fine silken twine." Why was that? Julie brought them. He was in the trouble now, sitting on the edge of the bed.

Amelia turned her head toward him: "Shall I die?" and he said, "No, you shall not die."

Amelia begins to wander.

"I am a rock thrown down, and heaviness is in me. I am alone. I put my feet apart and there is no silence. (Amelia observing Wendell:) Is this not he, the very he of it? How damned he seems, yet all my hate's not his. I shall be fond of him again in some way I know naught of. Oh, most lamentable hour! It is not enough to be a mother, but memory must bear down also? (Sophia comes in with a lamp.) What does she here? Sophia, make a distance and stay within it! Leave me alone with everyone. What is this matter that kills me with his craft of being? And takes my very horror for his spy? Out then, mole! Who taught you a woman's body had a way for you? Why, now I'll be afraid of you forever, for this road makes me most aware of you. Now I'll forget you never, never, never, but be wound in with you at every turn. If it were an animal of sorts, why, death had no sting."

* * * * * * *

"Oh, peaceful nothing, I cannot think of it! When the young lamb puts its head sidewise forever, and the herd is

short by four feet, when the fish goes no more in the way of
fins, when the feathered bird gives back the sky his part in it,
and comes fast climbing down to earth, grieve they? Yet I shall
grieve, for melancholy is mortality remembered. (Julie stands
by.) And if it is a girl, why, then Helen's a name, a sweet one
I've had fancies for! It was she who leaned from out the bar of
Heaven and rained down the imperishable stars. Or was it not?
No memory is apt when there's not yet what shall be soon. 1
fall to weeping for the two bare heels that took me for a nest
to ripen in. Be not yourself a moment till I get that moment's
peace in which to think of you! You do not trust me? It is well.
No mother would be mother ever an she could, in mid-fight,
throw herself a moment out of scent, so I, like any soldier in
any war, cry loud, 'Long live that which can in no wise be
stemmed!' And love you that you forged the coin of hate in
my own mint, and stamped it with my name. Out, monster,
this is love!"

(Dr. Matthew O'Connor holds the baby up, slaps it
resoundingly on its most unaccustomed bottom, turns it over,
glancing) "A boy!"

Amelia (taking Julie's hand), "I'm sorry, Julie, I thought
a girl. If threats could have sexed it as you wished, it would
have been well terrored into a sister. Dear, I'm sorry then, it
is as it is."

Wendell, regarding it—"The babe is black!"

"Bile alone is father of its colour," said Matthew O'Connor.

"Oh!" said Wendell.

At this moment Kate gave birth to a girl.

Chapter 20

Amelia Dreams of the Ox of a Black Beauty

That night, between pains that did much rack and torment her, Amelia dreamed a dream. Now it was, peradventure, an effort, naïve in its way, no doubt, and circuitous, as is the way of a woman who would set a mighty wrong to rights, to get the black man the attention of the Lord, and a place in his mercies, she having been troubled with the way Wendell had said of her last, "It's black." It was also perhaps, and who can deny but that she had justice on her side, an effort to retake Wendell in his own colours. Further than this, surely no mind can go, remembering that Amelia was a girl, country-born, all the days of her life, and well rounded in restrictions.

Amelia in the grip of her dream.

There I was, looking through a prodigious great keyhole, and a great fine room I beheld, celestial in build and high conceived as a nave, and the bells in the courtyard ringing out from three sides and three distances where stood three towers, and one side silent.

And I saw a long mahogany bed and a woman therein

sleeping, with pleasant hands crossed on small pleasant breasts, her fair hair about her thoughtless face. (For who can say that a woman dreams of aught when the Abbey bells are ringing; surely nothing uncomely, for the lambs of heaven bleat forward and upward.)

A night-light was burning before a Christ with down-drooping sweet head, and way down-falling body. And there were much books in a wall shelf, on the history of mankind, to remind her the way she had come and the way she must go. And from a balcony, all in dear woodwork, hung many pennants of many peoples, still in the still air, and there the breathless slow waning moon lay. Before the bed were slippers of down, and upon the bed there was a down-enriched robe, and upon a stand there was a heavy Bible open over a little litter of women's things, in the eddy her body had made shedding them. And there were pictures on the wall of women going nowhere to nothing, with snood and long leaning throats and hands held loose for lack of sorrow, and there was one grand tapestry in even stitches of Friars going from nowhere to nowhere, holily, and one huge panel of Adam and one huge panel of Eve. And the floor was a great distance from one thing to another, and the maid slept.

Then the deep doors moved and opened, and a great fair ox of a Black Beauty came through, lifting his feet, and climbed the three steps. His fine apexed quarters threw a shadow on the ceiling. He came to the doorway and he entered in, and he turned not this way or that, but went onward a great way toward the bed, and there he lifted up his four hoofs and laid him down beside her, saying: "I am also." And she unclasped her hands and cried aloud, and rose up beside him. And he said, "Give me a place in your Saviour." And his shadow was over the ceiling, mournful and splendid. And she said, "Go away and do not try to defile me, for I have time in which to think, but you must labour."

And the ox answered her, saying, "Give me a place in your God, or I go to acquaint him that I am, and he will damn himself in me, for there is need of that also."

And she rose up from beside him, her hair all about her, and went toward the candle and the crucifix, and could not go, and she turned and turned about in the chamber, taking things up and laying them down, and the Beast saw how it was with her.

And he let his feet down and went forth from the bed, and stood before the crucifix and knelt upon his knuckles. A slow downward way a shadow moved on the ceiling, which was his head going inward and downward, and he spoke for her, saying:

"Remember the woman." And he rose up and went out, down the long steps of the chamber, walking softly and closely, and his shadow went with him, and his feet.

Chapter 21

Wendell Dresses His Child

And he saw that it was small and red, and that its flesh was dry in the ear and the navel, and between the hands and between the feet; and between the nates it did perspire and give off a heat and a sourness, and between the thighs it did perspire and give off a heat and a sourness, and between its mouth it was dry, and its eyelids moved neither up nor down without great trouble and clinging, and the belly of it was great and the back of it was small, and it neither cried nor spoke, neither did it hear when spoken to, nor jump when shouted at, nor show surprise in its eyes nor its ears, nor its mouth, nor its hands, nor its feet, nor any of its organs or limbs, when the hands or feet of its parents sprung or jumped or started back or forward, or in any wise made sudden movement or unforeseen activity. Neither did a finger, or fingers, wagged in front of its eyes, or its belly, or its sides, cause it to move, or start or to show apprehension in any wise, or to contract its mouth or its ear, or its eye, or its vitals, or the openings of its body, so that Wendell had great grieving for that it saw not nor heard, neither knew anything, but confused sorrow and joy, for that it was born feet first, amid wailing and crying and great lamentation, from the midst of its mother.

And he cared for it greatly, and let it come to no harm. He took the band for the belly, the four corners thereof and the sides thereof, amid the whole thereof, stretching it and rubbing it between his knuckles, that the stiffness and the roughness might depart from thence, and fastened it upon her, end for end, the one over the other, crossed and about, and pinned it with three pins of equal length, and it was lapped over and held closely. And he made her a diaper of the finest bird's-eye, and he washed it and hung it out in the sun three days, and saw that it was dry and sweet smelling, and he folded it, one corner of the four corners cornerwise, unto the second corner of the three corners, and he placed it beneath the nates, and drew the best end over between its thighs, and over between its loins, and pinned it with three pins of equal length, one over the navel, with the laps enclosed, and one above the right knee, with the one edge above the other, and one above the left knee, with the one edge above the other. And over its head he drew a shirt of exceeding soft wool, and fastened it with three buttons, that it might not choke, or ruck, or tighten, or cause discomfort of any kind, and over that also he drew a gown that reached three cubits below the feet, and it was of white stuff, embroidered with fine needlework and with lace, purled and feather-stitched in all their kinds, and this he fastened also with three buttons, that it might not choke, or ruck, or tighten, or cause discomfort of any kind, and upon and above these he set a woollen jacket with the arms therein thrust, of open-work and pineapple design, and fine knitting, and it was of soft texture, and of a pink colour, and he fastened it loosely, nor tightly, with tasselled cords of wool chain-stitched, he fastened it, that it might not choke or strangle, or bind, or ruck, or cause discomfort of any kind. About her neck he set a bib of quilted percale, fine-wrought, with crenel-work and beading, and this he fastened with one button, that it might cause no discomfort of any kind. And upon its feet he put socks of wool, fastened one to the right knee, and one to the left knee, and he took her up in his arms, one hand behind the neck and head, that it might not hang, or dangle, or lop, or bend, or break, or lean sideways, or back or forward, or know danger of any kind or kinds, and one hand he put beneath the nates that it might know support and satisfaction and cherishing.

And he walked with it from the fire on the hearth to the door, five hundred paces, and spoke to it, and laid it down gently, for that he had forgotten its head-covering, and he brought its head-covering of tapes sewn across and about, many ways, in warp and in woof, and strapped it beneath the chin, that the ears might not bulge, or touse, or bend, or be deformed in any way. And over this he drew a bonnet of lace, and insertion, and drawn work, and with a caul of great smallness, and roundness, and a flower in the midst, and he walked with it from the fire on the hearth to the door, five hundred paces. And the tears fell from his eyes continually, like to a soft rain, for that it spoke not nor heard, nor showed confusion in the muscle, nor the eye, nor the ear, nor the mouth, nor in any of the openings of the body whatsoever; that it knew not joy or sorrow separately, for that it was born feet first, amid wailing and crying and great lamentation, from the midst of its mother.

Chapter 22

And Amelia Sings a Lullaby

Once upon an erstwhile day
There was a moral to this lay,
So listen well, though long gone hence
Is any reason, rhyme, or sense!
Fol di ril de re do!

'Tis truth there was in London-town
A silly woman running down
And up again, as wild, as wild!
For that she'd lost her only child!
Fol di ril de re do!

The child was lost, and there's no doubt;
For when a boy's more in than out
Of this world's gate, what can one do
But push the rest of him out too?
Fol di ril de re do!

He, in other words was—phut!
Head-first in the water-butt.

And as the most of him was in,
(Indeed, naught dry but his small shin!)
Fol di ril de re do!

She with true philosophy
Made no cry how it must be.
Since he was all three-quarters lost
She would make whole at any cost!
Fol di ril de re do!

She struggled not with mighty odds,
For what is good three-quarter God's
Is God indeed! So down she thrust
the lagging heels. Now dust to dust
And boy to boy, made all complete
By simply pushing on the feet!
What had been almost now was quite,
Good night, my little boy, good night!

Chapter 23

Wendell Tells the Mystery to Julie and to Timothy

"Then the man and the woman, being properly wrought up, took each the middle value of the other, he bestowing a little instinct, and she gathering it into her, and presently it put forth a great head with great eyes and no feet and no hands. And time passed and there were ears and a little willingness in the flesh to be a mouth, and time passed and gave it feet and hands, and it moved with them, and came upon its mother in every place, and she was brought to great pain and to bed, and she was in labour, and her belly was emptied of him, and was delivered of him, in the time of cries and blood, and that which was a bond was cut, and there was wailing and no one anywhere, and it found the breast, and it was comforted, and it whimpered, and it slept.

"And its name was called Timothy.

"And the second time these things were upon the man and upon the woman, and she went apart again and continued to the ninth month, and was again brought to bed and emptied of that which was affrighted, and comforted, and which whimpered and which slept.

"And its name was called Julie."

Chapter 24

Julie Becomes What She Had Read

In which Julie is many children, suffering the tortures of the damned, kneeling at the parent knee, in all ages, all times and all bindings, becoming what books make of a child.

———

Is this not she, the fair Arabella Lynn, coming down the cold and pillared stair, past the potted, odoriferous cyclamen, in a chaste and colourless gown of equal length, upheld by a childish hand, on which gleams, in fitful starts amid the crepuscular gloom, shot with the intermittent gloaming from the sepulchral foils and interlacings of the night, a cross of water diamonds set in a sweet bezelled ring?

Is this not she, barefoot, and with ashy pale down-falling aureole of curls, that leap softly upon her shoulders, tinct with holy radiance? Behold the gentle profile, turned and raised, the sempiternal glow from the interspaced, multicoloured leaded window, pouring its fancy upon her questioning features.

Is this not the young Arabella Lynn herself, with smoking taper held aloft, wending to the parent knee, where, kneeling, she will ask forgiveness for her multitudinous sins?

'Tis she in very deed, but now observe with what pellucid eye she searches among the shadows for the familiar figure of her mother, awaiting her with humble knees apart. See how the very doves upon the ledge, a good ten yards above the terrene tumult, fold their feathers for the coming of the night, and move but faintly on brittle feet, awaiting the pleasure of the settling shade!

Observe with what clear intensity Arabella Lynn comes forward, the smoking taper high above her girlish head! How swiftly and yet more swift she homes to the harbouring knee! See how she kneels in her figure-haunted gown, and lays her bright head upon the waiting lap. See how the small hands cleave and go up, and harken, as she lisps her tiny sin! "Oh, dear God, make me a better and a better girl. Yet have I not deserved so great a boon, for that my heart is a morass of evil, and my daily life a pitfall and a gin for my wayward feet! How small I am (five years), yet how great already is my iniquity! In my puny way, I too have said there is no God! For casting of my red and yellow ball amid the leafy splendour of my garden I said, as it rose on high: 'Were there a God, the ball would not return, for 'tis so dear a thing to play with, and withal so choice, that even He could not forswear it!'"

Now hark! how the sobs rack the little frame, observe the heaving shoulders! The feet upon the floor draw in for misery! See how tenderly the mother hand comes down and down upon the bowed, repentant head.

Arabella Lynn lifts her tear-stained face. Imploringly she cries: "Oh, leave me, mother, to my solitude, that I may set my soul to its most necessary order!" How noiselessly the mother glides from out that chamber! Now, once alone, Arabella Lynn stands before the casement, looking out upon the starry heavens. What must be her certain thought?

"How small, how infinitesimal, how insignificant I am!" For there before her looms the glistening pack of night, a brightly brindled horde, hounding down the dawn. "'Twas thou, and thou, and thou!" they seem to bay, and with a stifled shriek, the immature, impassioned heart wails at this accusing scroll, "Oh, empty out thy stars, and let the sky, in unpeopled multitude, take up my case!"

Throughout that long night she tosses on her bed. A thousand thousand children now is she, her sins tenfold multiplied. The baby brow is pearled with anguish dew, and fearfully she starts and throws the coverings from her fevered limbs, and moans, "Accuse me not, it was not I, nor I, nor I!"

And starting from her bed in a wide-eyed somnambulic sleep, she walks the floor, her groping hand playing madly over the features of the host that is her sleeping self, within that thrall.

Poor tortured soul! So short a while was she to tarry in this vale of tears! Before the night was delivered of the day, she, all unseen, has crept thrice about the coping of that her ancestral home, driving the flock of likeness on before.

And now, behold! Ere she could breathe out a last and trembling prayer, before indeed she awoke from her troubled herding, corruption had set in, death's unpeopled army had laid its icy hand upon her heart, and claimed her one!

The frail mould that but a moment gone housed a thousand impulses now holds but the long impulse of death! Oh, mortal clay!

But pause to think, dear reader. Is this, perhaps, not best? What might have been the dubious outcome of longer tarrying? What foul demon might have weakened that structure had it reared into full womanhood? What sin might have battened on that edifice, dragging it down into inevitable ruin? It is better, ah, far better, surely a thousand times better, that Arabella Lynn died while yet in bud! How comforting for her parents, the thought that this their daughter was snatched away into the great storehouse of heavenly tutelage before she had known stain of a baser world!

Now see the tiny casket decked with twining leaf and helix tendril, with lily of the field and Alpine eglantine, and harebell from the dale, being borne to its last resting-place, followed by an hundred little girls!

Ah, what a picture for the beholder! The long file of white-clad children in their smallest laces, with three-button, white cotton gloves, therein holding the diminutive prayer-books, the fair head and the dark bowed together in immature grief. The black shoes with the shin bones rounded, the fluttering pale ribbons at wrist and waist, the solemn octave of their falling feet, as they wend to take their last look at the waxen face amid its cambric, with downshut eyes and hand upon the silent heart. Arabella Lynn, the bell-wether, with her following flock!

Does not everything wear a muted aspect this bright spring morning? The very flowers hush their noisy trembling, the trees move no bough, and the birds warble but falteringly! Yet no sooner is Arabella laid beneath the unthinking sod than the thunders roll! The rain bursts in all its fury! The elements fling themselves across the mountain in epic sorrow! The heavens crack asunder, and the valleys are inundated! The fig tree fattens on the rain, and the fruit is whelmed!

Hark to the hurrying feet of the mourners! List to their fluttering voices, a treble this side of maturity, as they cast troubled eyes aloft. In the earth is the fair Arabella laid, and the living look upon the day!

Julie Grieve Ryder, Julie in multitude, follows that little body to the grave. It is Julie now lying on her bed, it is Julie snatched up and flung down into the market place, where they are selling Jesus for a price. It is Julie all horror, and terror, and great history. She becomes the shudder of the condemned. Her feet are all soles turned up, and her hands all backs for agony. Every man's heart is in her mouth, the bowels of the world kennel in her belly. Echo and its voice, screaming the scream incredible, comes homing to her throat The shadows of fore-shortened destinies fall down from about her, and pray beside her with the head of a man, and the head of a woman, and the head of a child, and the head of a beast, and she stands turning among them, her own thickening at their knees.

And is snatched up again and leans, all voluptuous sixteen, from the flowery casement, her young bosom warm to the warm sun. The doves cooing in their dovecot are not more innocent than she. Down she looses her hair as though it were the molten sluices from the gorged parapet melting in the noonday heat, flooding the garden, covering the roses with a web of brightness. A thousand birds sing in ecstasy for all she has yet to learn. Love shall be, never being, and life shall go ahead, a fine queen on a black-rumped mare, forging and breathing like a man; or in the dark of some forgotten close, life, like an idiot girl, smelling of neither puberty, shall finger the hem of her reverses, and count one, while, in the under-brush, and through the hot hedged day, a rabbit fleetly paws the earth, harkening the weather's inconstancy, and the chang-ing of the leaf.

Again it is Julie amid the children. She is the total of their running number, and they become mothers and are laden and are large, and the embedded face some this way and some that way. The little girls have little girls' heads, and little girls' hair, and it comes curling, and their feet are children's feet, balanc-ing a child. And they are falling slowly, this way and that way falling, silent and soft and docile, scourged and blasphemed;

rising and drifting sideways and over, uncoiling their destiny in a close sleep.

And the company grows old and they whisper among themselves, and Julie lies and looks up at Wendell, and Sophia running, weeping and crying: "Do not strike her, do not strike her! I had no daughter ever, and she is that daughter!"

"Keep her," says Wendell, "she is none of mine. Did I not hear her deriding me greatly?"

Chapter 25

Amelia Hears from Her Sister in Regard to a Pasty

The snows are here, dear sister, and the Thames is risen so that the House of Lords will soon be sitting in water, to say nothing of the inconvenience it will put them to for the comfortable framing of the next measure. It may set them to hurrying, in which case something may turn up this generation, and not lie over for another, and now I think on it, I shall pray for rain, to see what I may see, who have long waited.

A pretty matter came to my attention last Thursday week (I keep myself well travelled in mind). It is abroad in our good London that one of the Royal German family, the distaff side, while in Berlin, sent out for a pastrycook to make her up a Sunday pie, that she might be proud to set before her lord. She ordered it well crimped and browned, with a citron and gingerroot-rose atop, and in circumference no greater than three feet, to have filling of the choice parts of the hog, the foot and ear, the collop along the spine and a bit of the snout, garnished with parsley and winter apples.

What think you came to the eye an my lord had put a knife

thereto? Seven cuckoos, all in rank, and a sprig of mint on the breast of each!

Then was a to-do (for it did smack of cuckoldry)! My lord rose up, 'tis said, and looking on his seven sons (they do hold dearly by boys in Germany) wept aloud, saying to each, "Thou art none of mine, for I have seen a vision, and in it I have been as good as told that thy mother is thy father also!" No words beyond this can be torn from him. Those of the household who had temerity wandered up and down the corridor leading directly to his suite, but it is reported that he do say nothing now this week gone but "Alas and alack!" and sometimes varies the matter with "Tra la la la!" and "Fiddle-de-dee!" returning to "Alack and alas!" Which do prove his mind runs the gamut of misery. Do you dish up such things in your country? I think not, for here is the hub of the world, and you lie westward, and such things never spin loose, saving when at the nearest point of the greatest possible activity. Nor is this all the news (I am by this post mailing you two of our journals). I read much, for my bunion gives me pain; I can hardly set my foot to the floor, and never has that bunion hurt exceeding but the news had risen in like measure to a fearful climax of impropriety. 'Tis said that an old wound mourns when it is about to rain. Let me assure you then a bunion is the very weathercock of the morals, for when I do ache to the unbearable, at that moment you may be sure that in one quarter of the world or another some man or woman has run his or her head into a hornets' nest; if it is not your Wendell or your Timothy, or the horse Hisodalgus, then it is some king or citizen who takes up the case in the most outlandish of places, and I hear the echo of it in my bunion. Now I read that a fisherman in Sicily has netted a fish with a human eye, that a child in Wales was born with the foot of a kid and the foot of a lamb, and another paper do

say (though I put little stock in it, as it is not a church period-
ical) that pulp will give out, and that we will have to write on
something else in the near future. Well, let me tell you then,
dear sister, I have a good set of linen whatnots, a dozen of
cover-alls, and ten tidy cambric napkins, so while I've aught to
say, say it I will, until my privates are public, for I do believe to
the bone in freedom of speech, and in indignation to the last
pair, so you will hear from me, paper or no paper!

I have got me a new situation since last I wrote, and I cannot tell what I shall do, for I cannot yet see my way clear as to
what course to pursue. My lady is blind of an eye, halt, and
suffers a maggot in the joints, and though vast with gain, is
most stingy close to both the housemaid and myself, to say
nothing of her nieces and nephews, who come every Friday
to inquire of her health. Nevertheless, once a week, regular as
clockwork, my lady does drink a flagon of port, and becomes
immediately most boisterous unruly (though weekdays she is
as prim spoken as you could wish), so that I must sit me on
her right leg, while Susie, the housemaid, do place herself on
her left leg, and cook holds her by the shoulders to prevent her
from dashing herself against the priceless marines with which
her wall abounds, or carving out her temple on the leg of a
chiffonier or an Italian oak, which are beset with grape-leaves
and knobs of all sorts, such as they used to fashion with loving-kindness in the days of the Borgias and the Cencis. Now
should I sit and hold, or should I stand and let go? Abandon
her to her furniture, or listen to her tirade of wicked fancies?
For she do go at it with a will, and do laugh herself most
wantonly, and sets out to recount all the malpractices of man,
inventing most of them herself, I warrant me, for when she
has concocted a dreadful mire; thereinto does she drop the
most excellent personages, such as Roger Bacon and Alexander

Pope, and suchlike, to say nothing of what she do say in regard
to good women, like our Florence Nightingale and the queen
herself, if so it please her; until my very hair stands away from
my head. So tell me what you would do in this case,—to hold
the leg or not to hold? For though nothing can contaminate
a pure ear (as well I know), I am by no means for plaguing
that instrument, and so perhaps surprising it in a moment of
apathy, nor do I believe that Susie, the housemaid, is much
the better for it, she is yet young and wild with days, and what
must the poor girl have in her head after an hour or more of
such raving! 'Tis no wonder that on such days (Friday) her
beds are not fit to lie on.

In your last, you wrote but thinly of your children. Do
embrace them for their aunt, and tell them to mind their
mother, for this is the last generation, I take it, over which
anyone will have control whatsoever. So make the most of it,
my dear sister, and kiss or box their ears, as the case may be!

Your devoted sister.

Chapter 26

Kate and Amelia Go A-Dunging

"Owls would have hooted in St. Peter's choir
And foxes stunk and littered in St. Paul's."

———

It was a sweet spring morning, once upon a time, many, many, many years ago, when the two women, Amelia de Grier and Kate-Careless, went, as nature would have it (there being nothing new under the sun), upon their four feet to do up the dirty mess, and damn their infinitesimal-lime-squirting-never-stop-for-consideration-of-a-woman cloacæ (and she with the backache and the varicose veins climbing her legs), or whatever-you-call-the-backsides-of-a-pigeon, and to look into the matter of the eggs and casualties.

Up the dusty stairs they went, besoms in hand, a flower between Amelia's teeth, and with stomachs crawling (for alas! there's nothing new under the sun), into the thraldom of feathers, and there, strutting and cooing and bill-begging, round and round in a dance of death, went Blue-Wing and Sweet-Tuft, the metal rings on their twiggy ankles knocking out a convict's tune against the imbrication of their feet, round and round in a merry pigeon lust, squirting trouble as they went, and smelling most hideous insufficient, as is the way with a bird.

"Their young are most gruesome, and die by the million!" said Kate, as she pitched three out of the window. "And can you," she added, seating herself upon a log that Wendell had hewn for a perch, "tell me the reason that Wendell has fancies and we have the cleaning?"

"Most simple easy," said Amelia, piling up the dustpan with voidance and grain. "To man is the vision, to his wife the droppings!"

"Droppings, is it, you call it?" said Kate, perspiring. "Sometimes I'm angered by the use you put your British to, were you never at * * * * * ?"

"That I was," answered Amelia, still busy with the litter, casting a look of disdain upon her lounging co-worker. "And I may say it pleases me not at all in man, but that it pleases me mightily when it's done off an animal, for the thoughtless dunging of many birds is somehow a rest to my mind."

In the corner, two thin oat reeds in thin water went. Amelia leaned down: "Planting his grain in a dovecot," she said. "What will become of that man? In grave-clothes hurrying to the tarrying earth, and the tarrying stars, to give up his hurrying body, a little, not at all, forever, amen!" She came down the dusty length of the garret, pan in hand. She said:

"In the beginning was the jungle, and there you had turds of some account, beasts paying back the earth in coin new minted. And the Lord be praised said the trees, and the Lord be praised said the green grass, and the Lord be praised said the creeping vine, and the Lord be praised said the great rush, and the Lord be praised said the small rush and the lily and the buds in general that we know not of. And pray for us, said the great rush, and pray for us said the small rush, and pray for us said the great trees, and pray for us said the small trees, and pray for us said the short grass, and pray for us said the grass that was not yet, and down thudding came the supplication of the wild beasts. But what," she said, "can prevail now that we put floors and pots beneath it, and the mammoth goes down never from behind, but only man going head foremost, offering a word. And what is there in a word that is magnificent or of help to the land?" she added.

"Sometimes," said Kate, "I wish you were the mother of my children, for you have good fancies. Tell me yet more of the condition of the jungle before man, though how you know about it is more than I can understand."

"I never had much education," Amelia answered, "so the jungle was never scratched off my heart. Listen then. In the beginning was the jungle, with thick flowers and thick leaves, and the roots of things went down into a heavy tiger-pawed earth, and on the branches sat the puma, duke of the morning, and through blood-red lilies went the wild cat, and the slender-hoofed deer, and wild cows, whose teats had never served man, and the bellowings and the trumpetings and the roarings and the screechings, went forth in one sound that was a band of strength against the unknown quantity that was, one day, to be the slayer. There time rotted on the stem of night and day, and the water ripened on the branches of the ocean; there with weight of unseen swift flying, making terrible his feathers, came the nightbird through the thick groves, and clove them as oil is cloven and records not the break, and stood and pecked and pecked softly and swiftly at the earth that trembled under no footfall of man and, pecking, went his way, with little speckled feathers dwindling into the dark. And now," she added as a conclusion, "Wendell has a dog at heel and a floor beneath his birds, so you can't expect but that we'll have the dunging when he has such faulty fancies."

Chapter 27

The Beast Thingumbob

"Fish," said Wendell, "are cool and firm like the handshake of a friend. Let us go fishing."

So forth he went to the fishing, Julie and Timothy beside—a long net in case there were crabs, a box of matches on the hip, and a good dozen leaves of tissue, for Wendell would never be taken unaware.

Down they went along the sandy shore, lifting their feet hard and setting them down, Ryders all, and a wonderful time it was when little Julie, her three-ply stockings off and laid aside, and her skirts rolled up, and her panties crotched to sticking, went in wading and cried, out of the fear of maid-for-the-waters-of-the-world, "Oooooooo!" and flapped her arms and bottomed backward into the brine, feeling it come up over her with a round edge.

Made reed whistles, too, did Wendell Ryder, slipping the white wood out of its slippery bark, Timothy talking of the other days of his life, the one for instance when, moving once more, as was a Ryder habit, the van had overturned and Kate's machine fell into the roadway with all four legs in the air, as if to say, "My working days are over, and I lay me down to die,"

that was in the evening, and Timothy, in his Lord Fauntleroy, jumped up and down, screaming: "There she goes!"

Wendell presented a whistle to Julie, and she drew forth a long wailing, and went fiddling on it as if it were a thing of beauty. "That's no way to hold it," said Wendell, "and why don't you keep step?" And away he went, walking, tearing, at the pot of crabs and unhooking my-ladies'-chamber from their insides, and, "Come here and see," he said, and Timothy got there first, putting his dark head down to see, so that Julie could not see. And "Oh!" he said, and "Oh! she is sitting on her throne, and she has yellow hair!" And Wendell said, "Yes, that is the ladies' chamber."

"Now tell us a story," said Julie, as they sat on the bank, smelling strongly of fish.

"Once upon a time, then," said Wendell, never so well pleased as when idling away his life and making his offspring wonder at his fancy, "there was a great beast called the Beast Thingumbob, the same that slew the lions, that sought his life, by rhythm, as you may remember. Sitting on the top-most branch of the tree, he sang, 'Around and around and around,' to a neat measure, and around and around went the lions, as you recall, and died in the sleep of dizziness, all at the foot of the greenwood tree. And the Beast Thingumbob climbed down, the great basin of his head boiling and sending off a triumphant smoke, for that he had once again murdered the murder in others.

"But this story is about another day in the life of Thingumbob the Beast. For love was clinging to him, in his hide and his hair and his blood and his bone, in his claws and his heart, and in his boiling thoughts, and shone down from his eyes like flakes of fire. And it is a complicated thing," said Wendell, "when a great Beast like Thingumbob suffers the pangs of love, for it has no planned way, but must go what way it can.

"Now he was stricken for the love of a strange creature indeed. All through the hot night in the top-most branches of the greenwood tree, where was his nest—for he had wings, you remember, as well as paws, feathers as well as fur, and compassion as well as wrath—he dreamed of her whom he loved. And this was the likeness of his love: she was, as he was also, of large limbs and of a beauty outside of the imagination and quite beside what men would call the point. She was terrible in her ways, which simply means that her ways were not our ways,—and she was fettered to the earth for a season of harvesting, after which she was to return to the gods. Her feet were thinly hoofed, and her hair was many coils, and her face was not yet, and her breasts were ten.

"Now," said Wendell, "she was not virgin as other women are, or to be reckoned as other lives are, neither had she birth as we have, for many æons of moiling and fuming about in fur and feather, for the underworld had fathered and mothered her, one and the same, so that she had no seam in the soul, either on the one side or on the other side, as we have, so you can well imagine what the tasks of love for Thingumbob might be, for only a heart turned constantly in the fire of passion could undertake it, and not faint by the wayside.

"She had a valley of sheep and a valley of kine, and a little land where the goat was, and tilled earth beneath her. Above her, wherever she went, a thick covey of birds went also, crying, 'Vanity, vanity, vanity!' that she might be put to remember, in all parts of her forgetting body, that she too must some hour lie down all at once, and know death, for between her time to go and the time for the going of man and beast, was ten hundred and ten years. So that the passing away of man and beast was of no moment to her, for that they no sooner said, 'Here am I,' than they said also in the drawing back of their breath, 'Here I am not.' So it was said of her that she knew not pity, and very likely it was so," he added, "for pity is a matter of getting your breath between the 'Here am I' and the 'Here I am not,' and her breath was by no means as short as ours, but took a long way, and there was death laid on death about her, between the taking and putting, and no one has pity who has time otherwise than our time. So she was called 'the Cheerful.'

"No one had brought her a love of like years, so that she knew not what men said when they spoke of it. Thus was she a virgin, but not as other women, for because of these things, she had a greater share than any mortal woman could bear or possibly see to put up with, but to her the putting up was no great business; she had never thought of the matter until it was timed to her necessity, and that was when the love began to boil in the head of Thingumbob the Beast. So it came to pass that, when he spoke of the pain in his head and his heart, his hide and his wings, his blood and his bone, she said, 'Come to me, for I would talk with you.' And when he was come, she said, 'How am I to know that you have my love for me?'

"And he said: 'How shall you not know?'

"'Verily,' she said, 'this is the best that I may know. Then promise me a promise.' And he promised her a promise whatever she would, and she said: 'Promise me that you will bury me, then I shall know that you love me and are built of like years and one year stronger.' And he made promise, though the light of his eyes was as water.

"The rain came down steadily and softly where her orchard was, and her wheat and her corn, and there was no barbarity in it, yet the grass went down slowly before it, and the grapes gave it bosom, and the vine bowed, and she called him to her, and her coiled hair was many hairs going down, and there was a skin on the floor, and feathers on the floor, and the scythe forgotten, and she stood forth, and her past went backward from her, where the Beast Thingumbob was in that immense place, and where were horns of cattle, and antlers casting a long shadow, and grain scattered in the stalk, and an odour that was of love running hot among pelt and horn and wing, and the smoke there was thick. And she said to him: 'I began a long way before the beginning of your love, and there's that in my blood will cry halt when your blood but gets the whip, and go whining down a thin wind, while the tempest is yet another man's; and bed in dirt when his feet are lifting, and rot, when he is thinking of to-morrow.' She said, 'I shall die beneath you, yet from my body you shall garner ten sons, and they shall be harnessed of terribleness, and you shall bury me quickly, for I am burst asunder at their way within me, for they come marching, and I rejoice and go from this hour no further.' And she charged him well, saying: 'When you have dragged them forth by their iron locks, smite them with rain-water, and put my name on their tongues, and tell them thenceforth nothing of me, nor picture me to them in any way, saying, "She was tender-hoofed and her breasts were ten." For I am, and soon shall be as I am not, and they must know no deception. Nor cut their wings on the right side, nor cut their wings on the left side, nor metal their hoofs, for they are shod of me, at the forge of my heart, and they are.'

"And so it was that Thingumbob rose up in the dawn and plucked his sons from her belly, and carried them to his nest, and there daylong and nightlong he sits above them, the smoke of his sorrow boiling above the trees, his eyelids shaking under, for he knows her gift to him was the useless gift of love."

"Is that all?" said Julie.

"Isn't it enough?" answered Wendell.

"And what does it mean?" said Timothy.

"Well," answered Wendell, "much and little, like all wisdom." And he got to his feet. "We must go home now. We will go through the new sewer pipes before they lay them, for they are dark and mysterious, and you will like them." So down the dark tunnels of glazed ware they went, and they came upon a pair of dead green-grey trousers and a green-grey coat, and a pair of boots and suspenders. "Some tramp starved to death, no doubt," said Wendell, "turned up the white of his belly," he said, and moved on.

That night Sophia read aloud to them, as she always did, Wendell lying back on his spine, saying, "If there's a death-scene, skip it." Otherwise he would cry, the tears streaming like a woman's, as all men cry. "Ah, ah, indeed, here little Emily gives up the ghost," said Sophia, and turned to the next chapter. But that night, Julie on her breast, she read the death scene by the light of a round kerosene lamp, going word for word over the harrowing details, Julie's eye going over, too, but slowly, "'and here,' said Emily, 'take the needle from me, it is too heavy!' and she closed her sweet violet eyes and breathed no more—" And the darkness pulled at the lamp and at Julie and tore her away from her beloved while yet she lay upon her breast.

And the little seeds that go up and down in the dark died, and there was sleep.

And the cat jumped up on the fence, and from there into the bough, and the birds stood away from him and he leapt, and mystery took away the ledges and the places of the world utterly, and the cat fell, down falling, surprised, falling surprised forever, and no one to tell it to.

Chapter 28

If Some Strong Woman—

Dr. Matthew O'Connor was as nice and as good a man, and as pleasant spoken, outside of the confessional, as one would wish to meet. With children he was a jewel; all mothers whomsoever he had helped in child-bed swore by him, saying that he was a gifted creature, and as comforting as silk; and that his ways with the new-born were nothing short of magnificent.

"To see that man slap an unaccustomed bottom is a lesson in tenderness," said Amelia to Kate-Careless, and Kate agreed that indeed and indeed Dr. O'Connor was a man in a million. "For who," said she, "would rest content in the occasional acts of nature, if that man were not about to draw the rascals from their hiding-place when they are ready and willing to speak their parts?"

Molly Dance herself was not backward in giving him his due. He had helped at the birth of her last three, and each time he had said, "Molly, Molly, Molly!" (as everyone did). "And who, my dear, sent this infant down the road this year?" And she answered him as she had always answered, "You shall be father to it in spirit, for you've taken more trouble with it than its own. It's not the fox that sends the hare down the rabbit hole that is prized, but the hound that brings it out again by the scruff of its neck."

Dr. O'Connor was gentle with animals. He loved Molly's kennel to a dog, he stroked all cats within range, inquiring of every woman in a twelve miles how her young sows did, and how her ducks and drakes, and all women smiled to see him coming, and shook their heads as he departed. "For," said they, "such a pattern of the virtues should have him a wife."

One day, sitting over a dish of tea and a buttered loaf, Amelia broached the subject. She looked long and hard at the trees in the orchard that the doctor might set his intuition in order, then she spoke: "Matthew, it's time that you were assisting at the birth of your own, for never saw I such a man for loving-kindness, and such a way with little things. So if some good, strong woman . . ." But she got no further, for Dr. Matthew O'Connor had burst into tears. "It's always been my wish," he said, struggling with his emotions, "to be called Hesper, first star of the evening." And with that he arose and went away.

Chapter 29

The Psychology of Nicknames

In which Wendell gives his version of Amelia's courting.

———

"Nicknames," said Wendell, "give away the whole drama of man. They fall into many classes; the three most current are: those we invent to make a person what he should be—or names of persuasion; those we invent to make him appear as he is not—or names of cunning, and those we invent to more tightly wrap him in that which he is, and these are as various as our opinion of the person involved. Let us call them nicknames of opinion. Take my own case," he continued, "for philosophy, like charity, should begin at home. Let us tell then, the story of your mother's first reactions to your humble servant, and we shall have a case in hand. It will instruct you in the nicest turns and twists of such games, for and against, that you can think of, to say nothing of the abundant humours therein involved. It will be more to the point," he added, "than whole dissertations on nature, and will round out the inevitable end as you know it.

"During this soliloquy, heed well what she does, and what she does not call me, for therein lies the whole mad obscurity of the female heart. Observe where she might have mocked and did not, where again she might have placated and forbore, how, again, she might have had me swollen with pride, and spake not the word. Indeed, she might have said a number of things—but, enough!

"Love, 'tis said, has been known to bloom at first sight. Be that as it may, your good mother, to become better acquainted, pulled me down from a wall in Shepherd's Bush (for our yards adjoined) and here," he pursued, "be it recorded that she had never looked me in the face, but, seeing something in my posterior that tempted her to play with the future, she gave me a goodly jerk, whereupon I found myself sprawling, white rats and all (I was very fond of them)—on her side of the coping.

"'Bottoms-up!' she cried. I liked her well, I was never one to hesitate. I went to the business like a carpenter's apprentice, who, having learned to lathe well and to take the round, manages the subtler niceties of jointure.

"'Braggart-the-Britches!' says she, 'All-Woman's-Thumbs' and 'Bird-of-all-Bushes!' and any number of catch-words that I have lost from the bottomless pit of my memory, and very sorry I am for it," said Wendell. "So then I laid about me in other ways, and catching her soundly about the waist, kissed her fairly.

"'Pluck-of-my-Luck,' she cried, 'Try-Again-Thomas, Hot-Put-and-Hurry-o!'

"Now she might have said any dozen of things more to my liking; there are some that make a better creature of a man, but she kept at it in this vein, a scavenger, tossing words about my head like so many cudgels.

"'Hands-Off-My-Hard-Up,' and 'Babe's-Beginning-Spill-It-Less-Lightly,' and 'Trust-Not-to-Trifles!'

"Put to it, however, my pride and my possible prowess yelping in kennel, I continued the matter. 'Penny-Be-Priceless,' quoth she. 'Weigh-Yourself-Short-Pound' and 'Wrench-Away-Willie.' Here, scoring a little, she panted, 'Heigh-ho-ho-My-Hearty, Where-Away-Marching,' and 'Much-Beating-no-Music!' Till I liked her none so well, and would have desisted, yet hear now what came of the turn, for now she seasoned her scorning. 'Can-You-or-Can't-You? Will-You-or-Won't-You? Weary-Me-Kindly, Work-and-I'll-Worry, Upward-and-Onward, Tarry-No-Longer,' and 'The-Way-Is-Dark-but-the-Way-Is-Short!'

"So," continued Wendell, crossing his hands in his lap, "the play progressed, and within six months her burden had altered to windward again, as you shall presently hear. Now it was 'All-Women's-Gammon, Tip-Toe-and-Watch-Out, Hold-Breath-and-Short-Wind, Sneak-and-Snatch-It, Short-Work-of-All-Wenches, No-Woman's-Forever!' etc., etc. Thus the tirade rose, but life," said Wendell, "makes even a woman's fury weary a little and come down. Now she sighed where she had raged, 'Mr. No-Change-for-the-Better, Mr. All-for-the-Worse,' and 'Two-in-a-Bed-Makes-Four-in-a-House,' and 'Four-in-a-House-Makes-Eight-Eyes-to-Water!' Yet at times the smoke of her indignation rolled up thick and choking: 'Slogger-the-Beastie, Shaft-Pole-of-Cod's-Withers, Bedridden-Bertie,' and 'Teat-Drunken-Tom!' Yet how arrant is a woman's temper, for at times she murmured, 'Sweet-Driller and Dear-Damage!'

"In time, an a man and woman live it out to the bitter end," said he, unclasping his hands, "one of two roads is taken by the heart, and it goes, slowly but surely, in one of these two directions—wisdom or religion, so that she chose wisdom, and called me nothing all day but 'Oh!' and 'Ah!' saving in times of real anguish, then think you what she called me?"

"I cannot," said his listener.

"'Wendell,' just 'Wendell,'" he answered, "for all things end where they began, tail in mouth, like those little fish they serve to pretty gluttons."

Chapter 30

The Cat Comes Out of the Well

At times, of a frosty morning, when some woman buttoned her child into his coat and cuffed his ears and told him to run to school and learn his lessons like a gentleman, the idea came with the cuff that on the Ryder farm, called "Bulls'-Ease," there were two women who could eat their porridge abed, and never have to see to buttoning a thing, if they did not like the idea. For what sets the mind on duty as fast as the thought that someone has less trouble than ourselves, be it in buttoning or unbuttoning? Therefore, every six months or so, some farmer's wench soundly abused Ryder to her spouse, saying that Ryder's children did not go to school at all, but licked up comfort at home, growing more and more ignorant, probably developing, in their teacherless state, strange unscholarly notions which, in the end, might lead them, one day, to commit an unlettered and slovenly murder. The wives railed, and the school authorities, who had tried not to notice the delinquency, because it's easier to pretend ignorance than to sweep it up, were forced, by the growing discontent, to hold meeting and to question Ryder on his whys and wherefores.

By dint of much moving about the country, Timothy and

Julie had grown up without once setting foot under the lintel of learning; but well caught was Ryder with six yet younger. Some of them were, and others would be, ripe for straightness of curriculums before the mortgage on "Bulls'-Ease" fell due, and he could pick up his bed.

The authorities thought the matter over, for the cries of indignation had swelled along the valley, and some say it had even gone so far, and grown so bad, that, of Sundays, the phaetons and buggies that passed by on the way to church (the main road cut straightway before the Ryder farm) were whipped up of horse at this point with such fury that the animals leapt at the bit and whirled past this iniquity in a cloud of dust, on iron feet, speeding into the distance as if hell were buttoned to their cruppers.

Wendell, sitting in the bow window as they passed, went carefully over the score of a new sonata in quick time, whistling, "Swing Low, Sweet Chariot," but he knew the smell of the fumes rising from the pit, and set himself to think of a good way out.

The day was set for the castigation, in the autumn, the hour, four, the place, the school. The school-house stood on a hill, the culmination of seven roads. A village green lapped around it, the smoke of the smith's forge griming its windows. It stood, a blind mole of earth forgotten, leaning a little on its foundations. It was cold, it was ill furnished, the station-master's stove that stood in its centre never glowed. The blackboard was a smear of spit and errors, the books were tattered and falling into decay, the crayons of Washington and Lincoln, flanking the teacher's rickety desk, were fly-specked and warped. The only window looked out on the privy, and the privy gaped, doorless, its double-seated grandeur two black pits, the wood carved over with hearts and arrows, and successive generations' initials twined therein.

By two o'clock the seven roads were blocked by carriages, dogcarts, buggies, wagons and cultivators, anything that a horse would draw. By three, there was not a tree on the green that was not laced with reins, not an inch of turf not stood over by lean and sagging mares and geldings. By four, when Ryder drew up in his van with Hisodalgus in the shafts, there was only one seat left, his own. Ten deep at the windows faces peered and pressed, to hear the account that Wendell would give of his vagrant non-attending offspring.

It might have been the flood, for women in homespun held up their babies that they might see this monster at close range and be duly stricken, men whispered and spat, and slung themselves from left to right in their anticipation. The forms made low for children of five and ten saw great bony knees rising up to bearded faces, and black authority sat on the nearest form, looking upon Ryder, as he sat calmly upon his spine, his lamb's wool collar about his ears.

"Ryder," said the authority, eying him, "there is a grave charge laid to your door; your children are growing up in ignorance."

"Do you know," answered Wendell, irrelevantly, "what makes a man desperate and what makes him happy?"

The principal, turning his eyes aloft, answered:

"Religion makes him happy, my dear friend, and ignorance makes him desperate."

"Wait," snapped Ryder. "Religion makes him a coward, and education, as you understand it, makes him a monologuist in the presence of God, instead of a disciple."

The representative turned pale. He said, "Do you realize that you are bringing up your children like heathen?"

"Do you realize," quoth Wendell, "that your heathen put your Europe into that bed which is not your history?"

"They will grow up," continued the principal, ignoring this

sally, for he knew not what to do with it, "deflowering women, and defaming God."

"They will grow up," continued Wendell, clasping his hands in front of him, "neither with buck shot in the one man's part, nor with hymns in the other, but weighted evenly with the goods of their mortality, casting their shot one throw ahead, and one only, like man since the beginning of the seed. We have but one throw, sir, before we put our face to the earth, therefore don't come trampling along that road trying to make scrub-oak of my sons' trees."

"Equally, sir," thundered the representative, "this is procrastination! Do you know that there are laws in this country, and one of them is that children must attend school?"

Said Wendell, "The Board of Education provides dates and speeches, half forgotten, of dead statesmen. They feel that they have done their duty if a child can render Hamlet backward, and the Commandments sideways; so I keep my children at home and teach them better."

"Letting them do as they please," said the voice of someone in the back, which was instantly hushed.

"With reservations," conceded Wendell, looking in that direction.

"It's terrible nerve-racking that," remarked a woman at the door holding an infant-in-arms.

"My dear madame," said Wendell, pleased to have a woman in his midst, "I kill my own beef, pickle it, smoke it. At first my daughter, she is a gentle girl, was over-fond of the sight of blood; she used to toss in her sleep; but now she has calmed down, her ankles and her wrists are thickening, her hair is abundant and blond. My daughter is simple and great, like a Greek horror, her large pale head, with its wide-set uncalculating eyes, is that of a child begotten in a massacre and nursed on the guillotine, in other words, she can live gently from now on. Who can say as much?"

The superintendent leaned forward, "And the boys, sir, the boys!"

Wendell sank lower on his spine. For a moment he regarded his public, the uplifted children, the gaping women, the crowding men. "Splendid," he said softly, "splendid! Timothy, the eldest, and Hannel, the youngest, and Elisha, the in-between. Timothy is morose. I can't say how he will be useful to nature, but he will be useful. If he had been educated, if he had lived in a flourishing city, if he had been a dandy and come to wear a fashionable moustache, he would have committed some common crime, suffered grossly and have been redeemed by some debased side path of religion; you know there are such. As it is, he knows just enough of beauty and of beastliness to understand that he comprehends nothing. It will take him, as it will take the others, all his life to unravel the tangle of his upbringing. As for Elisha, he is another type and though but a child is thin, haggard, ridden by the heel of music. When he grows up he will resemble those priests who have found God too cheerful, and every woman in the audience will change her position—at least once, for you see I have planned immunity."

"From what?" said the authority, who had lost colour several times during Wendell's last speech, as it was Greek and a tomb to him.

"Immunity," said Wendell, "from the common and accepted conditions of life, as taught in the parochial schools. They know both more, and less. I've taken my children round by the side path where the truth lies rotting with the refuse, and they already look down upon you from a height."

"This," said the superintendent, "in no way explains why they are not attending school."

"Of course," said Wendell, rising to leave, "if you insist, I, being but a humble citizen, can but submit, but I may warn you that Ryder as an outlaw is less trouble than citizen Ryder. And to illustrate my point," he said, "I will ask this illustrious company to go outward toward the well, and leaning over with a little of that curiosity which they now direct towards me, to scrutinize that cistern,—abyss of disease and filth. For as I came up I observed three rats and one cat therein floating, and if they think that a child can stand your system of education with the admixture of contaminated well water, why then, my children, as the children not of outlaw Ryder but of citizen Ryder, will not come to this school until you have dug and furnished a well of pure water; nor," he added, to the back of the superintendent, who was now the only individual not leaning over the said cistern's brink, "can I permit my daughter to learn of love as it is written on yonder privy ring. So, gentlemen," here he bowed, "Ryder, citizen or outlaw, as you will, salutes you!"

And without a word in answer from the man sent to judge him (for he was now being of the mob well judged and almost hustled off his feet by loud cries of damnation for the condition of the pump; it had been in no other for at least forty years, and unnoticed until that moment), Wendell unswung Hisodalgus's halter from the bough and, getting into his canvas van, turned that animal's head toward home.

And this is how the cat came out of the well.

Chapter 31

No Greater Love Hath Any Man

Saying, exclaiming, quoting. A chapter on Timothy, and how it was with him and his Light-o'-Love, for he also came to be a man.

———

Quoth Timothy:

I adore thee, my rabbit, my coney, my pie, my charm, my finch, my pudding, my grouse!

Quoth Light-o'-Love:

I love thee, my love, my cabbage, my heart, my loins, my hig, my hog, my jenny, my jackass!

Quoth Timothy:

My cunny, my kitten, my body, my everlasting not any, my sorrow and glory! I love thy heart, its beating, its tottering, its striking, its ticking, its going and coming. I feed on thy fingers, their bending and binding, their closing and opening, their nipping and pinching, their plucking and holding, their keeping and losing, their softness and bone!

The wax in thy ear is as honey, as spice, as unguent, as

barley, as truffles and cake, as mead and as sleep, as slumber and death.

Quoth Light-o'-Love:

Thy small gut and great gut, thy liver and lights, thy tendons and muscles, thy tongue and its roots, thy belly and backsides, thy hands and thy feet, thy faults and thy fairness, are as pity and pride, as love and as hate, as I do and I don't, as I will and I won't, as I shall and I shan't, as I have and have not, damned and undamned, blessed and cursed, one and the same to me always and ever! (and from the earth the moon set forth, travelling low—the great moon! The glorious moon! The moon for a man!)

Quoth Timothy:

I hate and I loathe and I love and I mourn thy body and soul. The old and the new, the dying and living, the sign and the symbol, the follies and foibles, thy good and thy bad, thy sick and thy well, thy ups and thy downs, thy riches and wants. Thy thickness and thinness, thy roundness and flatness, thy wet and thy dry. Thy hair and thy skin, thy fat and thy lean, thy gristle and gravy, thy blood and thy bone. Thy brightness and darkness, thy laughter and tears. Thy noise and thy silence, thy standing and lying, thy bending and straightness, thy sleeping and waking, thy gulping and yawning, thy sneezing and coughing. Thy holy unholy. Thy trust and mistrust, thy fainting and feigning, thy sweet and thy stinking, thy functions and laving, clean and unclean. Praising, blaspheming in fairness and foulness, thy tricks and thy cunning, thy real and unreal. Thy madness and saneness, thy courage and fear, thy queries and quibbling, thy all and not any, my Judas, my Jesus!

(The sickle moon stands beneath her, and she, Lily of the Morning, stands above the sickle moon, and about the sickle moon roves the heaven, and about the heaven is a great light, and in the midst stands the Lily, her feet upon the sickle.)

I know thee as harmful, as sick and unstable, as mortal and ailing, as deadly as death, as tough and enduring, as fatal as life. I spew and upgorge thee, I drink and devour thee, I hold thee and keep thee, I renounce thee and cast thee away from my heart. I close thee and keep thee, guard thee and lock thee, chain and imprison thee deep in my soul!

(And from the midst of the water she came roving.)

Exclaiming and saying, quoting and sighing, they stood far asunder and clove to each other. Saying and sighing, exclaiming and talking, over and over, forever a little.

(And the moon rose—)

Chapter 32

The Soliloquy of Dr. Matthew O'Connor (Family Physician to the Ryders) on the Way to and from the Confessional of Father Lucas

Mine's a good family, mine. Thirteen of us when little brother Felix, who had the St. Vitus, dashed off into the arms, celestial arms, of Jesus, Lord rest his soul!—rocked in the cradle of the deep—thirteen around the table watching him throw his soup up into the air, dumbfounded at the ways of God—ask not His ways, for thou understandest nothing—and the St. Vitus leaves you with no ways of your own, and thirteen we were, crying like pissants into our soup and breaking wind for the poor bastard done in and out of his joys in life, and all his roads stopped up with dust, and the thumb of Father Lucas, and the seven senses and the seven pleasures gone out of him, and the seven times seven corruptions, and there we were, the thirteen little O'Connors, filing behind the coffin crying like anything into our gloves and our sleeves and our wrists and our handkerchiefs and our scarfs, and sniffling our noses, and all the light gone out of us drop by drop, and the black despair

creeping in and in, and the sky coming down and down, and the shovel going about and the earth falling and falling, and the coffin going under, and there we were, Nora and Molly and Maggie and Emily and Lucy and Jacob and Patrick and Timothy and William and John and Sara and Susie and me, howling and crying and throwing our gloves in the grave, and saying our prayers and calling on heaven and earth and the earth's earth, and the heaven's heaven, one within the other like a stack of cards, and Felix shuffled between and gone down to his death, and us understanding nothing. *Dominus vobiscum et cum spiritu tuo, ad infinitum*, one out of many, in God we trust, and turning round and round getting out of the cemetery gate, and turning round and round getting into our own house—I go to prepare thee many mansions—and everything all different, and him with no ways, and the candles going up into the air, when I first came down the aisles swinging my tin hips, see me, Matthew O'Connor, holding my satin robe about my backsides, tripping up to God like a good woman, and me only seventeen and taking on something scandalous for the ways my sins were with me! And Father Lucas, bless him, a Moll of God he was, saying kind things this way and that into his holy garments and out of them, stroking his hugeous great belly and telling me to keep it pure, and me crying like a baby. And were you never brought up in the Catholic Church? he says and No, and damn your eyes! says I, I've come to it with a free heart, once a lady always an acrobat, and him breathing in the dark of the box, our four knees with each other for the glory of God. Look up, he says, and there you will see the Lamb of the Lord trampling out the small clouds and the great clouds and the indifferent clouds of heaven, grazing without sin, go thou and do likewise. I'll do that, Father, says I, and please Moses it's in my strength, but what with a dilater on my hip and the diseases and distresses and distempers of man, and what they are prone to, coming into my mind, and before my eyes, and me restless, it's a devil a bit of peace I'll get, says I, banging my head against the scrofula and the tapeworm and the syphilis and the cancer and the pectoris and the mumps and the gleet and the pox of mankind, I says, and me with my susceptible orbs staring down into and up through the cavities and openings and fissures and entrances of my fellowmen, and following some, and continuing others, and increasing many, and them swelling and opening and contracting and pinching like the tides of the sea, and me a mortal like the sea with my ebb and flow, and my good heart, and my thundering parts and my appetites and my hungers. And such a way to be talking Kitty, and his ears in the Lord's service and my tongue rattling off with the mundane things of the world and the forbidden fruit still suave in my mouth, for, I says, I love the upright father, though I say it with tears in my drawers, and it is anathema. Go, my daughter, he says, and love thy fellowmen. And me beating my breast and lamenting the ways of my extras. Go and live in God and trust to thy better parts, says he, and think no evil and no evil shall befall thee. Visit me often, he says, and I'll give you comfort and kind words and a little consolation that shall inch thee on thy way a bit, and bring thee nearer the Celestial Gate, slip by slop, cleansing your soul as you go, that you may not enter altogether dusty and dirty and mucked before the Judgment Seat, with its two in front and its two behind and the four sighing Holy! Holy! Holy! God save the behind, I said, and staggered out into the life and traffic of my days. . . .

Yes, Father, and please you I've done it again, and this time it was with Fat Liz, him as keeps bar in a gophered boudoir cap, and smelling all zig-zag of patchouli, and as drunk as a

lord, and saying his prayers so fast that he hoped not a sailor
in Salem would so much as catch his eye, for he was giving
his inclinations the grand haughty O'Farrell, and him mad for
the gremial and the faldstool and the lambrequin of the mass,
and the grail and the surplice and the host, Kyrie eleison! and
the way the robes of the saints pass up from the righteousness of the feet and go under the righteousness of the cincture
and pass away under the holy beards, and saying his paternos-
ters and crying his te deums in a roaring whisper through his
nose, because the bridge of it is all gone and eaten away by the
whacking snuffing of coke he's done come forty years past, for
the temptations of man are not as pure as they were, and, please
you, Father, adulteration has conjured away many a best joint,
and there was Fat Liz staggering off to the fifteenth round when
I caught his eye, and he has travelled not one bead farther since,
please your honour, for my ways let no man forge at redemption. And night long there was his soul and mine tossing and
tossing, until the great wave came and receded, and there was
nothing for it but to beach upon our stranded shoals, says I,
and both of us rolling our eyes and praying fast and thick and
trying to scramble back into the grace of God, out of sight and
mind come twenty minutes, and breathing like we had been
pushing each other for all we were worth getting to absolution
and control, please Father, Son and Holy Ghost, it was a terrible race! And us coming in neck and neck, looking for the
score. Go, my child, and thank thy Saviour it came as high as
fifteen, and the earth rolling and plunging and tossing men
into all kinds and sorts of postures difficult to recover from
and puzzling to tell the good from the bad, and our minds
milled and addled by the Devil, and our noses and our eyes
thick with the dust that does pour out of hell like a storm cast
down to the boundaries of perdition and over and beyond,

and no stopping it, for man, he says, is a twig in a whirlwind, and this goes past him and that goes past him, some stinking and some sweet, and his net frail and his soul torn, wherefore then should we judge thee? but, my child, try thou to stand in that gale and catch neither finch nor fledgling, neither bramble nor chaff, but cling to the pillar of righteousness, and shut thy mouth against the flesh of thy brothers whirled down the vortex of time, and lo! thou shalt come to the peaceful lands where everything rises in still air, and the sun does not tremble and the planets are not mysterious, and the word goes forth forever from His Heart in a single uncorrupt stream and returns not, nor knows seasons in its mercy. Aye, he's a good man, as sweet a soul as ever dashed his hips across this world, and his disciple is a good man, as holy a Bitch as ever trod on the tail of my satins, and I'll keep it in mind, and bless him all the days of him, and his do-nothings within his doings, and let no man cast aspersions on me, for it's a good roasting and flaying and nipping and broiling and spitting and basting I've got on me by my own will in the Holy Catholic Church. For him who has not that goal in his heart and that light before his eyes and that fume within his nostrils and that breath in his mouth, is a bitch's miscarriage, and I, Matthew O'Connor, tells you as much, and I'll wipe no table top with you for a yes or a no, but go, thou, and do likewise, for when I'm lost in my bowels like a little child crying against the great darkness of myself, I think of that glorious Moll, and the incense going up like birds unto the seat of all thanksgiving, and a great peace is in me and my tears are caught up in light and heat and expectation, and my feet go with me, saying, Matthew O'Connor, you'll come to no bad end, for I'm a woman of a few thousand gestures and a hundred words, and they are going one by one into the ranks of the seraphim, and amid the mighty army of the church, and one by one they'll fly away into forgiveness, stock and shirt and breech, redeemed into the kingdom of heaven, and who am I that I should be damned forever and forever, Amen?

The candles took root and grew and rose toward the ceiling, and bloomed and wilted and died, and the ceiling grew and mounted and bloomed and wilted and died, and came down. And the stars came out on the great pillars of the candelabrum, and slid with them and dwindled and flickered and stood once more about the bier, the soft bodies of mourners in woolly clothing kneeling. And suddenly the lights poured and grew and rained down in the Dead March, *Omnia ad majorem Dei gloriam!* The figures at the altar blurred, crossed, melted into each other; fornication of the mass, parted and bred Death, Death's wailing child in wax, lying in a bowl of wine, mouth open for the gushing breast of grief, pouring forth the Word in an even belt of wrath. The sacred cow swam the shallow chancel, a garland on his brow, lowing, In peace let him rest! The church turned upside-down. Sorrow burst and the seeds fell and took root, and climbed about the stations of the cross and bore Him down to earth, and climbed on and on and bore Matthew and Nora and Jacob down to earth, and Sara and William and John, and Emily and Susie and Tim and Molly and Maggie and Lucy and Patrick down to earth, and climbed on and bore their children and their children's children down to earth, and the children of them begotten, and were not appeased, and climbed and bore man down utterly, and stretched out and took his works and bore them down also, and there was Nothing, and this, too, they reached for and closed on, trembling terribly and gently. . . .

Chapter 33

Be She What She May

It stands to reason, be she what she may, the mother of one son does not dote upon observing the son of another in the act of chiselling the head of her beloved offspring, though it would appear that Kate's bastard, Elisha, at the ripe age of seven, could employ that instrument impartially, and with the impersonal touch so dear to the heart of the artist.

Having, therefore, one fine morning, raised the said chisel and allowed it to find its poise upon the sconce of Amelia's youngest son, Hannel, she straightway screamed the mother scream and, plunging through the parsley-field, between herself and this inglorious act, snatched Kate's son by the collar and thereupon smacked and cuffed him well, while, in a steely swoon, Hannel lay face down, pouring blood from his top like an overturned ink-bottle.

Had her own son chiselled her own son, there the matter would have ended, but aflame with the indignation that must lie in a woman's breast, no matter how saintly, when the thing is done of a mistress's chit, she saw the act in the light of a malformation of anger; brother could not strike half-brother with that straight justice that descends from like to like.

"Scullion's rat!" she cried, and shook him soundly, cuffed him both back and front, top and bottom, and left him mute and still impartial, while she picked up her own child and tried to discover how much of her force in him had been spent and spilled.

Kate was not far behind her. With shaking stomach (it was always that portion of her body that expressed the most lively indignation, for she was a common woman and common women, be it observed, always express the heights of their emotions in that organ), she flew into the contest.

"See what your brat has done!" cried Amelia, pushing Hannel ahead of her that the world might mark his disfigured brow. "See what a beastly likeness that child is of its parent!" she continued, as Kate opened her mouth to deny something or other, and could not for the life of her think what. "That son of yours, that Elisha, has chiselled my son Hannel, and for nothing whatsoever" (though she had not inquired into this matter, and spoke from partiality, though in this case she was quite right, there had been no provocation whatsoever, beyond an innate desire on the part of Elisha, to see what steel and skull would do when mixed in the crucible of holy experiment).

"I was looking from the window," lied Kate fearlessly, for she was a mother also, even though not as she should have been, "and I saw it all. It was not Elisha who started it, but Hannel, your nasty, bad-tempered son. He struck my son first."

"What with?" screamed Amelia.

"With a pitchfork," answered Kate as loudly, mentioning the implement that came first into her head.

"Then where is the pitchfork?" said Amelia, with scorn and fury.

"Probably somewhere in my son!" answered Kate, and so frightened herself with her own lie and its culminating

imaginative probability, that she swooped down upon the still
mute Elisha, and began feeling of him in all directions, asking
him where he hurt, and if the tine were "here or there."

And now Wendell appeared, walking calmly, as was his
wont in such cases.

"What is all this rumpus about?" he demanded, and could
not hear a word that was said, for both Kate and Amelia began
talking at one and the same moment; the pitchfork and chisel
were so altogether amalgamated in their destruction, that he
could make nothing of the explanation, but came forward
nevertheless, and seeing Hannel the most bloody (for Elisha
was quite unruffled and unhurt), cuffed the poor mortal so
heartily that he again went down, for to him that hath, etc.,
and said, "There's nothing right in this house, or on this land,
because of you and your children!"

"Who and whose children?" both women exclaimed at
once, not too sure which side of the fence he was on.

"Yours," said Wendell, "and you," turning to Amelia, "they
have your nasty temper." He took Elisha by the hand as he
spoke, Kate radiating sudden joyous triumph, and Amelia,
cold, stark Saxon quiet, in the face of rank injustice, when Julie
hurled herself from the house and, without word or warning,
locked herself tooth, foot and nail on to the bounding front
of the triumphant and mollified Kate, who swayed beneath
the impact. Clinging there, all her hair about her, sobbing and
digging into that mountainous flesh, for the touchstone of its
feeling, crying loudly and wildly, for she was but fourteen,
and full of youth and right, "You, and you and you," to her
father, as she set her teeth into that which he had brought to
the house to the torment of her mother.

To this added bit of tragedy Wendell turned a charmed eye.
Cockfight or dog-fight, woman at woman, he had a liking for

the outcome. So mildly he stood by and counted round for round, while Amelia darted hither and thither, trying to save her Julie, until, with a Spartan grasp, he caught Amelia by the apron and made her a prisoner and an unwilling onlooker at the fight, Kate versus Julie.

Now Kate was a large woman, and had strength somewhere about her saved for such occasions (for never did she call upon this fund in the doing of the housework), and though her greatest glories had been captured by leaning on her opponent (she weighed nigh three hundred pounds), she could not at this moment lean, for can a person be said to lean on a splinter that has entered her flesh, and there is neither tree, nor table, nor chair, by to help? So still clinging, though her shoulders had come out of her gown, and her young breasts were mortally exposed, Julie fought on, saying over and over, nothing more nor less than, "You, you, you!" to her father, for she looked not so much upon Kate as the disease as the manifestation of such emanating directly from her father, and so drew blood, and would, undoubtedly, have inflicted mortal hurt but that Kate, in a moment of torment (the reflex action, indeed, of a horse flicking at a fly), struck her arm a sweep under Julie's chin, and sent her sprawling.

Here came Sophia onto the scene, and much and mightily torn between love for Julie (for was she not her favourite child?) and her duty, and thus stood, wringing her hands and calling on Wendell and on Julie alike, and not daring to move.

Now was the whole household on the scene. Timothy, and at his back Kate's other two, Elsie and Aaron, and Amelia's other two, Gaspard and Gaybert and all talking and crying together, when, with the most stark and cold realism, for which he was to be noted in after life, Elisha spoke up, standing with his hands behind him.

"You are all liars," he announced, "and not worth bothering about. And my mother is the worst liar of all. I chiselled Hannel to see what would happen, and that's that!" And so saying, he walked slowly, his hands still behind him, from the field of action, leaving even Amelia speechless, for so much truth out of a child she had herself chastised a moment gone did not put triumph into her, but a slow wonderment, and turning her head, she did look so hard and long at Kate that Kate, abashed at the scene's ending and not well for anything further, demanded, "What are you looking at me for?"

And Amelia answered quietly, and wrung of anger: "To see what in you can have gone to the making of such a lad as thy Elisha!"

Chapter 34

They Do Not Much Agree

Wherein Amelia and Kate-Careless leave home forever.

———

After this thumping bit of bad temper and battle, Kate-Careless went banging into her quarter (or, as she termed it, in fury of frustration, "my share") of the house, saying: "I will leave this place forever. Skinny Shanks (none other than Amelia, dear reader!) shall never again have the pleasure of telling me where I came from, and where I may go!"

After this thumping bit of bad temper and battle, Amelia de Grier stalked off to her quarter (or as she termed it, in patient scorn, "my hovel"), saying: "I will have no more of this, there is a limit to everything, and I'll not live another day in a sty that shelters that great pig's-bladder (Kate in another dress, dear reader!) of a woman!"

The day, apart from the quarrel, was one of those glories of autumn. Such a day as is good (an one is peaceful of heart) to take up with a book; such a day (as one is distempered) to take a horse's back and clatter to the world's end. And so did

Amelia, on raw-boned Hisodalgus, the horse-that-stood-in-need-of-coaxing, for she had breeched herself well in Wendell's cast-off huntings, and saddled the creature with the first best saddle inlaid with raddled leather; and she set a persistent and nowise motherly rowel into the flank, sending up a spiral of dust.

As she rode she turned her head from side to side, as was a way with her. She was grim and cheerful to think how long she had bided at home, listening to falling china and strife of children and mistress, her too often laden pelvis, jogging softly and pleasantly with the horse's galloping, for it was a free and flat affair from now on, and would nest no more trouble.

Holding the reins slack, she thought of Kate-Careless with her walloping great stomach, likely as lording it for a season at home, and "Be damned to her," said gentle Amelia.

She rode by cornfields and past men at logging, and rose up on the hill top and went down, whereby she had never passed in fifteen years, and saw the reapers reaping, and one lonely windmill working at water, and the plough turning up earth-worn matter. She was well pleased.

She dreamed to such purpose that she rode into a bog, unseeing, where skunk cabbages flourished fitly. She hummed to herself (a bar of the "Spring Song" as it had been sung in the Conservatory), trampling down the jack-in-the-pulpits, jogging over the green moss, and the grey moss, all under the boughs.

She turned into the Park Road. For more than a mile it stretched away in a thin vanishing, and at its far end she observed a speck in a cloud of dust. Thought she, "A fellow traveller, and I'll ride by singing to give him cheer."

So she went to it thus:

> A ha'pence worth of grog, my lads,
> A girl upon your knee.
> This rhyme is slung about my heart
> Like a bastard to a tree!

Singing loud and long, with her eyes shut in a thin line, she had most come upon the traveller from the other direction and had, perhaps, passed him, but that, upon the ending of her ditty, one so like in temper cut athwart it, that she sat staring.

> A thrippence worth was all I asked,
> And this is what they brought me—
> A skinny herring to the house
> To snarl and snap and thwart me!

And there, posting by her, at a pitching gait, went Kate-Careless on the red cow, sitting high and rolling on the top of the bonnet-of-a-saddle that Amelia had scorned but an hour ago.

"God Almighty!" said Kate.

"I'll return the compliment in no degree whatsoever!" said Amelia, and there they came to a stop.

"Goat-skin!" said Kate.

"Pig's-bladder!" said Amelia, and with a lean leap came thudding from her horse. Kate in like manner tried to pitch herself headlong from her steed, but whether it was that she was too fat of instep, and so clung to the stirrup like a bride to the wedding band or whether she was quite unable to lift such great weight of shaking and indignant flesh, would be hard to say, but there she clung, bottom out, until, with fingers ample in their fury, Amelia plucked her forth and set her up before her.

"Now," said Amelia, "we'll have a fair fight for the first time in our lives, for you've nobody but yourself to fall back on, and one of us shall not leave this spot alive. If it is I that have the preferment, I'll hang your heart up to yonder pig-nut tree, and set your liver alongside for company, as a warning to trolloping wenches. If it is you, you can do as you please, but I'll say this, for directing of your sluggish imagination and infertility of thought, that I have always had a fancy to be laid in the branch of a tree when all-soul's out of me, with neither rag nor stitch between me and the bird's pleasure!" And with that she started the matter by a clout to the face.

The horse, Hisodalgus, and the cow, Sally, knowing each other full well—had they not eaten side by side many a month?—stood by warming themselves in the heat of the battle that waged beneath that serene and untroubled autumn sky. First it was Kate that foundered, and then it was Amelia, and then it was black hair upon the wind and then mouse-brown; and then it was good English blood flowing, and then it was uncertain and sundry strains, taking their course down the nose side of No-Man's-Daughter. Then it was high yelp and low growl, and it was here and there and everywhere, until there was neither breech whole nor gingham gown, and each saw what in the other had charms for Wendell, before the most able-bodied and agile umpire could have flung himself into an opinion of how the game stood.

By this time, Amelia, who had Saxony to draw on, was a lean figure dried of aught but heavy breathing, but Kate, being of a Southern extraction and nothing stronger to call on than generations of Venice and a little County Cork, was burst into weeping and making plunges wide of the rub in any man. Amelia seeing, and being in no wise ungallant for a woman, put her hands into her pockets, gave over a neat linen handkerchief, and stood rocking on her heels.

"Thou art a wretch, undoubtedly," she said. "Think you to leave unprotected chick and child, and to desert all that you have come so unjustly by? Is there no shame in you, for well you know the bread is ready for the kneading, and it Thursday, and your turn? Oh, I think you in very deed, a most vile blot upon the escutcheon!"

"Nay, then," said Kate, weeping and blowing against the linen, "but what are you yourself doing upon this road, if not pelting it hot-foot, and warbling into the bargain, straight into kingdom-come, without, as far as I can see, a chick or a child of your own at the saddle-bow!"

"That," said Amelia, "nicely illustrates the difference between the legitimate and the illegitimate. As we've fought, it is meet to come upon philosophy. Take this, then, to your mind and mull it: the sole difference between the bastard, per se, and the child of wedlock is, that the wife may leave but the mistress cannot, yet but listen to the nice point of the argument, it is the wife who may enter a house and the mistress who should stay out. So had you any matter in your head, or any turn for mathematics whatsoever, you would never have made it necessary for me to worry myself on these points, and happier we both should have been, nor this day had I entered into the saddle of a horse, or you been scratched from a cow, an you had not gone the wrong direction all the days of your life."

"It's an ill wind that blows nobody any good," said Kate hotly.

"And what might you mean by that?" inquired Amelia.

"Had it not been for me, and my slightly vice versa mode of conduct, where would your philosophy have bedded? Not in your head, I warrant, but in the head of some other wife that I might have helped to it. For were it not for such as me, there would be no such as you."

"Girl," said Amelia, casting an amazed eye upon her, and yielding her by that appellation the most honour in fifteen years (for it had always been "that woman!" or "that creature!" with her),—"Girl, between cause, which is you, and effect, which is I, I do seem to see reason, and I've always held that, like a babe, it was born from between two women!"

With that she gave Kate a hoist into the saddle, and jockeying her own, they set their faces due north, for there was a taste of rain in the air and night not far off, to say nothing of the need in the bellies of the beasts, who lifted mournful tails, the one mooing and the other neighing, as they listed homewards under the trees.

"I'll see you to the gate, my dear," said Amelia.

"It's most good of you," answered Kate, hanging her head.

"It's ever the wife's place," said Amelia, "to warm the bed for the poacher, and to bring trouble home. Say no more."

"It's a deal more I'll say," cried Kate. "If you think it's all beer and skittles for the intruder, there's another way about of it that cries for vindication. I am a woman who likes to do my own warming, and, be what I may, to find no lean streak in a mattress that speaks of another build than my own, and to come upon a man unwetten by a forethought, even though it be legal. Think you that there is aught for me in this world or the next? For neither in this world nor yet in another, shall I rise to claim more than the half of a man!"

"What claim I," said Amelia bitterly, "because of you? Do you claim a right to be where you are? If you have the half, dolt, it is because it was another woman's whole!"

"In life or in death," answered Kate, "you can think on him as in one piece: your piece and the piece you had to relinquish. You can ever think in terms of charity; whereas I can only be comforted by the thought that you have had, and have not—two conditions—whereas I must sit and be thankful for one."

"Odds death!" exclaimed Amelia, "I do believe the woman argues the matter! Were you invited?"

"I was that," said Kate.

"When?" inquired Amelia, sticking a cruel spur.

"When," said Kate, "you looked not to the size in beds but housed one that would shelter three."

"This," said Amelia, "goes beyond a woman's bearing. In a moment I'll gather you down from that, and start this controversy from the other side of the nose! To build a bed that would keep you from shelving thereon, it would have to be as narrow as a knife, and even then, I doubt not, but that you would turn it to the flat and struggle aboard!"

Kate smiled. "I am a mother," she said, "but I'm none so sure that proves any great surface."

"Halt!" exclaimed Amelia, "you contradict yourself, bed or no bed, you now maintain yourself as inevitable?"

"'Tis only too true," admitted Kate, looking down, "perhaps it was not so much the bed as it might have been."

"Exactly," said Amelia. "1 should have thrust a spade into you when I first laid eyes on you!"

"That depends . . ." said Kate.

"On God's what?" asked her travelling companion.

"On your frame of mind. Had you been disposed to spade, spade you would, if not . . . well, here am I."

"Think you," said Amelia, lying low upon her beast, that the bulky form of her companion might be the nearer, "that I lacked courage?" "Or what?" said Kate, looking away into the distance where the old homestead hove into view.

"Vulgar, vulgar, vulgar!" breathed Amelia. "Te Deum, Te Deum, Te Deum! I spaded not because I faithed. I faithed me that Wendell was a large account, lost in a small and trifling balance; I spaded not, because I fancied him an inch higher than the steeple's highest inch; 1 spaded not, because I thought rich of life; I spaded not because 1 judged him greater than my judgment, honoured him above my honour, and loved him beyond my love; and I find . . ."

"Aye?" said Kate, listlessly enough.

"That he nests with vermin, that beneath the shadow of his wings, corruption breeds, that he moults bastards, and broods upon exceeding bad eggs!"

"I smell irony," said Kate.

"You smell judgment, 'tis the same thing," said Amelia, "to the common nose."

"I've as good blood as you!" said Kate, jogging slowly.

"If you've good blood it was pirated," said Amelia richly, "and therefore forfeit at every turn."

"Do I understand that you question my legitimacy?" inquired Kate, with deep indignation, rolling her eyes in Amelia's direction with fearful portent.

"There isn't a legal quiver in thy great bulk of mountanous flesh," said Amelia conclusively.

"I do think this has gone far enough," said Kate, "and as I am better at throwing than at the fist, and as I've nothing with me . . ."

"I cannot brawl beyond the duties of the hour," answered her companion. "As it is well upon supper-time, I shall wish you farewell, and jog ahead, if you, on your red cow, can make no better pace."

"Do I understand," said Kate terribly, "that you do not leave me at the gate, but that you yourself are returning to the fold?"

"I enter in," said Amelia nicely. "My steed is in need of oats, and yours in need of milking, and by this time Wendell will be calling for one or the other, or both of us."

"Speaking of Wendell," sighed Kate, "I do wish you would

use your influence with him to have him leave well enough alone."

"Meaning you, or what?"

"Me *and* what," said Kate. "Had he not a most high esteem for your irreproachable and correct nature, he would think twice before he hazarded so many tricks on me, and I sit this cow but sadly, for there is not so much as a single burning pepper, unguent or spice in the larder, that he has not burned and scourged me with, in order to bring me to, at least a local reason. But I can do no better at best," she added, sighing, "than faint in his arms. Now would you but speak to him . . ."

Here it is only fair to say Amelia broke into a British laugh. "Hot-Bottom, my poor trull," she said, "I'll have a word with him; he shall not abuse you."

"You are most good," said her companion, "at the oddest times."

"They are all we have," Amelia answered, and with this they both came into the yard, where all the children stood cheering, and both got down in manner according to their mounting, Amelia stabling both animals (for Kate was poor in most capacities), and as usual, calmly as can be imagined, preceded Kate into the house, both a little worn with their only (though many times threatened) treason.

Chapter 35

Amelia Hears from Her Sister in Regard to Timothy

What is this that you tell me, dear sister, that Timothy, your eldest, has already cracked his paint and is showing the grain of the Ryders?

Is this true that you write of, that he has taken up with a half-wit, white-haired Polish Lena, who lies at all hours beside the roadway in the underbrush for fouling of him? And he doing her honour in not honouring? Ah, what a pass indeed we have come to, and I think the world were better an it should cease this minute from whirling about the sun, or the sun about it, whichever is the way with it, and all the creatures thereon stopped before they do so disgrace it, root and branch, that the Lord will have none of it whatever in another generation or more! Why, is she then, this Lena, with child? And if so, what a kinless cry will be coming up from it, to say nothing of its two fatherless hands and two fatherless heels, and its smitten fatherless body in between, unless, indeed, a father be found, but as to that, are there honest blacksmiths in your country who, though smelling of the parings of horses, and blind of a spark, can be dragged up to the altar with the bride's belly

all out of shape, and smacked well to an angel and never be
the wiser?

We have some such in good London, or did have in the time
of our governess, for well I remember her saying that we get our
children where we can, and father them as we are able, though,
she added, "God knows I trust the thing is a boy, for if 'tis a
girl, the rhythm of the rape may lie in it." For she held that a
mother's tendencies run straight through a daughter, but halt
at a son. "So," said she, "I'll pray for a teakettle, and thumbs
down on a tea-cup," though what there was in that allusion I
have never been able to serve up to my mind's liking.

Yet, though I am sorry for you, my dear sister (I always
warned you against your man!), still, in the long run or the
short (whichever a man has with him) it's the lass who pays,
and if this be not true, then I should like to be shown where
I err, for not once do I remember a man as having ought of
discomfort out of these doings, saving in the instance of old
John,—you do remember him, no doubt—that same John that
had the little house between the hills. We used to watch the
smoke rising from his chimney when we climbed the rise, and
when we went down through the lane of Lovers. If we looked
over the pickets, we used to see him holding a copy of Bunyan
on his lap. Do you not recall his great figure, as he stood in
his doorway, holding a girl child up on his hand, mocking and
talking to her all by himself, and asking her where she came
from and why? Well, 'twas a pitiful sight! And so it is, I dare
say, that it's usual for the woman to pay, for in the Lord's sight
a lone man with a lone child makes two mysteries, whereas a
mother and her gettings seem to be all of the one batter. So
I've come to think that even injustice comes from justice, for
turn the ways of nature heel out, or right side up, it's all the
same, you find yourself in for what you should have; or why
is the Lord at all?

Ah, well, woman within woman and man within man are two different sorts of diminishings! My dear sister, if one could see the man-within-man, going down in its tiniest procession to his core, we would no doubt be well amazed at his great reputation. As for woman-within-woman, incongruous and impossible as it sounds, she is great at the core and dwindles as you reach her outer jacket, so that you see a monstrous little of a dire plot. As for the matter of nice sizes and woman-with-in-woman, I've come to think that the queen of hearts, or any other of a pack of cards, is a better way to be built than the way we are; for up one way, or up the other, they never have a troublesome end about them, but, as there are some who must live by a convulsion of the instincts rather than by well thought out manœuvring, what shall we hope to have upon our doorsteps but other people's children, asking, "Whither, whence?" and getting no better reply than, "Ask thy mother," as if she were to be trusted!

This, now I do think on it, is the matter with the world, that a man's greatness do come right out bang upon us, a woman's is in her flesh and hidden. How can one expect the ways of men to go right when things are so mixed up?

To illustrate my point, my dear sister, but think on what you have told me of your own daughter, Julie, in the matter of Mrs. Ryder Alexson's diaper ends. Would one, to see the child pulling at it, and the good lady running about trying to pin it out of sight and out of mind, incline to think on woman's splendour? Or say you, in the matter of the humours that do come upon that good woman when she is in the way of wind, would one think to see her (and I have your word for it, it is no unusual thing) placing upon that end a modulating finger, so that she toot in unison and with design (all the while the King of Sweden's ring upon that digit), that she was anywhere, in that act, near her great end? Or that, at other times, dressed as tidy as you please, and, smiling, with every muscle given over to convention, in the offices of Samuel Bowles, as she wrote her manly editorials for the *Springfield Republican*, that it were one and the same? Ah, well, the good lady spends herself at both ends, like the candle we heard tell on as children, which were better not lit from both, and I dare say it's a woman's way of coming sooner upon her grandeur.

I have discovered, dear sister, that what you do is to yourself only what you do, but to the public what they do not, and therefore all this great business of right and wrong, judges and juries, to say nothing of prisons and sentences. Life is too long as it is, my dear sister, for does it not find time in which to be unjust? Yet it is so short that we have no time for anything but religion. And until it is different, that is all we should try to stick by, for it was built to fit the years a man lives, or I do not read my Bible right.

So now, dear sister, do write to me soon and tell me what you are all doing with your time; for it is of much to me to have a little philosophy for my sleepless nights.

Thy Devoted Sister.

Chapter 36

Amelia Tells a Bed-Time Story

When Felice appeared in dimity her sister Alix appeared in voile. When Felice wore narrow shoulder ribbons of baby blue, Alix wore yet tinier ribbons of pink. When Felice flowered her hat with forget-me-nots, Alix bordered hers with violets, and when Felice gave up tea for tilleul, Alix took to kettle-tea and thought herself as neat.

Felice had little hands, Alix had smaller; Felice had a tiny waist and two breasts as delicate as the first setting of blanc mange. Alix's waist was only a hand's span and her bosom was no greater than two tears set low. Felice had golden hair, Alix's was fine and thin and curling.

Felice had a little skeleton as chipped of angles as a Ming, and as light as ash. Alix's flesh covered her bones as thinly as ice on a tree. Felice's ankles were faultless, Alix's were as weightless as cuttlebone and as fragile.

Felice was always running, Alix was always skipping. Felice was always laughing, Alix was always bubbling over with mirth. Felice was always breathless, Alix could never catch her own.

Felice was eighteen, Alix was seventeen. They always went hand in hand. They travelled close beside, they slept in the same bed, Felice with her face turned to the wall, Alix turned toward Felice.

When Felice awoke in tears, Alix was damp also; when Felice had no appetite for breakfast, Alix could not touch a morsel; when Felice was angry, Alix was ungovernable; Felice broke the tea-cup, Alix broke the saucer.

Felice went on the stage. Alix followed. Felice danced a song about a canary. Alix sang with her and was the feathers. Felice sang soprano, Alix sang higher. Felice wore almost no clothes at all, Alix appeared in less. Felice caught a little cold, Alix coughed.

Felice cried for a tiny doll, Alix got a smaller. They sat together in bed and the two dolls sat up before them. Felice's doll had china legs and an imperceptible china dimple, Alix's was of porcelain, and its feet were so small that two stitches of wool made it bootees.

The manager called and took Felice in his right arm and Alix in his left. He pinched them both at once and equally, and they both kissed him at the same moment, and he put them back to bed.

Felice said:

"At twenty minutes past ten, on April fourth, I shall be a mother."

Alix said:

"At twenty-one minutes past ten, on April fourth, I shall be a mother."

They took two tiny drinks of whiskey.

Two weeny little pinches of snuff.

They had four little circles under their four blue eyes.

And on April fourth, at twenty minutes past ten, Felice died. One minute later Alix died. And that's the end of the two little sisters, thank God, said Amelia.

Chapter 37

Sweetly Told

Wendell Grieve Ryder took off his overshoes softly, leaving on the felt, and came toward the music-room. The snow melting on the lamb's wool of his collar brought him a slight chill. He blew his nose, holding the handkerchief carefully, spat into its bellied whiteness sharply and definitely, put it back into his pocket and opened the door, coming in.

The two long windows looked out into the garden with its single box, and beyond, the twisted arms of the grape arbour on its twining mysterious journey to the privy. On the short stone balustrade surmounted by a tiny couched lion, Laura Twelvetree's husband sat, holding his bowler in his hands, staring in a mathematical dream.

Laura Twelvetree, unveiling, came toward Wendell, stretching out a hand, and sank down into the rag-covered cushions, blue and green. The fluted belly of the stove shone red at its girth, the dust of the wood-ash lay thick in its grooves.

"How are you to-day?" she said, the brown paper parcel in her lap ticking faintly against the fur of her coat. "It's cold for him out there," she added, "but he notices nothing, he knows but one thing, that one and one make two."

"He minds, or he does not?" inquired Wendell.

"He minds," she said, "and here is something for you." She gave him the brown paper parcel, and he, taking it, stepped back, placed his hand on the knob of the door, turned it, opened it, calling, "Amelia, Amelia, Kate!" And one of them came and took it, unwrapping behind the closed door.

These things occurred in the time when skirts were of many pleats stitched down from the waist-line to the bulge of the hips, and then no stitching. On her long neck went upward a collar of net, reinforced by four lengths of whalebone, the two longest reaching the ears, a plumed hat she had, delft blue and magnificent, and a long foot with laced vamp, and elbow-length glace gloves, with six rounded hooks to twist the braided cord upon, zig-zag going upward, with a dangling silver end.

"Where are the children?" he said, moving toward her, sitting against her.

"Away at school," she said. "The boy is learning Greek, but he brings home words that I feel are not dignified by time," and she looked tall and dignified and wounded with ignorance. "And I do so love your mother, she is such a sweet woman. I always call her the 'soldier,' she seems marching. How do you think of her?"

"The little general," he said. "That will do nicely." He sniffed, "What is that, rose or verbena?"

"Wild rose," she said, "and do you like it?"

"No," he said. He put his hand over hers, taking the glove off slowly, feeling the soft suède and the soft flesh. "No, nothing heathenish." She leaned upon his shoulder. "You have a little daughter," she said, "and she has no breasts. I've often noticed Julie—where," she said, rummaging in her scented case, "are those jujubes I brought for her?"

Wendell in the way, she got up, moving through the farm-house twilight, sweet smelling. The darkness came toward her meeting her halfway. On the piano stood an open book, at the head of the page two swallows etched holding a bar of music in their bills. Old music, sheet music, pale print, sepia brown, paper, cloth pulp, with a watermark like a ghost, showing through the grace notes. She looked around. A pair of shoes in the corner, Amelia's? Kate's? A lion in the house must bear the signs of the lions gone before. She went down crying softly, her arm under her breasts, her cheek upon her hand, the sweet twittering of birds gone out in silence in the dark of the lugubrious gardens with their umbriferous vines. A peewit called alone from across the lands, and no bird answered, "Watchman, what of the night?"

"Do you believe," she said, her dark hair a pleasant brown, "in the hereafter, in the spirits that our mothers saw and swore by, with a simple faith that transfigures ignorance?"

Through the twilight of the capacious room went the cohort of those gone, forgotten and remembered and forgotten again. Trailing regal garments, dust coloured and death worn, and threadbare of the grave—a lamb and a phantom, and the phantom's lamb, and the lamb of the lamb, and foremost, a prince in point-lace, with touching sweet honey-coloured curls, holding in the curve of a cradling velvet arm, the supine form of a girl-child with the blood of the rape flowing in a thin, fine, ever-widening stream, the slotted insertion of her communal dress, petal by petal, falling, the bride's bouquet in her betrayed hands, and passed out through the wall without cease. The lamb stopped at the corner and turned and ran against the wall and turned again and ran again, and turned his holy eyes, turned and turned and went through suddenly. She rose to scream and knelt to pray, and found her position in no wise altered.

"Kate," he said, "a girl brought up in penury, beached from the gutters, has been vouchsafed an offering from the shades. She was not three months gone with child when, awakening from the painful travail of her unconsciousness, she heard a voice, saying, 'Behold, I come to deliver thee!' and she saw walking down a continual mountain one who resembled her father, Father Watchman, in a never ceasing robe, with a lantern in his hand that flickered not, nor wavered, and behind him in never resting genuflexion, bowed the groves. In his beard was a voice, and the voice spake and said, 'Thou shalt not die!' And she awoke from her waking in a deep sweat. 'And handsomely I've been dealt with this night,' she said, 'and go you, and lie in a separate bed, and but me no buts, I am a woman to see a vision, and it no mean one neither, and from now on, I sleep my own sleep, and entertain my own prophets; so sleep you in a separate place of sleeping, for you've done your business, and now it's myself and my visions that are going to ward it from disaster and death, and devil a bit of a small proposition it is,' she said, turning over, 'for you know not what you do, and leave it to me to find out, and my father to guard.' And she went to sleep again, and I lay out in the cold the night long."

"If I should die to-night," Laura said, "what man would care?"

"Why then, I should," Wendell answered, "a little while."

"And after that?"

"After that there are your children," he said. "It is a matter of no doubt but that they never quite forget her who bore them, be it love or be it a chemical, so it is. For this I replenish the world. I have the spirit and the works. And though a child forget a father before a mother, between the lot of them I shall come to memory from time to time, if not with words of praise, why then of calumny," he added, "for be you wise or be you a doddering fool, the child will rate you in some manner, and lay something of his failure at your door."

"There is," she said, "an aristocracy in no outcome, and to this one should point the instrument, for otherwise it's a grave price to pay for a little talking when you are gone."

A child's hand, ringed with a simple band of turquoise, came through the door downward, holding the india red fountain-of-all-ladies'-hope, and held it, waiting: a child's offering at the gate.

"Oh," cried Laura Twelvetree, "if only I had faith I would scream aloud, but as it is, I shall visit Mme. Rodriguez Gomez and have her tell the cards for this thing!" She turned her eyes outward where, in lonely mathematics, her husband sat holding his bowler between his knees. "My God," she said, "poor Albert will freeze, for there's no organ in him but a sheep's kidney since this morning, and though the lad's a fool, there's mortality in his blood."

A little later she was taking her Albert's arm in her own. He said, "Did you have a good talk, my love?" And she breathed, "Merciful heaven, how irrelevant you can be!"

Sophia Grieve Ryder, the meanwhile, holding an ostler's lamp at arm's length beside the wicket gate, lighted them on their way.

"And what is this thing?" said Wendell, once back in the bosom of the family, as he looked upon the contents of the brown paper parcel.

"A hand-painted, Cheapside, porcelain timepiece, my love," Amelia answered, "with one hand. Some there are, and no names mentioned, who have no better time to give."

Chapter 38

Dr. Matthew O'Connor
and the Children

After the event described in the chapter on Some Strong Woman he showed a marked change. He was no longer comfortable in the presence of women. Yet many an afternoon he would sit in the pasture, Hannel and Elisha and Aaron about him, Elsie on his knee, laughing and talking and playing for hours, so that the women were more puzzled and astonished than ever.

"What would you do," he said to Hannel, "if all the stars came down and played about in the fields?"

"I should get my gun and shoot them," said Hannel, "because they would be a pest, and all pests, father says, should be shot at sight."

"But," the doctor said, "you like them up where they are?"

"That's because they are out of the way," said Hannel.

"Ah, well," said the doctor, "perhaps you are right. Now," he said to Elsie, "what are you going to be when you grow up into a fine strapping woman, and have a house to yourself, with curtains to every window, a new calico gown with tucks all over it, and six eggs in the cupboard?"

"I shall run away," said Elsie sweetly.

"Shall you now?" said the doctor. "And what will you do when you are a man, Hannel?"

Said Hannel, "I shall get me a girl, and beat her with the warming pan until she gives up the ghost, then I'll settle down. But a fellow must see the world first."

"Indeed and indeed," said the doctor sadly, "I'm afraid you are a little unnatural, Hannel, my son, you should never hit a woman."

"All right," said Hannel, "but a fellow should see the world, at all costs, before he gets old."

"See the world and welcome," said Dr. O'Connor, "but don't blast your foundations by whacking a woman."

"Dad says," Hannel went on, "that one should regard all the miracles of nature with an impartial eye; 'observe,' he says, 'that slaughter makes the shoulders rise and the head descend. See,' he says, 'the little girls stumbling to school; it's their future maternity that makes them stare into the hedges like that. Mark,' he says, 'the squirrels lifting their tails unabashed;' he calls that pure reason and unobstructed inner vision."

"Does he?" remarked the doctor.

"He does, and he says, 'All women are worthy of attention.'"

"That's all deviltry," said Dr. Matthew O'Connor, "wind and water, signifying a horse of another colour, and not for a child. Never listen to a man when he is talking loud; such sounds are not for little ears. You may listen with profit only when he is asleep, or in pain; all the rest is the coming forth of that discomfort he has sown in himself, before he knew which end he stood on."

"There's a woman comes to our house," broke in Elsie. "She is tall and full of braids and smouldering passion. 'Play me a war-song,' she says to Dad, 'because,' she says, 'it fills me with beautiful terror, especially when I am eating.'"

"The Beast of Bashan, no doubt," said the doctor.

"And she said," went on Elsie, lifting her voice into a mincing treble, 'Life was so terrible, Wendell, when I was born, the cows calved and the bodkin ran like mad, and the buskin cracked in the pains of labour, but now I have known you, a strumpet gathers light feet at forty and thanks God for you between one thing and another.'"

"Heels over head," said the doctor, "never makes a pretty down-coming. That's a part of history that, if I were you, I should not repeat."

"I," said Aaron, "should like to do something."

"What about?" said the doctor.

"My life," said Aaron, "like this. It began to rain, like that, simple. It was dark and it began to rain. A man, a young man, is walking along the road. It is summer. He listens to the frogs croaking in the valley, one, two, three, many. He does not turn his head, but goes straight on, breathing the cool air from the mountain. A carriage passes him. It is the school teacher, he knows by the colour and pattern of her dress. She bounds from side to side, going over the heavy ruts, into puddles, through the mud, thinking of the early settlers. The people in the town begin to light their lamps, the church-bell rings, and a pack of dogs fight in the dark. . . . I am that man."

Dr. O'Connor was silent a long time, then he said: "That's the best wish of the generation, and I defy the Lord to better it." And with that he got up and walked away hurriedly, and ran himself straight into the confessional, and went bang down upon his knees, and began whispering: "Lord, Lord, a wicked grimy soul has this day been cleaned by a child. He opened his mouth, all set about with new teeth, and said great things simply, and made a way for himself with his words, and went down the quality of it, his heart beating in both breasts from clearness of purpose, and nothing rose up to snare his heel. And he shot through the murk of this generation, a bird on the wing, clean over the mark, and there he sits on high, saying nothing but, 'Holy, Holy, Holy,' always, and I, Matthew O'Connor, wallowing in the pit, have been vouchsafed this vision. May I rot like a duchess if it do not reline me with sweetness and light. Amen!"

Chapter 39

Wendell Discusses Himself
with His Mother

"My dear mother," said Wendell, "you know better than I the things that went to make me, but the little face that came forth from between your feet, has it a look now that you would care to see, an it were just putting forth from that place?"

"God forbid!" said Sophia, tucking the end of her lace fichu under her bosom.

"Exactly," said Wendell, "I sport a changing countenance. I am all things to all men, and all women's woman. At one moment I am a young and tender girl, with close-held legs, and light bones becoming used to the still, sweet pain that is a girl's flesh, metaphorically speaking, of course. At other times this face, is it not a dowager's? Sometimes I am a whore in ruffled petticoat, playing madly at a pack of ruffians, and getting thrippence for my pains; a smartly boxed ear, or, a bottom-tingling clap a-hind. Yet again, I am a man-with-a-trowel, digging at the edge of my life for the tangible substance of re-creation; and once I was a bird who flew down my own throat, twanging at the heart chord, to get the pitch of my own mate-call. And once I was a deer stalking myself,

202

and it was then (I know well the hour when I called myself a dyspeptic), for my son's good, that I thought up a name that would keep him in stomach and make him definitely a child of destiny, giving him, in place of your gift to me (which was a too gentle, twofold, many-sided instability), the appellation of 'Cock o' the Walk' or * * * "

"Have you forgotten," said Sophia, curtly, "that you have changed your own name a thousand times and never gave yourself such an antonomia?"

"A very simple matter," replied her son; "I date from a sentimental period, and, accordingly, I name myself as I find myself. What I would be, that I say I am, and thus, eventually, I become. What need have I of such a cognomen as 'Cock o' the Walk' when the evidence of it sits at my table with sixteen legs? Do I not, I ask you, sit apart at my own humble board, just to be in such a position that this stupendous fact may be a constant joy, as I drink my ale and finger my kipper? I am myself a company apart, for no man is born abnormal; the diverse soul is as pleasing, I dare say, to the universal, as he who can play but one tune upon a comb."

"You forget, my dear boy, that you play a number of instruments not at all necessary to the soul of any one single creature, be he seven men in himself, and as many women; it is not necessary to take up the wood instruments, and the wind instruments, and thunder away at organ and harp, all in one lifetime."

"True," said Wendell, "the angels play the tympanum, the devils twang, with pleasure, the human gut, the humble Scotsman wheezes at his bags, and the Austrian thumps his mandoline; and I amuse me with half-a-dozen instruments, but it is only diversion and a practice, for my real glory is in the merry music I've struck up with my spherical, timbersome pipe of a single stop, the core of the codpiece. How many notes fly through a woman at its orchestration! Grave notes, and half notes, and demi-semiquavers, all clinging to the beam of her interior, and ripening after the nine months, to fly forth duly harmonized, like a good war-song of the early pagans, or those rollicking dances that set peasants bobbing and flinging many a shapely leg up in a hornpipe, or," he added, with a melancholy pause, "stillborn like a rush of grace notes, too hurried for the voice to catch, and then silence and a Christian burial."

"Do you remember," said his mother, "the good Herr Gustave, who treated you to your first mortal music?"

"Do I remember God?" he said with pleasure. "A fugue player of the first water, a harmonist and a lover of the metronome, catching it up with a flurry of great notes that made Beethoven seem like a small water trout, bubbling in the brook. Lying in bed, early of a morning, when the milkmaid, far away in the Cornish Country, was bringing down her first teat full, when the letter carriers on the Margate Road were not yet to B, and the first confessions of less than a sin were rising from the heart of the convert (a sin as sinless as that of a doll), Herr Gustave lay abed, spectacles on nose, demonstrating the great uses of the metronome, and of time, with the fair baton of his own powerful anatomy. 'Up, Jocko!' he cried, and up it started like a dog from sleep. Or to prove himself no-man's-less, hanging therefrom an empty broth cup. The very morning that I, in full haste, ran to him with the Times to inform him of his winning of the prize for the most full-bellied cantata, I found him in dressing-gown and wellingtons, in the middle of the room, saying, 'It is not justified,' yet his timepiece told a different tale, standing buck-high with glory."

"Do you recall," said his mother, "any unbristling days?"

"Never a one," cried Wendell, bringing his hands down on his knees, "and it's for that that I love him!"

"I have been ribald and hearty myself," said Sophia, "and in my own way have distempered many a wife, yet never with a wish to hurt, but to hear laughter, and to go about my days in little shoes, to the sound of men reaching and missing by a hair."

"Ace by ace," said her son, "you've bred up to the final covey, where lies the speckled bird of prey."

"Ace by ace," said Sophia, "we've won many a game."

"And ace by ace," said Wendell, "lost many. Oscar Wilde was a man of beauty, who looked through a privy-ring at the stars. A man of imagination, a man of parts, a man's man. I saw him once, and was less a one myself, for that I, seeing him lean from out a cab in the days of his trouble, turned my head away, and listened unlistening to that voice that had slid over every woman's blandishments, from Oxford to Reading, like a mighty cod on his way to sea. I turned away, my hams shrinking. The scandal had burst, and though he was the core, the fragrant centre of a rousing stench, in a month he was a changed man, not changing, sitting within his cell, weeping, writhing, plotting 'De Profundis,' his fingers outside his mouth, shuddering in all his soft female body, direct suffering in his breasts; a bull caught and captured, sentenced, hamstrung, marauded, peered at, peeped upon, regarded and discovered to be a gentle sobbing cow, giving self-suck at the fountain of self, that he might die in his own image, a soft pain chartered she, a girl cast out of heaven, harnessed for a stallion's turn; tremolo to his own swan-song. I turned away and was matchlessly damned."

"Now that we come to that," said Sophia, "you might as well tell me what possessed Polly, some twenty years ago, and she a good serving wench, and never showing arrogance in her life before, to come, with all bold unfeeling impudence right into the music-room and, before my very nose, to play a deafening war-song, or something mighty to its shape, at a clip and

a gallop, with the most uncommon sauce, upon the upright
that stood beside the picture of Dante going down into hell?"

"Every man," said Wendell willingly, "has been initiated
into these matters either by a kitchen slut or an elder aunt,
who remains a maiden for all of that. Why then, with Poll it
was but short work. I had often seen where her feet came from,
but not where her legs went to, and going about, in a voyage
of discovery, I found her one day upon the back stairs, I, getting for my pains, a 'You may touch but you mustn't look,'
for love is in direct opposition to religion, where it is, 'You
may look but you mustn't touch.' Yet for all of that, I arose
damned within the hour for that her flesh was the flesh of all
wild things, too mournful for a man. So it is, perhaps, that
she went thus triumphantly at the upright. I was Christian in
the Slough of Despond, I dropped, untimely, my load, and
she, snatching it up, went and played it upon your instrument;
thus I rode on to polygamy. . . ."

Sophia said, "Polygamy exactly."

"No man," said Wendell, "can judge this world an he had
risen from one bed only, for according to that bed will he arise,
and a one-bed judge never made a lenient judge, for look you,"
added her son, "be it a bed of bleating, he will go forth therefrom baaing and making a what-to-do about nothing at all,
and if it be from a bed of laughter, he will be stretching his
face into all manner of things not pleasant to his next-door
neighbour, or be it a bed of tears, he will walk forth lamenting;
hell she or heaven she, it will leave its mark upon him. But if,
on the other hand, his character has been moulded by a multitude of beds, why, a multitude of persons he will be, better as a
father, better as a citizen, and better as a debtor, for polygamy
is the only bed a man rolls out of, conditioned to meet the
world, and in fettle for the midwife or the grave-digger, and

that, thank God, gets me back to the why of calling my son Cock o' the Walk or * * * It is not only a sonorous, deafening, pulsating, ponderous, Latin-sounding affair, a very hurrah! huzzah! halloa! rattat to the world, but it is something to lean back upon in the face of a suspicious, inglorious life; it will pull him through! A name is a battalion to walk beside you, weak or strong, according to its wording."

"And the consequences?"

"Of what?"

"Polygamy, in the long run."

"There was Amelia going up, and Jane coming down, the grand staircase," said her son. "My first trial of that noble philosophy in the home. 'Beast!' said Amelia, for the smoke of the shot was not yet cleared. Can one blame her? It was not her breach, and she a wife of but three summers and great with the second."

Sophia said, rising and seating herself beside her son, her small feet thrust into juliets, and her general's hands in her lap: "Think you not dyspepsia may have had a great deal to do with your particular turn of mind?"

"Your wardens, your statesmen, your priests, your vandals, your saints, your courtesans, your doctors, your generals, your queens and your courtiers, all, all have at one moment what they would by no means crave the next; only a dog returns to his losses, and only a Catholic keeps for better or for worse."

"It is very advanced, very old, and very nice, perhaps," said Sophia, safe in her sixties from the personal element involved, "but we must keep it from the public, at all costs, until you are prepared . . ."

"It is magnificent when you think," observed her son, "how ignorant you can make the public with one great thought— untold . . ." and he laughed heartily.

"The number of fools is indefinite," said his mother.

"No, seriously," said Wendell, as they sat thus together like two old politicians who no longer found politics enough, "what is to become of me? Certain warmths have made me, like any good cockerel in an oven, but the final basting . . . whither, whence?"

"To what do you refer?" inquired Sophia, regarding, with pleasure, the neatness of her feet.

"I have been tempered, cooked, made what I am, by the various heats emanating from the body of woman," said her son, his long upper lip set. "There was, for instance, the preliminary basting, the warmth of the mother breast, there was the first scorching of a sweet girl bottom upon my knee at fourteen, and there followed the various and peculiar cookings incurred by the married state, but I may say that I was never fully roasted, frizzled, and come to a good crisp, until I knew the fair Kate, for there were heats in her like to no woman simmering, and now that I am done to a nice turn, who is to eat me? The authorities of the state and the wiseacres of the nation? For I tell thee, mother, they smell a well-done fowl, my aroma is ripe to the nose of justice, and like a pack of hounds, all slavering at the jaws, with bloody eye and wind in the ears, they snarl down the road of my destiny."

"Do I not stand between you and retribution always?" inquired his mother magnificently.

"Always," he said, and laid his hand on hers. "Always, my most good mother, my courageous spirit, my beginning and my end. You know," he added, "I have always wanted to do you homage." He looked upon her tenderly. "I have always wanted to save you for a better hour, but I spend you minute by minute, and I fear I shall become beggared of your quantity, at the pitch of fate. I am the life, you are the suffering; I am the insulted, you are the injured; I am the note, but you are the instrument."

She was gay of a sudden. "Look," she said, "I love my family. I have told each child here that I would guard it. There were eight to tell, and to each I went and I said, 'I love you,' and to each it was exceeding easy to say, to Timothy, to Hannel, to Gaspard, to Elisha, to Aaron, to Gaybert, to Elsie, I said, 'I love you, and I will take care of you,' and I went further where was Julie in the deep of the garden, and I said, 'I love you,' and I could not kiss her, as I had kissed the others, because she was thinking something outside the family. Therefore I leaned my head upon her little breast, and she said, 'You have betrayed me,' and she held me with her arm, and because she doubts me, and because there is trouble in the house, I shall remember her always, and she will walk to my grave, and will doubt me long, until I am a memory with her, as long as I was a life, and then she will condemn herself, and I shall not be there to comfort her. So I must say, many times, that one of the sayings will live after me, 'I love you and will take care of you.'"

"Um," said Wendell, "but she has always been a hussy and a stubborn girl. . . ."

"She has always been you," Sophia answered; "I have seen you from the seed," she continued, "and I have seen her, and you are exactly alike, except"—she made a period in the air with one of her Jesuitical hands—"that she is unhung, and you are slung like a man; it will make the difference."

"To get back to me," said Wendell

"To go beyond you," said Sophia.

"To get back to me," pursued Wendell. "There is, for instance, the undoubted fact—" But at this moment they were interrupted by the entrance of Kate. She was evidently both extremely excited and angry, for she was gulping and trembling in a most furious manner. "Look at me!" she cried, advancing into the room and straight up to Sophia, who hurriedly placed herself in a reclining position on her bed, awaiting the onslaught: "Look, both of you," she continued, trembling all over. "Here you sit, like buzzards, and I sit downstairs, yes, and Amelia also, carrion waiting your hunger! And my flesh trembles," she continued with flashing eye, "to think of that indignity." She turned about as she spoke, and both Sophia and her son jumped in their outer flesh as she continued, in a hiss: "I'll have my children, as many as I like, and that for you!" She snapped her fingers under Sophia's nose. "Do I care that you have to feed them, that you are sixty and in your old age? No, they are my right, and I will have them. So don't you," she added, flinging an angry look at Wendell, "talk to me of your economies. You should have thought of that before you got yourself into the matter. A fine way out of it you have tumbled upon with your great mind," she said, sneering. "You deprive the cows of their fodder, by the panful, and come trapesing in with: 'Here, this should make most excellent bran-bread for the children!' Faugh, you think in terms of the ranchman, not the father. Well, you've taken me, you've brought me to your house, you've bred with me, and I've got the taste." Here she laughed. "I've become infatuated with the flavour of mother-hood; you poked it under my nose, and I've learned to like it. It makes me ill, and there's no pleasure at either end, but I'm an addict, and it's your fault, keeper of the shop, and madame of the keeper!" She was now quite beyond herself with fury. "I'll kill it the minute it's born, but I'll bear it! There's humour for you, and you can't prevent me! I'll stand over it like a dis-tempered bitch before a wailing litter, and I'll stamp it to the ground, and be done with your filth! But you can't prevent me having that moment, you can't take away my revenge, even though it is I who have to give it birth! I'll spew out my own heart in my own way, but you shall be father to it, and," she continued in a loud voice, "I can do more than that. I have gone to Amelia's muck and begged it forgiveness in the cupboard there, where she had flown when we quarrelled, and she knew that I was sorry and was following to beg her forgiveness and to ask her to kiss me, in human love. And because she is decent, she went into that filthy cupboard and hid her face, and would not kiss me, and would not forgive; because she has a spirit and a clean heart, and would not soil herself with the conditions of an imperfect soul. But I will, and I'll have my children, one, two, three, a dozen! until the mould breaks, and I'll stamp on them, as I said I would! And be clean, and sing again about my house, as I used to, before you and your son came forward with his notions about women loving one another when they were not meant to love one another, or to get their children from the same spigot, or to wail under the same doom, with skeletons got from the same box, or to wind up sister flash on separate spools,—it's disgusting! I'll have my fill of it, and that for you, my ramping lusty!" she added, and up with her hand and smacked Wendell well on both faces, "and that for you, 'mother,'" she added, casting down at Sophia's feet a tumbler snatched from the table, and bursting into tears, rushed from the room.

Sophia wet a handkerchief with a little cologne and passed it across her face. "She suffers, poor creature," she said. "I judge from this onslaught, that you have been at work again."

Wendell looked up at his mother and he looked down. "Yes," he said, matching his thumbs, "God forgive me. What shall you do?"

"What have I always done?" said his mother. "I have supported, in some manner, twelve, what is to prevent the manner stretching to take on thirteen?"

Wendell came to her. "I wish, I wish," he said, "I could be humble." He said it like a man preoccupied.

"But you can't, you don't understand, it's all right," she answered. "And after all, children are a blessing, even if you do manage more than the necessary number of blessings a year. What of Amelia?"

"That's the devil of it," said Wendell. "The sore point, as you might say, neither of them knows which is to be a mother first."

"And don't you know?" said Sophia.

"Not an idea in the world," he answered proudly; "you see it was an experiment."

"Again!" exclaimed his mother.

"Again. . . . This was the way of it. Amelia lay on one side, and Kate on the other, only a hate apart, so what the one left, the other claimed, and what with their plucking and squabbling, and my mighty flying hither and thither (I being the bodkin), if there are two babes, one will be the half of the other, one will mother the body, the other give suck to the soul."

"My God!" said Sophia, and lay down, "really, my son, you go past comprehension."

"Mother," he said, "what does one do with nature?"

"A humane man," she answered, "would occasionally give it respite." And she turned over wearily.

He went on tip-toe.

Chapter 40

Old Wives' Tale, or
The Knit Codpieces

Now Amelia sat on one side of the fire, and Kate the other, Amelia with her two feet well on the boards, and Kate with hers firmly upon the comfort of a hassock.

"What is it that you are doing, Amelia?"

"What is it that you are doing yourself, Kate? It has the same stitch, and when I turn to take the round, I see your needles slant for the same journey. And though what I knit is red, and what you knit is blue, there's nothing to prohibit them from the same destination."

"Mine," quoth Kate, "is for all-man's-work."

"And mine," quoth Amelia, "is for all-woman's-luck."

"For two such things," said Kate, "there is but one homing. What a trouble it is suiting the stitch to a thing so circumspect in the cold."

"And never more than Greek, no matter the provocation."

"Nay, and never," quoth Kate, "at peace with itself, in snow or in sun, but must be forever charging and retreating, winter and summer, and coddled it must be, with craft of one kind or another, day in and day out."

"There's laughter in the case," said Amelia, coming up on the curve with a flurry of steel.

"If it were only laughter," said Kate, "I'd have no complaint. Laughter I've always liked since the clouds took the shape of a camel, or a bitten crust resembled, in no small way, the head of Napoleon, but it's a fruit that shakes down trouble."

Quoth Amelia, "Fruit, is it, or climber?"

"Be it either," spake Kate, "there's been two women in the bough, more than once in my day."

"One was owner," said Amelia, "and one was poacher."

"One was gift fruit, and one was gotten," quoth Kate.

Therewith, a doughty clout Amelia fetched her alongside of her head, setting her mousing among the cinders, and as good as was sent she gave in return, till blood flowed, and hair fell, and there were tears amid the equal anger.

"Filthy slut!" cried Kate.

"That and its sister," quoth Amelia, "that and its brother, that and its cousin, that and its halter, that and its litter, on hoof and on wing, on fin and on foot, lying and walking, there's not another as perfect, or may I sit on cold iron all the days of my life!" And at it they went again, in most good earnest, until habit, rising in them, overflowed, telling them it was past the hour of dinner, whereto the master of all nosebags, done and undone, would be coming, tempered with rage at a slight to his stomach.

Chapter 41

Wherein Sophia Goes A-Begging

Sophia (echo of her familie's despair),
Wrapped close within her sombre warring cloak
Of pauper stuff, well rounded to her case,
Made forth, a firey spirit, yet in thrall
Of webby death, and muted with decay—
To sit, and watch, and catch the golden fly
That should be bled into a buzzing use.

———

SCENE: The large sanctum of a magnate's office. Book-shelves, with false books, reach up to the ceiling. A portrait of the magnate's great-great-great-grandfather, in political tights, and scaled with the ornaments of civic appreciation, hangs over the desk.

At the head of the table, flanked with great ink-horns and enormous quills, sits the magnate, his disciples, twelve in number, ranging away on either side, an ink-horn apiece, nibbling their quills. The magnate is dressed in snuff-coloured garments, he has iron-grey whiskers brushed, in the approved mid-Victorian sweep, from mid-chin to mid-ear. He breathes with difficulty, the hair of his nose is exceeding swampish.

A little figure enters, walking with a good walk the length of the gallery, a three-tier caped dolman of twilled stuff, envelopes from chin to heel, surmounted by a shovel-shaped hat, embraced with close-clipped Dijon roses, and swaddled in black lace, a multistoned, ballheaded hatpin securing the whole. The eyeglass laces dangling over the full soft breast, laced boots three-quarters up the well-turned leg, encased in grey hose with a beaded list. Hand in glove, a large fine head on a small fine body, eagle on the rock, pink-pored, and everyone's-mother, smiling. The just pauper calling in a just cause, but underneath a double set of real Irish linens, scolloped and braided with satin-back grosgrain, and a falbala of lace; a railroad magnate's love-name in the back of the stem-wind, gun-metal breast-watch, dangling from a silver bow. A railroad pass in the reticule. A seat, by courtesy set, is taken by Sophia.

Sophia. Ah, and what ho, my dear Boots!

Boots (or the magnate, as he is to his friends). What ho! my very good general!

Sophia (drawing down her gloves, exposing a soft-skinned, capable hand, thereon the Swedish bloodstone ring in form of a heart). I was a girl once. (She smiles in turn, upon the magnate's co-workers.) My cradle rocked with applause at my coming. I had planned well. I had a handwriting, a most superb script. Body of me, what a rare girl is this! said I, and set about to house her. It was a good and canny house, my lords, well built and with everything that heart could desire or body need. Pictures on the walls of Hamlet thinking the thought, and of Leda doing the deed, and small daguerreotypes of my babes in duffle. He who came from between my feet, and fell downward into the grave, and he who came from between my feet and rose up into a man. And was I in any way a reckless woman, or a thoughtless? Nay, for I had tea-cups, and saucers, and a service of sweet matching; and linens by sizes. So was I, in the days of my life, but do we live forever? We do not, yet there is a world without end, and I firmly believe in it. And what is there in that world for you, my dear, what shall I promise you? Beauty is there for you, cubbed from the mating of gold, gold that cannot be earned, but must be won other ways. (Carefully she unhooks her pince-nez from its body chain, and holds up the bifurcated lenses to her motherly eye, scanning.) My son is weak, he has great gifts, but do we live forever? Life is strange for him. He is like the criminal in a famous murder case, that had been forgotten. So I, who gave him birth, have seen his sleeping at forty, the ageing symbol of a forgotten action. He plays, he writes, he can do many things; he has, only imagine! operas to his credit, with full orchestral directions planned, and executed amid the din of hungry children, on a deal table, littered with nothing more than the never-out-of-sight-of-the-hungry-and-the-distressed, bread and water. Alone and not alone, for a man always has a lively follower, if only one, an he walks backward, or a scout an he walks forward, but what has a woman? A pew to stable him in. What comfort an the pew be empty, and the stall uninhabited? (She stands up.) In a pool of rain water Simon denied Peter, and the cock crew, but who lives forever?

The Twelve. She is a beggar! A superlative, an assiduous and most astounding type, multifaced, multifeathered, but her breech-string, for all that, ties with a running bow. Toss her from wall to wall, and from the midst of her nefarious skirts you'll hear the mother cry, but let her stand, all her garments hanging to the earth, and you shall not know her!

Boots (reddening to his finger-tips but smoothing, with master touch, the hairs of his beard). O infamy! a mendicant and a woman in our midst! With what words has she not come, in times past, calling for our succour (turning to his right-hand partner, as he rubs forefinger and spatulate thumb across the grain of his ribbons of honour). Perhaps it were well to try her. An there be a battle and no old woman found among her clothes, connivance and no mother look,—for even praying you can tell the mother bottom,—why, we will set her out at the gate, that the citizens may witness so heinous a thing! I am all charity an the supplicant be truly tattered to the skin and the skin well parched, but whole cloth estranges me, as a patch of well-fed stomach throws me off scent!

Sophia (kneeling quickly). Come down, Sophia, even down from that your little height! This is the hour when men seek a girl among your skirts! Why, find her then, catch her on the flicker, for she asks forever only help, and reeks of that condition. Tear her into pieces adequate for the glutting of your suspicion, and every rag will speak the selfsame story, for there's nothing else about.

The Twelve. Need is a vulgar thing!

Sophia. And here's its very damn!

Boots (fingering a bill of no mean proportions in the left trouser pocket). Has it not been said by some philosopher, or man of that kidney, that sound stopped, echo is nowhere? If this is need's crying echo, why, we, like all great gentlemen, can experiment, though not too often, in the matter, and see if we agree. (He gives Sophia the by-no-means-mean bill.)

Sophia (rising—a little creature in an ageing dolman, going in a good walk up the stately corridors). Need is no longer need, shall the leaf tell of the tree? Who is pauper here now? Not I, though I've been, so the two conditions have buzzed within the hour. I bring you, Boots, my most dear, many things therefor. Farewell, then, and cry, "Mother, mother, mother!" for it is a word that comes up to me ever.

Chapter 42

Amelia Hears from Her Sister
on the Misfortunes of Women

This last week, my dear sister, have I looked into every nook and cranny of good London for a suitable position. Thirteen letters have I answered to no purpose, and perused as many more. At my time of life, I find that the ladies who would employ me (in answer to my advertisement, nicely placed in the *Church Times*, stating myself most certainly a companion) have so degraded that appellation and condition as to deem it one including back-scratching, nursing of halt and of lame, reading to the feeble of mind, fetching and carrying for strangurized nobles, dusting arms and putting the match to fifty chandeliers, stitching and sewing and mending, to say nothing of seating trousers, and touching up flaps to suit the vanity of the generation; in cooking and boiling, and steaming and roasting, spitting and pulling of fowls, woodcock and the like, that no decent woman would put her hand to. Scouring of pots and commodes, outhouses and night-vases, binding up wounds, and in general, so disporting oneself, as to relieve from embarrassment all the mishaps of nature and his wife. And it has but this morning been put to me, in a fifteen-page note, to wait

on an old lady in Putney, who knows not which end to put
the spoon to, and has continual gripes and is, beside, in nice
need of being read to in the tortures of the inquisition, that she
may sleep of night. And now, why is it, my dear sister, that the
holy Roman candles in such people's houses are good sturdy
dips in the evening, and nothing in the morning but a wick?
So fearfully do these things prey upon my mind that I am all
riddled looking for the cause. Neither will she bed alone, but
must be bedded with it seems, in order, she says, that econ-
omy may be practised in the way of these very same candles,
for they are exceeding expensive, coming as high as two and
sixpence, and, as she says, out of sight out of mind. Now where
can they be to be out of sight, and where placed to be out of
mind? It is more than I can comprehend. So bedded with, she
must be, and many nights she does but strangle one with fears
and agonies, needing much reassurance as: neither murdered
nor papist, nor foot-boy nor friar, be about to wait upon her
with request to hie her hence, in the cruellest manner, there
being (as she does most truly point out) many uses and ways of
religion, but that perhaps her dips do go too far into the matter.
Now this I lay you, I shall never become so neat to my soul's
end, that I shall forfeit my nightly freedom; my own bed I will
have, and one room therefore set aside to lay me in, no matter
what the house I go to of necessity, and by no means will I
lie with the old, or push out a bath-chair, ever so cunningly
devised to resemble a chariot, for I am neither horse nor lint,
nor crutches nor sponge; and where all these troubles come
from, unless it is a rare visitation in this our generation for its
sins and unbelieving, I know not, but you have my word on
it, there are so many terrible women, so hideously mated, so
many cripples and disjointed in our fine city, that you would
not know it for the healthy bouncing wench it was in our

time, without so much as a seed in the ear, or a bean up the nose, nor any malady, such as goitre and lumbago, rickets or hernia, to say nothing of those running distempers that so put one out of countenance. And though I be nearing two score and ten, I'll not get me to any habitation whatsoever, be it in Bond Street or Chelsea, that has for master or mistress some creature who cannot hold his, or her, wind like gentleman or lady, but needs must be blowing you up and down the corridors like any shuttlecock.

At one time, if my memory serves me, I was taken for her ladyship, the good Queen Alexandra, and not so many tens of years ago, neither. When my issue was most boisterous and I was in the bloom, I was presented with a pair of Queen Elizabeth's finest silk hose, and as I am within a pound tuppence of my alternatives, I may turn a royal leg to some account. Therefore I'll not stoop to change the rot in Denmark, nor so much as slap a plaster on the rheum of any lady as has sighed Heigh-ho! in her youth, and never thought twice before she flounced her person about in the December fogs with nothing more upon her lowers than handkerchief linen, and that falling a scant half-inch below her what-not, for though I suffer from the quinsy, and have the devil's own fancy in my left arm, well I know how it was come by, and that in leaning on the cold pews of our Church of England, and not from trolloping all over Kensington Gardens in a ruffled diaper! And though I must confess a monstrous bulging bunion, it's not shaped by wantonness, nor running here and there after cock and spur, or lance and gusset, or wig and fly, for not an ounce of chrism could be squeezed, tortured or blotted from off one such, if she were pounded and rolled a six months. Now such, dear sister, as you well know, I've ever had an abhorrence for, and never I got into my wincey but

I told myself no flimsier stuff should ever come between me and my philosophies, be they ever so High Church, and while I have the breath of life, I shall incline ever to the sturdy and the hearty side of faith, leaving to the somewhat game of my contemporaries to fancy that they are immersed in holiness an they but touch a pyx or a holy flower, or scrutinize the lace upon the altar cloth, for the autumn and the drift, and the fallen leaf of these things, is too like the vanities of the stuff, and not the substance.

Nor is this all, could I but tell you how the times have battened on the present, so that the day is overrun with dandies, swollen like sacks of pudding, how now you cannot drop into a dairy for a sup of beef-juice but you hear the critics, or those who profess to that grade, declaiming that the times have come to such a pretty pass that their wives' garters must go without their rosettes, and never so much as a shoulder-ribbon for the bunching of my lady's nightshift, or a buckle for her shoe, when she sets foot into the opera, as if these things were meet to a nation, then or now. Yet if I hold out, I shall not be numbered among my contemporaries, for a lot of beggars they are, that prate and prate, and come to no meaning word.

So I have come to think of times, an this condition do not stop, I shall lay most violent hands upon myself, though what a grievous sin it is! And come unto my judgment out of time, for I tell thee, sister, these times are not to be borne. What ins and outs there are to man I cannot turn my mind to understand.

Now that it is winter, I have some touching troubles to think upon. My winter wools are gone at the knees and where I do most sit, so that the inclement air does find me wanting in those spots I hold most dear. I go to bed these nights and have great trouble at the warming of them, what with chafing and rubbing and laying on of hands, however, I do well before

the clock strikes out the hour of midnight, but so much good
time lost in waking when the pillow calls, I hold as so much
time pilfered from a nice release.

And here to-day I made a fearful error. In passing up and
out of the Tube at Shepherd's Bush, nature so called and called
and whined within, I thought a penny-worth would set me
straight, and went to do that business. But so it befell, either
because I was so inner harried, or because my eyes begin to fail,
I lost a shilling, and it nightfall before I got the proper guard
to fish it back for me; and by that time, what with worry and
amazement, another penny went the selfsame way, so that I
am tuppence short, and my room not more than a mile from
the spot I stopped to give nature parole. 'Twas ever thus! I trust
that all these matters are quite unknown in the country where
you live, and yet I doubt for all the cunning of the American
but that he puts the penny to the slot somewhere along the
road. Now but tell me if I err, for these be things that I would
know of; their difference is what sets us so much a world apart,
and if it is the same, I shall feel that much nearer you, my
dearest sister. Therefore take your pen in hand to spare me a
word of your condition.

                              Thy most devoted sister.

Chapter 43

Timothy Strives Greatly with a Whore

"Have you ever repented a little," he asked, "either by night or by day, either walking, standing, reclining, looking up, bending down, reaching forward or sideways, over or under, singing or dancing, riding or trotting, running or panting, sleeping or waking, laughing or crying?" (She was well into her forties, and many a man had summered upon her.)

"No," quoth she.

"When bending to garter, to pick up a needle, to look under a bed, to search in a placket, to lament for a pin, to lay a cloth straight, a rug or a mat, to search for a button, a poker or wrench, a glove or a coin, for ratchet or whip, for a bodkin or feather, for a counter or dice, for a grid or a candle, for a stone or a stick, for spool or for scissors, for a hair-net or wimple, for thimble or spindle, for a tract or a treatise, for a thousand-and-one things that will fall on the floor?"

"Neither," quoth she.

"In reaching to fasten a cloak on its peg, a shirt on its arm, a bonnet in cupboard, a jar in the pantry, in hanging a picture, a curtain or motto, a fountain, a bird's cage, a shoe-bag or lantern, a rope or a flag, or calendar valentine, stocking, come Christmas?"

"Nor this," quoth she.

"Then in reaching," he said, "to lift down a volume, a mug or a jug, a shiny bed warmer or tumbler or caddy, those thousand-and-one things that dangle on wall and slumber on ledge? Think well, for it is a weight and a burden to my patience and forbearing."

"Nay."

"Perchance," he continued, "it was in doing of those million-and-one things that require circumlocution, travail and caution, such as cooking a feast for guest and for God's folks, for taking to font the bedwetting begotten, in a health to the married, or in grief for the dead; in dusting the parlour, in scouring a pantry, in sweeping and moiling, and pain of all sorts, in planning a season, in sewing or reaping, in running a tandem or stitching a gay seam, or taking a tuck, in dressing a foot, or easing a groin, in peeing the baby or neating its vent, in scouring a leg, or in care of all kind, for the sores of the flesh?"

"Not so."

"Then," he said in great perturbation, "in some small thing that goes not for employment. In wiping your nose, in lacing your boot, in pinning a left sleeve, or drawing a sigh, in gulping or sneezing, in coughing or spitting, in catching a lock from the nape of your neck; in changing your posture, in flexing a muscle, in turning a ring; in moving your eyebrows, in changing your focus from far to near by, in turning your body in one way or another?"

"No."

"God's trouble!" he cried, "wherein shall I find you! Was it in praying?"

"No."

"In travel?"

"No."

"At home?"

"No."

"At a window?"

"No."

"In your bed?"

"No."

"In another's?"

"No."

"In going upstairs?"

"No."

"In coming down?"

"No."

"In the morning?"

"No."

"At noon?"

"No."

"At even?"

"No."

"At midnight?"

"No."

"Then when, in God's name?" he said, in a great sweat, bringing his fist down on the table.

"Never at all," she answered, "and much trouble you'd have saved yourself and me had you been civil enough, in the beginning, before you loosed the deluge and dumbfounding, if you'd asked, 'Have you or no?'"

Timothy wiped his face with his handkerchief, and looked at her in wonder.

"I'd never have thought it sufficient," he answered, "or well and appropriate for the case as it stands."

"Ah, then," quoth she, "'tis because you are flouted and mauled by your pros and your cons. A pro and a con, my good fellow, never turned a woman in bed. But as you've been to such a pother, as you've put yourself to such heat, I'll go you one better, and show you what a deal such windiness gets you in the long and the hard run, by telling you the moment when I *almost* fancied I smelt repentance on the path to my door. . . ."

"When was that?" he said heartily, easing himself for the moment of surfeit.

"When," she said, curling her hair on her finger, "neither lying nor sitting, neither standing nor walking, neither in morning nor noon, nor at even nor night, neither in dusting nor sweeping, neither yawning nor sneezing, nor coughing and weeping, in wedding or shriving, or bending to capture, in looking from window, in easing a child, but when I sensed that my nine months of my mother were over and ended, I took a haul at the bell-cord, and swung down for the world."

"Was it then!" he cried joyfully. "And what way were you posed when the thought came into your head?"

"Pox on the fellow!" she exclaimed, and sat down in despair.

Now he lifts the girl's face up, and now he recalls her many things. "Remember," he said, "the day in autumn when I found you, befouled by man, lying where the last fling of fate had cast you, on the greensward, between the panther and the lion? The birds in the aviary were making squall, their feathers falling, lost and coloured, through the height of their cage, and the eagle gazed downward, the earth a million miles alien to his heart, and yet a prey, and you said, 'His flesh haunts him,' and that was our story. And," he continued, "in the days that are not, there were great men and great women and great sins, and great chariots and horses,—ways different from ours in beginning and ending. Then people went up a great way greatly in fire and in chariots and amid wings, blaspheming and praying, and some came downward, for they were becalmed, and the spirit shed them. There were then fables, and the history of them was written in the clouds, and the passage they had there, and the gods and their customs were beneath and above, but the times have come down, and eating and drinking and quarrel and peacemaking are not what they were. Therefore be not astonished that I, merchant, smelling of coffees and spices, should speak to you of the sins that are on us, for, my dear, there is no better in these days, where all wisdom has shrunken and the gods are dwindled and their chariots no longer smoke on the wheel. We are unlearned of our greatness and lost of our destiny and foredone of our inheritance so, do what we will, redemption is a small thing and no wonder." He continued, "The features of beauty have passed from man's face, but an animal, here and there, recalls them. All beasts have the holy look who have their eyes on either side, for they are apart and contrive not together, and the one sees not what is seen by the other, and mix not their roots—the ox and the goat, the lamb and the deer—"

"What of the fish?" says she * * * * * * * *

"The fish," he says, "have the eye on one side and the eye on the other often, even to the whale, who moves with an eyeless front, but they have not the holy look, for that they stare into waters where no man has trod with his Bible or sword, and the one eye sees water, and the other eye sees water, and there is nothing for discussion—and I would," he added, "that your own eyes were not so dumbfounded acquainted, for it's a terrible time I'm having setting holiness between them; and there, I fear me, it will meet with its death of tight strangulation."

And she was wroth, and rose up from the midst of him and held argument, saying: "It's no use the bridge of my nose is coming to, and it's because of the two eyes of me contriving this close that I've stockings and shirts and a shift to my bottom, so God be praised, and I'll say my amen."

And he wept sorely, for the place the devil occupied in her

blood-cells, and her bone-marrow, and her arteries, and her cavities, the cavity of her mouth and the cavity of her womb, and cavities of her mind. He wrestled with her greatly, smoking and talking.

"No more shall you come in the night-dark and have me, nor be drunken and wanton, as hithertofore. For I'll shut my sheets against you truly, and draw up together against our ways with each other, and the things that we do there, and I'll speak to you, saying: 'We are sinner and sinning, yet now and henceforward we'll not play at the business, for you, though a whore, shall turn aside and be whole in the small ways left over, and go to your daily encounter, a good girl and unrummaged, all the days of your life.' Get up now," he said, "for I've lost the art of high pleading." And the tears fell down continually from his brown eyes, unlearned. "But even a dog may turn twice for his sleeping," and he stroked her and told her he would give her up for the width of her soul. And she laughed all about him as he talked and wept, and her hands were upon him, cunning and cautious. His watch-chain and cuff-links, and his roll of a hundred, she took for her case of oncoming virgin, and she went from his chamber with soft feet and with sighing: "I'll do better, my love, most exceptional better, and prosper most hugely, and the world and its wife shall murmur amen!"

And in the morning he arose and, lo and behold! he discovered his loss in her, and tore at his hair as he sat on his bed, older and poorer, and he swore a great oath then, as great as he was able.

"God damn her and all whores from one end to another! Nowise can I tell a good woman from bad, for they distract and confuse me, and pluck and bedamn me, and open and shut me like a bag on a string. So I'll take my good wishes this day to the races, and the horses shall have what I've wasted on women, and the cards shall have what I've wantoned on women, and dice shall have what I've squandered on woman, and drink shall have what I've offered on woman, and the devil shall have what I've saved from a woman, and no man shall say that Timothy went further, for that childhood's upon me all the days of my life, and nothing could mind but the first war recorded, and nothing could add but the first two in figures, and nothing could learn past its very beginning. From the days of the famine I've nothing to fill me, and only the manna for a meal and a half. Curse my father and mother, their children and mine! and the people behind us, in millions and millions that have made me, Timothy, last crust to the world, a fool of a prophet without a forthcoming!"

And he arose and put on his clothing. Now a fine striped vest of a wonderful colour, with corded revers, and buttons and binding, he set about his body, and socks to match of a lovely plum colour he put on his legs, with high varnished boots to make a smart finish, and a coat that made a song of the lot And walking well paced, with his knees wide set, he turned to the races. And here, sitting, he waved his hat at the horses as they went over the hurdles, now up and now down, and he shouted and gambled and stood up with the crowd, and when a filly ran in by a leg and a half, he brought his hand down with a thundering thwack alongside of his groin, as is the way with a man when a beast is stupendous, and he sweated and laughed. . . .

And he saw an hundred women sleeping a low, soft sleep toward morning, when the spirit is going out at one end of the body, and a small fire is coming in, and the hundred slept on their hearts, and did not turn, and he said, "Is the sleep of virgins like the sleep of other women?" And they all turned over on their backs and laughed, and the sound was everywhere and even, that no one took more cadence to herself than her sister. And he cried: "God shames himself in me!"

Chapter 44

Fine Bitches All, and Molly Dance

Dance was a dog fancier; fine bitches all, with a sire to each, and to each sire and bitch a pedigree that would put a king to shame for its lack of straying, done in blue and red ink, and with marginal decorations representing intertwined ivy, and very infrequently a black cross against a name. For whenever, on whatsoever dark night it befell, that some grand dame of dogs so far forgot herself as to break loose in another breed (thereby bringing disgrace down upon her head, and unto her children forever and ever, like any erring girl) this one suffered the stigma of a black ink cross, with hour and date of the downfall, could Molly discover it, by peeping from between her blinds, as was her wont, at odd moments throughout the murky time allotted to slumber, for she chaperoned her kennel assiduously, and it was no easy pastime. Her ears could tell, to a howl, that which heralded, in the future, a brindle with a hound's ear.

Molly, it must be writ, was no better than her dogs, and seldom as good, for she got her children where and when it pleased her. There were some ten, and no one looked like, nor could one have pointed, with any certain finger, to its sire, or have penned it a tree of any proportions, above the sturdy root which was Molly.

Molly said that the human breed was of no importance anyhow and so what mattered it if they came from the ends of the earth? She herself was torn between two gentlemen, both of whom, at times, she called father, and at others, no father at all, for her mother before her had been stricken of a cast in the eye, which led her into all manner of mistakes, for that she could never see but half a man at best, and the halves that she saw, were, she said, as identical as peas in a pod, and how could God hold her responsible, if he made so small difference in such important instruments?

Molly Dance was a wench of a high water, with much flesh roundabouts, well shaped and lively to a touch. Molly drank a bit, not enough, it is true, to trouble her accustomed way of walking, but sufficient to make her healthily heedless when the youngest was overdemanding of the nipple. Molly had borne six sons and four daughters. Every one of the six was a liar, thief, drunkard and pickpocket. A merry household it made of an evening, as they whittled away the legs of the tables and chairs, boasting of this and of that, with many stolen watches as a basis. By the week's end, the increase of time-pieces produced a thumping lot of ticking about the premises, to say nothing of the brawling over who should profit therefrom.

Molly would say, as she was their mother, so their watches were also hers, but Molly was only fooling. For, as she said, she had been an honest woman all the days of her life, and had a wholesome picture of the likeness of the Lord, of damnation and hell-fire. The Lord she could have drawn with her left hand, and did many the time her sons were blaspheming, in a long gunny-sack, and, with a halo that reached clean round him, for safety, said Molly, and with a beautiful beard. As for hell, it blazed on the kitchen oilcloth in piercing flames, six in all, impaled on each, a naked, shrieking human, much like, in appearance, to her six sons. But touch a watch, or the gains of a watch? Not she! She had kept herself, and her children, up to that age appropriated for self-support, by the good round prices her well-mannered kennel netted her, and slept in the assurance that her sins, if any, would be forgiven her, as she had done her best with a very bad tangle, had cheated no one, and had paid her way.

The four girls (one was but a suckling babe, another but six) were promising much trouble. And do what she would, "Can I," asked Molly, "stand at the window all night through, watching for the thread of scarlet in both my girls and my dogs? So if there be a turn to Emma's leg that has a look of precocity, what can I do about it? They must bring their price as they may, but the bitches I sell to gentlemen, these be blooded straight, for when a dog goes wrong, you can tell it in an instant, and where will he be for a blue ribbon on dog-show day? With girls 'tis different, they may do many a wanton turn, and marry a count in the end, so where's the harm?" she said, and added, "Often and often's the time that the more astray they go in the beginning, the more ribbons dangle from them in the end, so there's an end to the business!"

The house of Molly Dance and the grounds around were as rambling as the trade. A great outhouse stunk and sounded with this breed and that; the kitchen stunk and sounded with her own. There was not a dry plank in the two buildings that one could put foot to, what with the youth and the care-free spirits within.

Molly pleased to term herself, "A little begotten of good, and a bit pushed by knowledge." She could read, and did, by the light of a blue-bellied lamp, feet on table. She consumed one after another some hundreds of shilling shockers, laughing with hearty delight when a knave got his mouth clean slitten, or a damsel suffered rape: "For at least," she said, "it never hurts in the reading."

Molly's eyes were also thirsty for beauty, and, like the head from which they looked, were not too particular. Her walls were somewhat covered with cheaply-framed lithographs in high bleeding colours, battle scenes and infants' pictures, trulls and virgins. Molly thought nothing of hanging the "Little Maid Crossing the Brook" next to the gentleman who got out of bed one second too late, of placing "Tears, Idle Tears" smack beside "Three Dead Men on a Dead Man's Chest." No, Molly Dance loved life and its miscarriage, but for arrangements she had no eye, save in the exact and narrow road of dogs.

Withal, you could not come at her with good or evil; these two things were thought out by someone in the beginning who had no liking for all things, of all kinds, all at once, in the same place. Molly had liking for just that. So what would your good and evil have meant to her, or how could she have understood it?

Molly Dance she put her children to bed, and listened carelessly, and good-natured, when they said, "Now I lay me down to sleep, I pray the Lord my soul to keep"; and just as good-humoured and careless she listened when, for variety, one of them would say, "Now I lay me down to wet me, will the Lord for this forget me?" It was all one and the same to Molly: they were praying, and that was well. They prayed one night as she wished, and the next as they wished. Well, and was that not comely to the universe, seeing that it made no two heads alike?

Dog thieves were common, and that one should have bumped into another, and have resented it, was nothing odd. When Molly fell over the body in the morning, she said, "Poor fellow," and meant both. It did not impair her appetite. Were there not life and death always, and was one not either in the one condition or in the other? Surely every inch of the earth must see a man go down, who cannot pick himself up again, and if it was her yard to-day, it would be someone's else to-morrow, just as it rained in at her chimney one night, and in at another's the night after.

Molly Dance believed, more or less, everything that was told her. "For if it's a lie," said she, "what do I care? It was good enough for the man that told it, and that suits me."

In this way, as may well be imagined, Molly Dance had a number of things mixed up in her education, so mixed, indeed, that another would have considered it a lack. Not so Molly. She said that she had knowledge both sides, back and front, and when Wendell struggled with her in these things (he had come to buy a bitch, and stayed to talk), she could not be got, on any account, to see what was wrong with her information, though on the other hand, she would have been the last to cry Wendell's down. "For," she said, "I've one way in my head and you have another, and the world's the world for all that, and what you think is fine, and what I think is fine, and better suited to my purpose, so where's the harm?"

"But, my dear," argued Wendell, not hot on the track of making Molly something—for everyone of every kind could not help but like her,—"how can it be well with you, when you think Henry James was a horse-thief, and Caesar the betrayer of Jesus?"

"And marry come up!" cried Molly Dance, "and what and who is Henry James that he should not be a horse-thief in his spare time, an I like to make him so? And what of Caesar that he might have betrayed Jesus? Somebody had to do the business, he had as good a right as the next fellow. You are always for taking away the divine privileges."

"Molly," said Wendell, regarding her with a sorrowful eye, "do you know the fundamentals of anything?"

"They scream about the place," said Molly calmly, "what better proof?"

"Molly," once again said Wendell sorrowfully, "do you know where hell is?"

"Sure enough," said Molly, "I do; it's let down from heaven on a string, and you no sooner grab it, than it's snatched up again."

"How do you know?" said Wendell, now ready to make a catch of her in this.

"By seeing it," said Molly shamelessly. "Many's the time I've seen it dangling just in front of my nose, and as I made to reach, it was snatched up again as quick as lightning!"

Now Molly was cantering. "In the beginning, this was a great world, so the history tells us, and what we can pick and glean, from the peelings and pits left scattered about, of its first days. Water was all over the place, and not a strip of land to put a train to, or a spot to build a store on. Then one day came Jonah, out of a whale's mouth. And now you think you are going to catch me on the matter of land! Well, it was this way," said Molly, "no sooner had the whale put Jonah down (and he was a sight, for he was the First Man, all decked out in olive branches and briars, and a crown of thorns, and his underneath all scaled, for everything was fish in that time), so, as I said, no sooner had the whale put him forth, than down four angels, each holding to a corner of land about the size of an acre, came, and unrolled the ends, and laid it where Jonah could put his hand to it. And it was stuck full of grass and flowers of all sorts and kinds, and the trees on it making a whistling, as they came through the air, and waving their branches for all to see, and the birds hanging on like grim death, all singing: 'Glory, glory, hallelujah, here's a wonder!'"

And it was a hundred and five inches thick in any place, that the moles, and the worms, and the ants might not fall out, and the edges were sealed up with roots, that it might not bleed in the waters, and might find foothold, and stay where it was placed, for a sign.

"When Jonah's scales dried in the sun, they turned to feathers, and a bit later, the feathers turned into furs of all sorts and kinds, and after the fur Jonah got down to his skin, which was as good as a hint at the human. Now Jonah had the wick of the Lord running in the midst of him like a candle, so that a vision came toward him and lit him quickly. And in his vision he saw a lake of crystal, and out of it coming a woman all dressed up in ribbons, and hee-hawing like an ass, which is the sirens' song. So Jonah waded out into the lake of crystal, and had word with her, and before you could say nip and tuck, the place was swarming with the human race. There immediately was the tribe of Dance, and likely enough the Ryders, and the MacMullens, and O'Ruaks, and the Norsemen, and the French, and the Germans, all talking with a difference. The Romans riding around and around in chariots, and martyrs playing the lyre, and the Jesuits tuning up on their jew's-harps, and Rome burning, and flags rising and falling like chaff in the wind, the Egyptians a thousand thousand years dead, all in the wink of an eyelash, and God tossing up the sun every minute, which was a day, and it falling back again, which was a night, because things moved swiftly, that the nations might get started. And the Jews all running up and down and wailing and rending their clothes, because they could not play with it also. Then the Italians began breeding for themselves, and the Norsemen began talking of age and of death, and down in the cornfield Cain suddenly slew Abel, and no sooner had murder been discovered, than Cain's frontal bone split asunder, and poetry began walking up and out of the place, and everyone began to sing, and the animals came down."

"Now what do you mean?" asked Wendell, hopelessly.

"Why, the animals had always herded in the sky, because there was no land. It was no uncommon sight then to see horses and cows and bison cropping the clouds, to say nothing of all those bigger animals that are not now, for that they broke up coming down—you've seen the pictures of it, no doubt—and the lambs and the ducks and drakes all going orderly in the clouds; the wild ducks remember it still," she said, "for do they not fly in team going South? All beasts used to do the same, like an army, for when the banded ox met with a hundred horse, there was a mighty battle above, that they might keep the paths that they had trodden there, but when they heard Jonah reciting, they came down, and stood about him, listening and wondering mightily to hear such lovely matter, and before you could believe the evidence of your eyes, Jonah had domesticated many of them, so that the lion lay down with the lamb, their faces on their paws, and nothing frightened, and Jonah was well pleased. But there was one animal who did not come down, and he was the Hound of Heaven, as you probably know, being somewhat in the way of learning yourself, and he ran a beaten path, his nose to the stars, hunting down the Star of the North, which was surnamed 'Knowledge of good and evil,' because it had run from the hem of the Lord when he was a-walking. So the hound put his ear back, and listened, but he would not come down, for there was a thing in heaven yet for him to do. This bothered Jonah greatly, and he set to ways and means for snaring him."

"And did he?" asked Wendell eagerly, forgetting himself.

"How is it that you do not know?" cried Molly, "for wasn't it by the discovery of the miracle of fire? Jonah struck the first match and set a blazing faggot before his cave, and down came the hound like a whirlwind, and snapped the fire up in his mouth—for he thought so bright a thing must be the truant star—and Jonah put him in chains before he could yelp himself clean of the blunder; and because he was caught by cunning and not by beauty, he has been man's slave ever since."

"Is that all you know of the stars?" said Wendell.

"No," said Molly, "but the other matter I'm not telling."

"And what was the end of it all?" asked Wendell.

"The end of it all," said Molly, none daunted, "was Britain. Up sprang John Bull, England on his right hand and Ireland on his left, and there's never been peace since, with the two of them reaching across him to grab at each other. It's why we have fish on Friday, in a blind effort to eat up the seat of the trouble, for you remember the whale was the fish that began it all."

"Molly," said Wendell, "is that all you know of original sin?"

"Original sin," answered Molly instantly, "was not at all as your biographers make it, no more than half the queens in the story-books died as they are said to, for I have the truth direct from her as got it, in a vision new laid—so I dare say it's the best—none other than Mary Flynn, the midwife, she who has fits. She says she was drinking one night, and playing a hand of cards with Michael, and every card an ace, when she fell off her chair and hit the fender, and as quick as that," Molly snapped her fingers, "she was right up to the ears in a vision. She says she saw a light, sharp and fine, shining as if through the bung-hole of a barrel, and that, she says, was probably due to the difficulty it had in entering her at all. And a calf's-foot came toward her, with wings on the shin bones, and little wings fluttering all about it, and a mouth speaking from the midst, saying: 'Mary, tell your people, and the people of them begotten, that the original sin was not a woman's.'

"'Had it to do with an apple at all?' inquired Mary, and there was a commotion in the wings, and the foot lifted itself up, so that it was all sole, and a voice came from the side of it, saying: 'It was an apple, surely, but man it was who snapped it up, scattering the seeds, and these he uses to this day to get his sons by.'"

"Oh, Molly, Molly, Molly!" said Wendell, "what is to become of you, you are all manners of mixed up in all things!"

"Bottom up or head up," said Molly, "it's all one to the Lord. He never said we were all to come to, in one position. Molly Dance I am, whichever way you take me, and that's saying more than most. My heart's nearer to my history than yours, that's the bone of contention," she concluded.

"Molly, Molly, you are as mixed as a pack of cards!" said Wendell.

"I'm hard to catch, and that's the truth," said Molly, draining her glass.

Said Wendell, "How is a man to have pride of his ways in you, when he cannot find them ten minutes later?"

"They'll come around in turn, my dear," answered Molly, and that's all the misery she would have of it.

"Molly," said Wendell, "who was Judas?"

"A man without friends," said Molly.

Wendell gave up with, "Molly, do you, for instance (not to perplex you unduly), know who is the father of, say, your last born?"

"As to that," said Molly, in no way distressed, "who cares? He didn't, I don't, and the child won't have to, and that's simplification."

"Molly," said Wendell, "what do you say to knowing, for once, who is the father of your next child?"

"It's a good idea," said Molly, "but how is it to be?"

"Here am I," said Wendell, "and there are you, Molly, and there's certainty in that."

"Do you think," asked Molly, "that it would be a way of setting things in order?"

"I think it a mighty fine way indeed," said Wendell.

"In that case," said Molly, well pleased, "we can but try the question."

* * * * * * *

"And now," said Molly, with a yawn, reaching for "Dick-Dead-Eye" in yellow covers, "there's only one thing that might make something uncertain of this certainty."

"What?" said Wendell, and stood stock still.

"Whether the child shall know you for its father or no," said Molly pleasantly.

"What do you mean, woman?" said Wendell sternly.

"Well," said Molly, stretching herself for comfort, "how shall she, or I, or you, or another know but that Dan, the corner policeman, be he? For not two nights ago he had the same idea, and that only goes to show you," she added, "that one man's thoughts are not worth much more than another's."

"Oh, my dear," sighed Wendell, "you are then, just as I found you, and I leave you no better and no worse."

"Bottom up or head up," said Molly, "it's Molly Dance to the end, and that's more than most people can say!"

Chapter 45

Dr. Matthew O'Connor Talks to Wendell on Holy Inspiration

One day, coming out of Molly Dance's gate, Dr. O'Connor ran into Wendell, who was coming in. Now, Dr. O'Connor had been but helping Molly at her eleventh, the same that might, or might not, set the tangle of her knowledge straight; and Wendell was come that way to inquire how things stood.

"Does the child look like anything you've ever seen before?" he asked the doctor, and the doctor, looking well past Wendell, answered: "Very like indeed."

Wendell, standing just without the now closed bars, said, with a touch of hesitation: "Boy or girl?"

"Girl," said the doctor, changing his grip from his left to his right hand, also looking preoccupied.

"Ah!" said Wendell, and touched a stone in the roadway with his boot, moving it an inch to one side, then moving it back. "And whom does she look like, to be exact?"

"She looks," said Dr. Matthew O'Connor, also manœuvring a pebble, "extremely childish."

"It's to be expected," said Wendell, "in one so young."

The doctor took out his watch. "Twenty minutes," he said, "to be precise."

"What sort of nose has she, now, for instance?" said Wendell, and turned him about, pretending to look at a billboard.

"Nose?" said the doctor, "nose? I don't think I noticed."

"Ah," said Wendell, regarding the poster with acute attention, "then it can't be, or you would have noticed."

"I dare say," said the doctor, and they both swung round and stood facing.

"What are you looking at me for?" said Wendell haughtily.

"For precisely the opposite reason that you are looking at me," answered the doctor, and took a step down the road.

"Wait a minute," cried Wendell. "I'll walk part way with you. Do you believe in heredity?"

"I would be an ass if I didn't," said the doctor. "Heredity is absolute and conclusive proof of God and the father."

"What?" said Wendell.

"God and the father," said the doctor, "that likeness is in all children, it is what produces trouble in families; when there is more of God in the child than there is father, that gentleman invariably accuses his wife of adultery, instead of faith, as he should, and a great deal more becoming it would be, and a saver of the peace of the home."

"Is she yonder, then," said Wendell, "God's child or the father's?"

"She is God's," said the doctor quietly; so quietly and hushed did he say it, that the heart of Wendell smote him and he clasped his hands together and cried aloud.

"You are pained?" said Dr. O'Connor, and looked away into the horizon.

"I am pained indeed," admitted Wendell, "for I now, for the first time, taste this jealousy that you spoke of. Is God the only thing man may be sure of?"

"When he cannot be sure of himself," said the doctor, "that's what he is there for."

"I," said Wendell humbly, "have never before had to believe. Perhaps that accounts for my lack of faith."

"It comes to all men, sooner or later," said Dr. Matthew O'Connor, "if they have manners; God is the only refinement of the masses."

Wendell pushed his hair back, and stood a minute in the roadway, thinking. "You know," he said presently, when he observed that he had kept the doctor standing a good five minutes, "I believe in another life, yet I do not believe in God; that is a contradiction, but I don't see why it is not possible that there should be another world and yet no God in it."

"It is impossible," returned the doctor, "for the reason that in another world man will be man, and will also have need, perhaps in increasing proportion, of behaviour; for when you reach subtleties, and fine shades of conduct, manners become still closer to the heart's need; therefore you will find God there also."

Wendell once again clasped his hands, but this time behind his back. "Dr. O'Connor," he said, "I perceive, in some dim way, that you are not as other men. I have loved many women, I have always been the undeniable father of my children until this day. So if I am not the father, on your own premises, why am I not then God?"

The doctor smiled. "Ryder," he answered, "you are not God because you tremble in the balance. God does not tremble."

"All women," said Wendell, leaving the argument for the moment, "are equal, until one dies in child-bed, then she becomes as near to saints as my mind can conceive. Why is that? you ask; because they died at the apex of their ability. But short of that they are, as we are, only now and again, great, for if they live, they come down, as we all come down, from their nobility, and must pursue life again in its own rounds, and for such a part," he added. "Give me the ugly woman, beautiful women do not make divine martyrs. I knew one such; she played the part of a drummer in the Haymarket, she was young then, and had a long, melancholy face, like the faces of kings that have not ruled. I could see in the way she lifted her legs that she wanted to settle down, to become gross, to be a mother, to drink strong coffee, to sleep in the daytime, and at night to pore over the destiny of the Corsican. She was very simple, very lewd, she laughed at one time and not at another. She was strong but not healthy, she was pure but much handled, she had dignity but she was powerless—the perfect mother!"

"It is much," said the doctor, "but what of that child?"

"She," said Wendell, "will follow her mother, she will become both buxom and coarse. It will have saved her from the pale existence of those women who, from the cradle to the grave, have but two odours—celibacy and monogamy. My daughter will be frank, neither promiscuous nor child-less: those two things are appropriated by flat-chested women whose hearts beat sideways for want of room. She will eat, function and die, looking neither backward nor forward."

"What," asked the doctor suddenly, "will she do with that ecstatic moment when she lies for the first time with her lover?"

"The simple," answered Wendell, "put no claims on ecstasy."

They now came out upon a grassy knoll overlooking extensive farm-lands. The doctor sat down, and Wendell was not slow to follow his example.

"Are you," said the doctor, leaning back, his arms behind his head, "what might be termed a good father?"

"Excellent. I keep my children well occupied, mentally and physically. When it is hot they are without need of instruction; something in their blood tells them what to do; but when it is cold—and we have inordinately cold winters, by the way—" he added, interrupting himself, "I tell them everything."

"Ah!" said the doctor.

"And I add," said Wendell, "that women, with some unknown dexterity, take comfort from anything that has no evidence."

"It's God in them," said Matthew O'Connor. "It accounts, I think, for the peculiar difference in the suicides of man and woman. A man may commit suicide for any number of the same reasons that a woman commits suicide, but he never lets the effect seal the cause, he reasons it out, he leaves notes, he says it was this, or that, or the other, in an endeavour to place himself on an equal footing with God. It is to him death of God and the father. Say the young man is about to kill himself (and for what manner of things do not young men kill themselves!); he has, perhaps, been outwitted by a woman; very well, he goes up to his room, he plans not only the end but the means to an end, he goes upstairs with a special and prolonged tip-toeing; he turns the handle with a difference, he closes the door with the feeling in closing it that he shall never open it again. It must be a painful sound! He goes to his mirror. He looked into that mirror when he was a growing lad— in that room he was born—well, he looked into that mirror as a lad, and understood that face. What must it be, when he looks and sees a face he does not understand? Troubled—why? Because he cannot kill himself without including his will in that action. He knows that if he kills himself, he is the slave of that action, so with the soul of the slave he bargains, and makes great argument about a thing that has not only no base for argument but no way but the way including its will. He says to himself, 'I must abandon you. How shall I abandon you?' Thus, he makes for himself a pact. If I kill me, my corpse shall be, in my terms absolute, and by myself, myself made not myself—voilà! With a woman, take what woman you like, the virgin in her nightshift, the mother in her maternity gown, the actress in her beaded buskins and ruff, the queen in her leg-o'-mutton sleeves, the peasant girl among her wheat, the shop girl among her percales, the market harridan in her filth and degradation, the whore in the stews; one and all commit, in that act, their body to death's custom, neither making bargain nor asking for precepts and points of departure, nor platforms for philosophy, because women know that there is God only, but man knows that there is God and the father."

Wendell looked at the doctor for a long time, in silence. He said: "How would you die, Matthew?"

And Matthew answered, "I should die like a woman."

"I," said Wendell simply, "should die like a child, most terribly frightened."

"Ah!" answered the doctor. "The child! That death is terrible indeed, the child knows neither of God nor the father!"

"Then I have you!" exclaimed Wendell, rising up. "If there is neither God nor father for the child, where then is your justice?"

Said the doctor in a low voice, plucking at the grass, "It lies in that grave with that infant"

"Why," cried Wendell, exasperated, "do you, of the Catholic faith, juggle so with words? Justice is a terrible, an irrefutable, and a colossal thing."

"Well?" said the doctor, and raised his eyes and looked at him.

"Oh," answered Wendell, for a moment bereft of anger, "yes, I see. Still," he said presently, coming back into his wind, "I don't see how you get comfort from your religion. The child, you say, stands without it then why not a man?"

"Because," said the doctor, "a man is what, think you? Only a child who has walked within the circle of the need of God. It is the difference between them."

"Am I a child that I know that I shall die like a child?"

"Yes, God help you," said the doctor fervently. "I fear that you are a child, and that like a child you will die."

"It is the worst death?"

"The very worst—for a man," said the doctor, "but," he added, "I will try to be there," and put his arm about him. "I serve children of all sorts," he said gently.

Chapter 46

Ryder—His Race

With a treatise on carnivora, the schools of love; a digression wherein Wendell explains his mission in life with an expose of much nothing.

———

Of all carnivora man holds woman most dear.

To see some sweet creature, couched in splendour, putting away sides of ox, fills him with pure ravishment. Does he not exclaim: "How prettily she becomes replenished! Goes she not about this business with gestures perfectly timed to the temporal art of gourmandism, setting it, with her exalted fancy, above that which it appears, as the vulture, by mounting the air, makes of his carrion something divine by that ascension?"

In like manner, consuming whole lamb, trawls of fish, an hundred guinea fowl, woodcock and grouse per annum, does she not eat, that through her office slaughter may be transfigured?

With what a gaming foot comes she to bed, lying upon her spotless linens, awaiting possibility! With what aqueous felicity does she slip and swim into slumber!

Has not wild venison rhymed her coquetries of throbbing bosom, spaced the heaving stomach to a strophe, as she lies dreaming in all capacities, mundane yet meticulous?

Has not some ox closed its great and downy eye, that she might fix an orb of disquietude upon her lover? Some fin, in dark water ceased to wave, that she, with beckoning hand, might take some gallant prisoner?

What rib could do that for itself which she has done? What kidney ever laid a nation's dust, as lightly as she will lightly lay that nation's dust, when that same kidney is relieved of its vain days of miring, by her reprieve?

Did ever brain of ewe fling a noose of desire beyond the next green leaf, until she raised it to a cast that brought down the stars, or turned a knot or two of it to trickery and treason?

What bullock heart made aught of its august proportion, till she consumed it to the deed?

How many a carcass has fallen to the axe that she might rise indignantly upon some cockscomb who did misconstrue her, setting her tearing among the tearing curtains, crying out familiar justice in an unfamiliar voice? Has not some dove cooed loose its perch, to give her the voice in which she says, "Lovest thou me?"

Aye, what brisket, shoulder, leg, rump, brought her to her knees crying, "I am thine, O Lord!" What snaring turned her on the lathe of gentleness? What cloven hoof tramped out her vintage of dark melancholy, to bring her down with mortal lowing?

All things whatsoever prey upon all things, and for man there is nothing that on him preys but God, and He upon him preys night and day, dreaming of greatness, threaded on the human agony, as man sets his game spinning on the helix of a vixen's whim.

A thousand times, in as many tongues, men have asked: "What is woman? Wherein comes that of her which we are not? What destroys our reason in her, when we see it enter her as we would, and come forth as she will? What in her, like a shadow jackal, preys upon the mound of our accomplishment, dragging off that of it we thought most rotten with defeat, to make of it an halter and a noose? For man rides the monster civilization, but to woman goes the shoe cast of it, in which is the exact record of that journey."

Such an one was Lady Bertha Bridesleep, Lady Terrance Bridesleep, and so Wendell came upon her in his crusading. "For," said he, "what's worth doing at all, is worth doing in all ways," and undoubtedly Lady Terrance would be a way undreamt of. She was near her final trick, for she was well into her sixties, and, being a woman of wit, could be counted on to turn her last somersault well within the shadow of the *chef-d'œuvre*.

Her home lay between two immense hills. It was shingled, wall and roof. Two verandahs ran its huge girth, and smoke issued from three of its six chimneys winter and summer. In this building were some eighteen rooms. Over an hundred perfectly paned windows opened out into the customs of North, South, East and West, and the polished floor was speckled with the sun shining amid the leaves of many a potted plant.

In the massive oak bed with its dark panels lay two warming pans, for Lady Terrance's blood was cooling, "And," she said, "no woman should chill too swiftly, for it kills the memory."

The small chapel, opening out into this her favourite room, had the look of a much used lair, where the beast has gone in to rest and sprung out to capture. It was somewhat of Lady Bridesleep's manner.

A night light burned and flickered in its bowl of ruby glass.

Above it the Lady of Heaven loomed amid her lilies, looking down imperishably upon the sixty years of the perishing flesh of the lady of the house, a little high with humour.

Against a black velvet curtain hung a Christ upon the cross, with bare breast, crowned head, and bloody hands and feet. But there was no Christian loin-cloth, for he was the Christ of the Spanish, and about him, to cover his blasphemed body, a little ballet skirt of gold.

Amid this setting Lady Bridesleep took Wendell's devotion, much as a rich beggar the last offering, which he shall not live to spend, dropping it among her heavier coin with pleasure.

When he spoke of children, she forbore to laugh, for though Sarah bore at ninety, Lady Terrance knew her furrows too well to suffer apprehension.

To Wendell there was no age to a willing woman, the willingness spoke of fecundity. He had known her long. Had she not, when he was but a youth, chucked him beneath the chin? How old she was he never thought. When she first swept into his mother's *salon* she had become but lately Lady Bridesleep, for she had married that estimable Lord Terrance of Bridesleep the winter before, she being then forty, and he nearing sixty-nine. In all due justice to her it must be admitted that she was ignorant just how much of him was nature and how much artifice. She feared that all that he then appeared was not plot of the womb, for his left eye was particularly estranged and fixed, and he walked well to one side.

The wedding night found her faced with the necessity of helping him to bed. When the noble was winnowed down, she found that she had married a head and trunk, and little more.

She said later, with casual greatness, that there was just enough left of him to Lord, for upon the dresser were his wig and teeth, upon the Chippendale sofa his leg and arm, his corsets lay upon the floor. The world said that she had married well: her wolf was drawn of fang. As he drowsed beside her in his tasselled nightcap, she read to him from the glories of the French revolution, and when, ever so often, he said "Ah!" she did not turn to inquire what had struck his fancy, for she said: "It could only interest the past." Though Wendell was undoubtedly Lady Terrance's last play (she had been widowed ten summers), she was yet too gamesome to take the hand at par. She was both epicure and gustator. At five she had eaten her porridge simply enough, but at sixty there was scarcely a bird or beast that held adequate intricacies; for she would nothing but the by-paths of a bird, the afterthoughts of a beast. These fashioned into a malign concoction by the blasé art of the French chef (who was as unnecessary to the continuance of nature as a capon) were her delight. For thirty odd years he had served up rudiments and hidden parts to her stomach's exact proclivity, never by so much as a parson's-nose overstocking the nice exactness of her desire. Therefore she could remember to a tripe to what she was beholden.

Men had come to her as men, and had left as little girls. Wendell had come Wendell, and as yet he had left Wendell. Who was she at sixty that upon the turnspit of her attraction a man should baste and be a man for all that?

She was not, however, as the reader may suspect, merely a "sport." She was vastly pleased with nature at its most natural, she itched to put the oysterman's tie in order, and to smarten up the bows on sundry chambermaids. She liked the simple reiteration in a stream of nuns, the monotonous tolling of mortuary bells, for it told of those who make of something unfamiliar the long custom. She sent the newborn layettes, and held many a dying pauper by the hand, and though she never wept, she had the thick eyelids that make tears unnecessary.

Now upon the advent of Wendell she thought long. Said she to herself, "What is man, and what his love? Men saw me in my youth, and love spoke thus—for I am the one to know the schools—putting his finger to the wing of his nose, he coughed, hawked, spat, sneezed, changed the hanging of his prowess from left to right, and walking not three steps behind, made a roaring wind, all good craftsman, to catch my amorous attention." She took up her first finger counting one: "Let us call that the School of Love Cough versus Sneeze, for dames in the first blush of lovely womanhood, for what less can a gallant offer an he has any sensitiveness at all." She took the second finger: "I begin to fade. He still coughs, sneezes, hems and haws. This shall be known as the School H. versus H. for dames in their fair thirties, for here his wind comes down." She took a third finger: "Then I am well within the shade. He still stands at attention, but he neither coughs, hawks, nor spits, for such cannot be expected, they belong alone to spring's idyll. Nay, now he saves his wind and water, and simply says, 'Alack, and Alas!' School of A. versus A. So here I am at sixty. What is the school come to now? Boast versus Brag! I shall be mistress of it."

That night she went down in her chapel, leaning her head against the mahogany foot of the cross, and said to her unseen confessor, herself confessor confessing (the thrifty heart), "How shall I make of me, in this my last play, a double six!

"In youth," she said, "the suffering of the mother is compared to the suffering of Christ; one becomes older, and the suffering is like another's, and one becomes old and the suffering is like everyone's: and one comes to die," she paused, looking at her hands, crossed and cunning, "and the suffering is less than one's own. But Terrance," she added thoughtfully, "was mother of none. Hark ye, lads and lassies, this was

I! Daughter of Bess, daughter of Jess, daughter of Hannah, daughter of Anna, daughter of May, daughter of Eve, daughter of Tilly-turn-spit, daughter of Kitty-the-Handle, daughter of Alice-be-Quick, daughter of Sally-Strong-Hand, daughter of Fanny-the-Faint, daughter of Winny-the-Haughty, daughter of High-Girl and Low-Girl, daughter of Kit-Here, daughter of Kat-There, daughter of Fool-Nowhere! So let it be a merry jest, for sorrow's company is full of kin, and let there be irony, that men may rock to think of what I thought one night in fall, when I was but an oldish Girl, and spreading at the end."

She pressed the bell. "Bring me," she said, "the thesaurus and a warming pan. I am old, and I must contrive."

Wendell, being a methodical and gentle soul, had placed a date upon his lying with her, as good debtors give day for paying of bills. It fell on a windy Sunday, when there was snow in the air, and Lady Terrance's servants were out walking with their hearts on their sleeves.

And Wendell was as good as his word. By ten he was divested of all but an argument.

"The time has come," said he, "when it is necessary that I should boast to you a little, and though it boot you nothing, it may explain all kinds of things that you will see from now on. I, my love, am to be Father of All Things. For this was I created, and to this will I cleave. Now this is the Race that shall be Ryder—those who can sing like the lark, coo like the dove, moo like the cow, buzz like the bee, cheep like the cricket, bark like the dog, mew like the cat, neigh like the stallion, roar like the bull, crow like the cock, bray like the ass, sob like the owl, bleat like the lamb, growl like the lion, whine like the seal, to say nothing of screeching like the parrots and all sundry cryings, wailings, belchings, gnashing, sighing, sobbing, screaming, such as one hears the world over, but from a thousand several throats. Never before have all these sounds been common to the human, but I shall accomplish it; some shall have the milk-tooth, and some the canine. Some shall be prophets, some sophists, some scoundrels, some virgins, some bawds, some priests, some doxies, some vassals, some freemen, some slaves, some mongers, some pamphleteers, some eunuchs, some hermaphrodites, some nobles, some pussywinks, some panders, some jades, some lawyers, some doctors, some presidents, some thieves; pro and con, for and against, though never one bourgeois or like to other men as we now know them, but at the fertile pitch of genius. For this was I created, and to this will I cleave. My children shall come forth, grow, rise, decline and fall in a manner hithertofore unknown to man, nor one so timid of spirit that he shall put a foot out of the womb, as children have since the beginning, inquiring, 'Is there whereon to stand?' but shall stride forth like those who have been nine months struggling in a net of sleep, wherein they did great deeds impaled upon slow, balking time. They shall be legend and folk-tale, and stories told at sundown. They shall follow the hounds, and herd with the beasts and know the way of birds and fish. They shall be fleshed with all fleshes now alien to man and unknown, and shall be by that flesh made so tender with wisdom that they shall know how the hoof strikes, the fin cleaves, the wing soars, the paw runs, the claw clings, and the web swims. No heart shall strike with a difference, for they shall have hearts within hearts; ox heart and robin heart."

"How do you accomplish all this?" inquired Lady Bridesleep.

"By bedding in all beds, and in bedding, sow no seed of doubt, and this," he added, "takes might and a will!"

"Shall they," inquired Lady Terrance, "know for what they were born?"

Said Wendell, "Does not the passing bell know of the corse, the wedding bell of the bride; and the fête bell of the thanksgiving? In a thousand several shapes shall they be created, and named all things!"

"So be it," said Lady Terrance, and there was no talk.

◆　◆　◆　◆　◆　◆　◆

In the dawn, where Wendell lay crowing like a cock, and most extraordinary pleased, Lady Terrance arose, and turned to him smiling. "What shall we call him?" inquired Wendell in huge pride.

"Nothing and Never," said Lady Terrance sweetly. "He shall accomplish all the others leave undone. You need No Child also, my good man, all fathers have one. On him you shall hang that part of your ambition too heavy for mortal. And now," she said to the maid, who answered her ring, "bring me the calf's head that you'll find on the ice."

Wendell opened his mouth, but no sound came.

Chapter 47

Going To, and Coming From

In which Wendell tells the authorities about the unaccount-able children.

You can well imagine, there was a deal of trouble in keeping Ryder's life out of the papers; the mayor said, gallantly enough, that Wendell should go to jail, felt boots and all; the school authorities said, still more gallantly, that unless the various children now living on what was known as "Bulls'-Ease" farm did not attend school, it would be not only much worse for them, but for their parents, *whoever* they were!

A delegation called, headed by a social worker, a small woman in Nelson tweeds, carrying a copy of the Christian Hymnal.

Wendell skipped about in his lamb's-wool coat (worn summer and winter alike), and said, before bearding the lions, to Amelia, his wife:

"Dress yourself in your black silk, my love, and as for Kate, keep her in the cupboard, for I am about to be infested with scrutiny." He then sallied forth.

"Wendell Grieve Ryder?" questioned the leader.

"The same," said Wendell, plucking a rose, his red hair shining in the sun.

"We hear," pursued the foremost of the party, a stoop-shouldered creature in a dun-coloured duster, "that there are two families in this house (he pointed); there are said to be as many children hereabouts as eight, and," he continued, looking from beneath heavy brows at Wendell, as if to see how it were possible, "as there is no account of more than one man, we have come to reconnoitre . . ."

"What?" said Wendell.

"The conditions," replied the questioner.

"Insinuate . . ." said Wendell.

"Is there not more than one woman here?"

"Oh, there are several," said Wendell.

"Whose are they?"

"They belong eminently," said Wendell, casting his eyes up, "to themselves. Now there is my mother, a most extraordinary woman, there's also my wife, no less in her way, and there's one Kate-Careless . . ."

"That's the party," said the creature in the dun-coloured duster, lunging forward on his cane.

"What?" said Wendell.

"That's her, that's the other wife, that's the mother of three . . ."

"True," said Wendell, "three exactly . . ."

The dun-coloured person brought his face closer. "Whose," he demanded in a sepulchral voice, "are they?"

"Hers," said Wendell.

"And?"

"Undoubtedly his."

"His?"

"Did you never," said Wendell, in astonishment, plucking the rose apart, "see him?"

"Who?"

Wendell looked carefully around the rose-bush, and then whispered behind his hand, "The cherry-coloured individual, name Arthur . . . ."

"Never!" said the interlocutor, leaning back on his heels. "What has he done, and who is he?"

"Damned good man," said Wendell; "he did the extra children, one trip apiece. He's a travelling salesman, sells water filters. Once every year, as regular as clockwork, he climbs over the gate; he won't open it, he's different in every way; he comes over the gate stroking his beard, a most beautiful affair, long and loose of hair, like a prophet's, only in better condition, goes around to the pump, and there meets Mrs. Arthur. 'What has been your occupation these last twelve months, minus one day only?' he inquires. 'Go on!' she says. 'What do you suppose but that I've finished that bit of tatting, and am well into the darker shades of the rose.' 'Will you take a short walk with me?' he says. 'I'll go no further than the cornfield,' she answers. 'The cornfield it is,' he says, and off they go. The corn is high and in the ear, and the meadow larks are singing. She is a big woman and she sits down, and he is a thin man and he sits beside her."

"Then . . . ?"

"Then," pursued Wendell, "as I have the account of it, he puts his arm around her. 'Have you asked God for anything this summer?' he says. 'I have not,' she answers. 'And why not?' he asks. 'Because,' she says, 'I want there should be one person in the world that loves Him for Himself, and not for His influence.' And there's a bit of silence. The green corn waves and the earth-worms are turning up a bit of a hill. 'Since the beginning of creation,' she continues, 'men have said: Give me, and now I am, and I say nothing. It's hard when you know, spitting sure, there's things being handed out, and your name's not down, but here I am, and I'll ask for nothing, just to show that I love that man.'

"'And what do you think of justice?' he says.

"'That's what I think of it,' she answers, 'justice is all compact of letting the justifier have a moment's peace! When I came to bed,' she added, looking at the sky, 'with that last child of yours, I had a vision.'

"'You had!' he says.

"'There were many people in it,' she says, 'all in a continuous stream, so that you knew something was going to be done without a personal bias; they bury people like that, and like that they go to mass, and like that they came to reassure me.'

"'Of what?' says he.

"'Of a good delivery, to be sure! And how am I to be certain they'll do as much a second time? And without it, how am I to have courage?'

"'I'll tell you a story,' he says, putting his other arm around her, 'and while it's piling up into a thing of beauty, there's no knowing what, unthinking like, we may be doing with the next generation. So,' he says, 'you lie comfortable on my arm, and I'll shade you, and the corn will shade you from the excessive rigours of the heat,' he says. 'And we'll find a way.

"'Now,' he begins, 'in Patagonia . . .'

"'Don't make it so far outland,' she says.

"'Well, for that matter, the same thing took place in Sparta.'

"'Nor among the heathen,' she says. 'I won't have my children all which ways from the start.'

"'Then how is the country of Connecticut?' he inquired.

"'It will do fine,' she answers, and lies quiet.

"'Well, it was in New England that it happened,' he says, beginning easy, and breathing through his nostrils. 'Once upon a time there lived two fine women . . .'

"'Ah, you devil!' she says, and half rises up.

"'Halt!' he cries out loudly. 'In the year before I was born . . .'

"'Oh,' she answers, and is quiet as you please. 'There lived two fine women . . .'

"'Though how you know about it,' she adds, 'is more than I can see!'

"'Hearsay,' he says, 'and hearsay is mighty gentle on women. But listen now, there were two fine women, and one of them was very pious and religious, and did everything as it is pleasant and good, and the other was a hussy, and a wanton, and a baggage, and her clothing was held together on a running thread, and the most private garments were chain stitch, so now you know how it was with her.

"'Molly was the good one, and Eva was the bad one. I'm thinking their names should have been vice versa, but it's too late now. Moll and Eva they were, and so they lie side by side in the same earth. Well, as I was saying, one was always going to and the other always coming from church—which was which I guess it's not difficult for you to imagine—anyway, it caused a deal of trouble in the town, for there arose a controversy that finally drew in the whole shire for miles around; everybody with a troublesome mind was caught up into the matter, and it ended in the death of the one, and the disappearance of the other. Well, it was Moll who was always seen coming from church, and it was Eva who was always seen going to church, so people began to say, "Which is the holier, she who is always going to, or she who is always coming from?" Some of them had it that Eva was the better, for said they, it stands to reason that going to is more pleasant to the Lord than coming from. But, said others, how can you tell where Moll goes, when she is coming from, or where Eva goes when she is going to? Some maintained that, though it was true that Moll had been in devotion a moment before, as is necessary and preliminary to coming from, no one could say, once in the way of going from, where she was, or where her mind. Others said, that while Eva had never, to anyone's knowledge, been seen on the inside of a church during her whole life, and that somehow, in her going to, she always went further, still it was with a mind turned toward, and not away from, the holy sanctuary.

"'Well, as you would suppose, the whole town became one seething mass of speculation, for what do men like better,' he says, 'than a rag to chew on, and tatter between them, so long as it has a philosophic savour?

"'Be that as it may, wives forgot to put the pot on, husbands forgot to come home; and it is recorded that the town went one whole night without light, because the lamplighter was having it out with the milkman, who never delivered the morning's milk. And all as to whether Moll or Eva was the most wholesome.

"'When this terrible argument started, it was just after evening service, and, as usual, Moll was seen coming from, and Eva going to. Now, because a garrison of officers was stationed there for a day or so, the town had made great preparations for a celebration. Women were cooking prodigious great puddings, men were fitting bung-holes with spigots of superb roundness; the mistresses and the daughters of the house were tearing tapestries to pieces, in the most touching sections of the design, where doves mated, and lovers trysted, and Venus sported with the waves, hands everywhere committing indiscretions, for evening pelts and stomachers, twining everything in their hair that they could lay their fingers to, snatching crystal drops from chandeliers for earrings, knocking off china flowers from jewel cases for buckles to their slippers, and running up and down with tussocks of hair now on this side now on that to secure the most bewitching angle, others hiding in corners, and under chairs with pretty white doe-skin volumes of the poets, trying to get a verse by heart before the making of the dressing and the jellies; the balustrades, and balconies, and gardens full of them, with busts arranged just to the point of strategy when, as I said, the argument began, and there they were a good full week later, never having changed their position, in kitchens and bedrooms, in garret and in cellar, in house and in street, all rucked and rumpled with the heat of the matter, and no solution in sight.

"'Of course, they finally saw that something must be done to end the question, therefore a delegation, including everyone, men, women and children, old ladies with crutches, beggar and rich man alike, set out to the house of a philosopher renowned for his great wisdom and learning, a holy man, but tinct with wizardry, and there they streamed up and down before his house, still arguing and squabbling, so that to this day many of the families are estranged.

"'The learned man in a nightcap put his head out of his casement, and would know of the matter. When he was become conversant of the dilemma, he so mightily liked the case that he discussed it with them full three days and nights from his window, talking sometimes to the Great Bear and sometimes to the House of Lords, and yet again to Jehovah, for these fellows, by means of their linguistic abilities, can commune with all peoples.

"'Well, the upshot of it was, that they bore him back on their shoulders, and set him down before the door of the two sisters, Eva and Moll, saying, "Now solve this riddle, or come not out from this house alive, for thus we cannot go on."

"'Now the house of Eva and Moll, the two fine women, was in darkness, though it was broad daylight, for the blinds were down at the windows on the road-side, so the multitude had to content themselves with seeing and knowing nothing. Therefore they set themselves down to wait in the gutters, and about the wall, some even climbing up on the ledge to try to secure a peep within.

"'When the learned man got himself into the hall, he looked about him, but his eyes saw only as far as their eye-balls, for it was so pitchy dark that he had trouble knowing if it was his own hand before him or another's. Stumbling along in this quandary (for anything is kidney for speculation to the mind of a man open to argument), he came to a flight of stairs which, with great difficulty, he managed to ascend. A dim light shone across the dust of the sill to the inner alcove, and upon knocking, he was bidden to enter, in a faint voice.

"'And therein he entered, and saw before him a great truckle bed, with two full horsehair mattresses thereon, for going to, or coming from, they believed in having it comfortable. In the bed lay Moll, and at her side lay Eva, and a babe between them. There were candles, alight and burning, at the four cor-ners of the bed, and candles burning about on ledges, for the room was full of little women virgins, in pink and blue robes, and each had a candle burning, and there were curtains to the bed drawn back and fastened with faded baby ribbon, and there was a smell in the room of wax, and of oil, and of incense, and the bed was full of pictures of the saints and the bleeding heart, and they made a great bleating when Eva moved, for she moved a little, and Moll moved never at all.

"'"And now," said Eva, rising up, and looking upon him with great quiet, "tell the people, who make a rabble in the town, and sound at all times in my gutters, that they can go home to their own ways of living, for the matter is settled as to whether Moll is the most righteous, or Eva, in that Moll goes to, and Eva comes from, for the thing is reversed. Moll has gone to the Lord, and I have come from the Lord, so let them change their rag for another. Moll is dead, and I'm a mother, and be damned to you and the rest!"

"'And with that, out he went. And now,' said Arthur, 'there's a good deal of coming and going for you, and how do you feel, my love?' She answers him, 'It was a good story, and one that I'm not likely to forget the moral of this nine months.'"

"Wasn't he rather long about it?" remarked the man in the dun-coloured duster, regarding Wendell, as he stood beside the rose-bush.

"A great, long time," quoth Wendell.

"How do you account for it," remarked the man in the dun-coloured duster, "that a person so willing to forge in two or more ways for so long a time, should leave on the same day, and never show up until the next harvest?"

"Why," said Wendell, "that's a simple matter. Arthur is a most fastidious creature."

"How?" prompted the dun coat.

"You see," said Wendell, "he is timorous, he is fearful, he is possessed—"

"What of?" inquired the social worker, lowering the psalms.

"Of a certainty," said Wendell.

"Come to the point," remarked the dun coat, lunging forward on his cane, "if you please."

"Then," said Wendell, "if you must have the man's whole character and history, he is afraid that, if he waits longer, say some nine months or more, the sleeve of his left cuff may be pissed upon."

"Good God!" exclaimed the man. "It's perfectly clear. I beg your pardon a thousand times for putting you to an inconvenience, and for my, shall I say for our, unjust apprehensions." And he bowed.

"Not at all," said Wendell, "for I am a great entertainer of gentlemen."

And upon that everyone left the garden.

Now when Wendell left the garden, he so well liked his own story that it pained him greatly that it was a fabrication, and not in the way of its happening. "For," said he to himself, "I've talked to that woman many times, in a number of ways, but never in that way, and I'm a number of men in myself, no doubt, but I've never been Arthur, and it's a great shame," he said to himself, and went a little way into the woods, and sat down among the underbrush, and thought a long while.

"When next I come to lie with my Kate," he said, thinking, "will I tell her that story, or won't I? That's the question. And if I do, will she so answer me that it would run as I said, or will she switch me off in another direction?" He brought his hand down with a bang. "Another direction it is, or I know her not!" he said, and lay back looking up into the gnarled oak, where hung the roan carcass of the nannygoat he had hanged but yesterday for that the scrofula was on her, and she suffered in her hide more than she-goat can bear. "And it's damned what a sensitive man is brought to," he said, talking to the swinging body, "when he's racked with women, and with beasts."

Chapter 48

Elisha in Love with the Maiden

The candles shook slightly in their sockets. His knuckles, coming forward toward him out of the high glaze of the piano, went up slowly on Beethoven sonata, Beethoven, Ludwig van, born at Bonn on December 17, 1770; at four he began the study of music—at nine—About the neck, the white neckcloth, down coming, the unlovely thinking eyes—Dad's eyes—He played on.

Love and the maiden, that was life and beauty mingled! Two wings folded over her feet, and two over her eyes, and two to fly with—that was the maiden. But he was Elisha, bastard of Kate-Careless, bastard. But his father was Wendell, and what was his father's real name—Peel? He had never liked that, a bad good name. He, Elisha, playing Beethoven; that had something to do with his father again. It was said that the story lay somewhere bitten into a razor blade, but the razor could never be found. Was that the secret place in his father, not telling, hiding it forever, hinting the story and hiding the proof?

Death and the Maiden. So painfully mingled, two wings folded over her feet, and two over her eyes, and two that would not fly. What had he said to her? Half-formed mind informing a girl child. Was it a half-formed mind that cut the world-weary heads from queens' shoulders?

What could he tell her? What had he told her? "I do not know myself." Sinned to set her apart to sin and to know. And she sitting apart, forsaken, to sin and to know. In him was the cloak of protection, half formed and not rainworthy; but one must shelter before one is able.

He played on softly, all fourteen and in youth's love, played not as his father wished, loud, loud, for the pleasure of knowing icy splendour of volume, but softly, softly, as his work-hardened hands would go. Would he have been thus had he gone away like other children? Been brought out of Egypt? But Egypt was the mother wound, the festering that gave off music, and whining, and the power to withstand.

Now the jury of his thoughts came to sit upon his case:

You are, to all intent and purpose, a road-mender for the county; I declare there is yet the muck of clay upon your knees.

I shall play for the people in the town hall, nevertheless.

You are in love; what kind of woman is it? Look her well over in your mind's eye. Is she as young, as lovely, as innocent as you make her? Is she not perhaps, at bottom, as well dregged with life as a bottle of wine?

She is death and the maiden.

That is your fancy. Where is reality in you?

I am young, my masters.

You will be old, my son.

I shall play in the town hall for the people, nevertheless. Gently and softly, as in a dream, he went among the cows, the little heifer faintly hoofed, with eyes of kingdom-come, drank, tearing at the rag of the mother teat, sprawling on spindly legs like a slackened instrument Elisha took up the guinea pigs, kneeling, smiling to see them blindly rooting in his pocket, the open places of his coat, the quick noses flickering, with the shaft of wheat outthrust from the fragile furred jaws, rodent and not rodent, fearful and helpless.

Looking past the sand-pit he could see the red of Wendell's hair above the furze, the dusty brown coat, his bent arm pluck-ing some herb or root that should be dinner's experiment. He thought of his mother's experiment-shocked body, heavy of belly, the stiff legs, a distorted shape of death. He went out under the trees of the orchard, stumbling against roots, looking up into the branches. It was beginning to rain, new rain, but his mother said the morrow would be fair, and she had strange wisdom, because she needed a recompense, for that she went off into trances, seeing men at war, and her will-of-the-wisp dead sister in a long white gown,—the dead will not supply colours. Right buxom was that sister when she died, folding her hands over a well-turned breast, but she came back a maiden, death and the maiden. Who doubts this matter? Who doubts the word and the testimony of the common woman? She alone who is too ignorant for beauty alone may see beauty; she who is too vulgar for religion may be vouchsafed the word. Who doubts one's mother whose beauty is gone, but whose humour is lasting? Who doubts the word of the mother who sees that which compensates the condition? Not I! And who can doubt the word of the mother when she is shameless in her nakedness before you, to show you how a body goes down into death?

On the morrow he plays, his hair about his boy's face. Touchingly the ungainly body leans forward under the first frock coat, his chin trembles on the unhappy arrangement of stock embellished with horse-shoe tie pin; his hardened hands come living from his cuffs, his hobnailed boot slithers on the pedal, his hands requite him. On the road they worked for Dad, now they work for himself,—death and the maiden so painfully mingled.

He does not look about him into the hall where the people are, or up at the ghastly bowl of light hanging irregularly on three chains. The sound of feet, and then no sound, and then his sound and Beethoven's sound. He bends over, he jerks his body up, he is with himself alone, he has thrown off the people, a drowning mass about a drowning man's neck, and plays loud, and is liberated to himself, softly, softly for my soul's sake, says he, and plays softly. And he is weeping, and he rises, bows, weeps and bows, and the people thunder applause.

That night he lay with his little brother; his father lay in a bed beside. Rising up in the night, he looked at his father where he lay, the heavy odour of pine that was his body's smell thick about him. His father awoke and looked and saw, and called him. And Elisha got into bed beside him, and put his arm over his father and said:

"It is all right."

And Wendell answered: "What is to prevent you from becoming a great man? After this there is greatness. It is well to be great, it keeps the people off. Live for the people and you keep them off. It is the secret; otherwise they swarm over you and you perish. But the great man lives and dies alone. If he is one with the people he is apart, and knows no one,—and has no brother. One who has reached the people and touched the people has finished with the people. But for that you must play loud, your whole weight, you must buy your freedom with great tumult. Later you can play softly, softly. Man is only bought with tumult, there is no quiet price, you shall see."

In the dark Elisha wet his lips, and said softly, "Tell me, what is a woman?"

"Passion, of a kind," said Wendell.

Elisha said, "What is the kind?"

"She has seen a man tremble," said Wendell, preparing himself for a discourse, for he liked nothing better, even though it came up in the pit of night. 'What is this?' says she. 'This is yours,' he answers. She comes toward him with a lively step, perhaps there are tears in her eyes, for she is submissive. 'Give me something no one has ever given a woman.' And he answers, 'I have only that which has been given since the beginning of the world.' 'What is that?' she asks, and he answers, trembling still more, clasping his hands on which the veins stand out, 'Grossness!' With humid eyes she sees him approaching her, looking," said Wendell, "very divine and very ugly. 'Wait!' she cries, and he begins to breathe heavily. He knocks over a chair, and she regains her equilibrium. There is always some disaster in the walk of a man that gives back safety, if it is wanted. 'Beast!' she says. 'Mate of that!' he answers, and comes down upon her."

"Then . . . ?"

"Then," said Wendell, "she knows still more."

"What more does she know?" said Elisha.

"Injustice," said his father. "The curtain goes up on injustice, she is in the pit dressed for the scene. A low white gown, a corsage of lilies, a band of brilliants, a fallen fur wrap. She settles herself in her chair, she has a feeling of expectation,—warm, comforting, ecstatic. This is what she sees—one man betraying another. She does not take sides, she pities; she does not judge, she waits, like a child, for the dénouement.

"Citizens A and B are acting out the travesty of emotion. Citizen A cries to the jury, 'Behold the man! He has cheated me! He came to buy a sheep, and he stole a cow!'

"'He lies!' retorts Citizen B. 'I ordered a cow and he sends me a sheep!' And all the while your woman, my son, smiles behind her opera glasses, best German make, covered with leather, sold in quantities, and does not take sides. She said to herself, 'What is this divine difference between cow and sheep that makes the one a prize and the other a default? Was the cow sick and the sheep healthy? or were both ailing, or were both of select stock?' And the injustice continues.

"'Lock the man up,' says the jury. 'Give the dealer six months for the lack of a cow, and the purchaser seven for the acquisition of a sheep.'

"'What!' says your woman, 'is one man's injustice valuable to the extent of six months, and the other to seven? If so, which injustice is the most just?' And once again she knows more."

"Then . . . ?"

"She goes from one scene to another, the scenes are the worlds, but the end is her own."

"Why?" asked Elisha, lying still.

"Because," said his father, "one dies of oneself. She has observed that also."

Elisha said, "How?"

"By death in others. Passion in others. Injustice in others. A man dies, let us say; she is once again the spectator. She sits beside the bed. 'Open the window,' says the dying man, and she opens the window. 'Are you comfortable?' she inquires, and he says that he is comfortable. And in saying it, he recalls his youth when comfort was a thing so comfortable that he could not have claimed it. His mind wanders, he is sick of himself, spent and past. He is dying now, and he is selfish as only the dying are selfish. He has lived up all his disinterested days and now, with the last hour, he counts himself one last drop of water in the sun. With a maniacal effort he tries to re-establish himself. He demands another pillow, he sends it away. He asks for air, and when she opens the window, he would that it were closed, and in the dark, trying to recollect when he was a sum unspent, he dies. And all the while your woman sighs and dabs her eyes with her lace handkerchief, and is not troubled overmuch. Yet she waits for the last sentence that shall fall from those lips for, like the world, she puts some value, which is a gross error, on the last word. It is important to her because there will be none other to cover it up."

Said Elisha, "Is woman good or evil?"

"There are no good women," says Wendell. "They see too much from the start. If you locked them in a dungeon, in solitary confinement, from the cradle to the grave, they see too much."

"How?" said his son.

"They look into their hearts," said Wendell, "and in their hearts is the whole drama of man. Confinement would, in fact, only make the matter worse, for alone, they act it before God. That is religion."

Elisha slept, his childish man's face turned back. With open mouth he slept, and nightlong played down his father's leg the second movement of the "Sonata Pathétique," his father's hand twitching in the midnight scale, sleeping too, breathing down his hairy nostrils, his red hair spread like a girl's upon the pillow. Sister in her room sleeping with her good hawk nose close to her mother Kate's bulk. Sleeping all, sleeping sleep, dreaming things they never thought of. Sleeping through the night.

Chapter 49

Three Great Moments of History

As told by Dr. Matthew O'Connor to a young man he saw legging it over a fence with an earthenware pot in his arm, whereupon Dr. O'Connor did catch him amid his crotches, and brought him down to partake of a sup of such education in the ways of the world as might, in some hereafter, set him in the strait path once again. For that good man did hold strongly by wit and wisdom where it drops off the thin edge of the centuries, and had held argument on this business in the portico of many a church from land's end to land's end.

So says he: "Listen, my lad, for I'll give you what is better than stealing, as a young girl is better than an old, a boy better than a girl, and a goat the best of the lot; to wit, the matter of the three great moments of history, for I think I see about you that which is ill gotten, and never so is it when gotten of the pure wisdom of nations. I am no scantling, and do not haggle with a man's soul, for some come one way and some another, and all are not hung head up on the line when they are set out to dry, but must, of a dozen or so, be one who hangs by his heels, and thus is addle-pated. Or being pegged by his member cannot in after life forget it, and do put much pride

279

by it, and boasting alongside of it, praising and offering it at the most unpropitious moments, seeing nothing else of value all his life. Some so magnify its importance to themselves that they leave instructions to have their bodies placed beside it in the grave, as if it were a bride or a soul, and some have gone so far as to leave codicils that it be not taped nor swaddled, but left four good round days bared in the coffin, that the breath of life shall not be cut from out it, an it should take it into its head to revive and bespeak itself as still a citizen. Wherefore be you more reasonable and listen to the true foundation of man's pride, that which has made you what you now are, though hot put to get out upon the road, never so much as giving a thought to whence you came, or where you go, above this place you would leave, for the place you would hide in; for certainly it is of more import where you came from, out of the eternal whim of time, and whereto you go, into the eternal maw of its caprice, than that you should be home with whole cloth and with a pot that looks to me to be filled with Lady Drawbreeches best and pinkest honey, for I know the shine of it to a bud, and could almost lay me to the very flower each drop breathes of, and yearns to, but let that rest, and lend ear."

So thus he began:

"The first great moment of history that I shall recount to you was when Cleopatra, wearied to tears with her Antony, longed for the obliterating peace of sleep. Yet, for such is the way of women who have been of service overlong, she thought to have diversion of one kind or another to rest her ravelled ends. In those days women, and men for that matter, were never so solaced as when observing the movements of some dance. So thinking of her dancing girls, she clapped her hands, and they were forthcoming, and did, I dare affirm, many a pretty turn for her amusement. But do what they would—and it was a plenty—they could not amuse her, she was at that excessive pitch of boredom that not Copernicus himself nor his theories could have caused her a moment's speculative pleasure, she had so thinned to weariness and thickened for the pillow. But one thing was yet in her mind—that to remain beautiful one must visit the stools somewhat. Therewith she called for her masseuse and a basket of figs, for what thumping, pinching and rolling could not effect their salubrious medication might perform.

"When, therefore (being well rubbed down and kneaded to a perfection), she languidly reached for a fig, and, lifting the fattest and most pompous of all these laxatives, saw beneath it the cunningest of asps, neatly curled: She said 'Ah,' and set it toward her with that remnant, or I should say rudiment, of mother instinct which was allotted to her at birth, placing it to her left dug. Presto! No sooner had she so done, than the little animal kicked her with a mighty kick, or bit her with a wicked tooth, for I know not which is its deadly custom and, closing her eyes, as she drew her breath backward through her teeth, said, 'oooooooOOOO *Jesus*!'"

And that was the first great moment of history.

"Now," said Dr. Matthew O'Connor, "listen well to the second, for though it clips but a short road and could be put in a handkerchief, or tucked in the corner of an eye, it holds more wisdom on that complaint called humour than thirty volumes that might have been written, and have, no doubt, by some ageing scholar with more wrinkles in his testes than a sow's dug, for the lengthy time they have rested on the stool of learning, the while he searched for wisdom among the ancients in dead languages, and so far forgot his own life and its calling and whining (for a man's member is like a mighty bloodhound, and a man's body, forsooth, nothing but the staple it tugs at), that, do what it would, rested on the selfsame crease

from dawn to dusk, as he searched great tomes for the cause
that made lesser men so inordinately proud of it,—as I told
you of at the outset.

"Thus, when Stonewall Jackson went riding by, Barbara
Frietchie, putting her head out of the window, shrieked,
'UUUUh, HHHu, Stonewall!'"

And that was the second great moment of history. "Now,"
said he, "we bear down upon the third, and, my lad, it is a
lesson in that simple dignity and honour that contents itself in
plain linens, uncoloured with woad or other haughty and satiric
dye, with which many a young fop paints his breeches or vest,
or stains his nails, come, I doubt not, from plain eating and
sweet slumber. For honest fare makes an honest coil of guts; and
what can one expect from those young blades who incarnadine
their intestines, like an Easter egg, with the unlovely vagaries
of a Trimalchio, and cannot taste a lie (an it comes gurgling
up from their midst) for the herbs and vintage that baste it
about like a caul, and whose girth is swollen with puddings
and pasties more fit for a vomiting whore than a man. For a
whore takes in all things and vomits as she takes, but not so
should it be with a gentleman. Now a gentleman was General
Lee, whom I trust you have heard of, a gentleman whichever way you sliced him, and nothing else whatsoever in the
grain; but Grant was a kind of old sow. Be that as it may, Lee,
knowing that he had to surrender, polished up his medals,
reswung his epaulets, tightened his girdle, and burnishing up
the old blade, walked into the courthouse with the step of a
Caesar, though in his eye many an unshed tear glittered like
the dickens. Drawing himself up to his full height, he said,
as he unsheathed his trusty blade, presenting it hilt first: 'You
know what you can do with this, don't you?' And that," said
Dr. Matthew O'Connor, "was the third great moment."

The lad become somewhat restive, the good doctor, plucking

him upon the hot point of the bottom's cusp, brought him
to ground with: "As yet, my boy, your withers are unwrung,
therefore you should take good counsel easily, nor be in such
haste to withdraw yourself from it. History," continued he,
toying with the boy's spirit, "is not, to be sure, the only thing
a man is good for, though there are those who would have it
so. In my opinion 'tis not so amazing to contemplate what
man has done, at times, as it is to reflect on how much he has
left undone. How his history has gone one way and his heart
another, to illustrate my point, take the matter of tombs—"

At this, the lad burst into tears, "For," said he, "a tomb is a
thing I cannot behold without grief, and indeed the thought of
the amount of them in the world turns my bowels into a mare's
nest of woe, for to it all things come, whatsoever, so that I am
good for nothing and cannot get my lessons for the thought
that so much charming and good work will be a worm's snack
some midnight, and make him none the better, or draw aught
upon his skin that a beggar's carcass might not limn; for the
grin of one skull is no better than another, and cynic and sen-
timentalist alike show their back teeth in the grave. So what is
the use of my best efforts above another's worst?"

Lamenting in this way, he had set the good doctor to deep
concern.

"'Tis a point," said Dr. Matthew, "and one that I were ill
able to refute, were I not of the opinion that you are madly and
fantastically wrong. For look you, what does one man get from
wenching above another's not, saving the woman in the case,
and so it is with learning. You get no more good by diligent
thought than another by no thought at all, saving the thought
which you have, and he has not, and while 'tis true that you
must give it up at death and loose it on the wind again, like a
caged pigeon, it was yours once, and may go croaking of the

difference, with somewhat of your voice, to be heard by yet another ear, for a remembrance. Whereas, he who never had the bird, will have no bird cawing at his passing, nor, which I think a greater sorrow, anything to set loose as he goes down into his last resting place. It is, in a manner of speaking," concluded the doctor, "very small comfort, perchance, but small though it be, yet 'tis comfort."

"Truly," said the lad, "comfort it is, but 'tis small!"

"Thou art a niggard," returned the good doctor, "and would have much where no one has had above thrippence worth; yet I'll tell you of a man I know who is most wondrous fine at this business of nothing and small. His name is Wendell, and a Ryder, and though fear of extinction is undoubtedly the cause, he is none too mean to bang away at the effect, and is never above a book or an argument of kinds, nor wastes he his hour, but goes about making the most of a poor conclusion, by multiplying his own nothing by as many more as he can get, in wedlock or out, and pisses him the while for the simple joy of seeing his own vapour hot against a stone, while there be an ember in his body to bring it to warmth, nor, like you, would save it cold and unshed for the very uselessness of spouting. For though knowing well there will be a day when his fountain shall run no water, nor fling forth that which shall rise up and call him father, it does gush well while it may, for no pipe of whatsoever metal lasts forever, but should play while 'tis hollow for the purpose; and though he knows his brains will yet be as pointless as putty, and in no lobe good for aught but an ant's whim, he do nevertheless burden it in both panels like a mule's pack, that while it is on foot it shall be observed by his neighbours as the ass of a man of no poverty. But you, my lad, an you go on at this rate, will be a starved, ill-caparisoned beast, whom no man shall see passing without a 'tick, tick!

That poor animal has naught about his ribs, nor need whatsoever of the two holes given him by the good Lord.' For as
nothing disappears in the one end, how shall aught come forth
at the other? His belly is a crying pit that weeps for that which
enters not at the mouth, and whines piteously for that which,
on that account, is not there to go forth at the vent. So back
and front you go cheated, and there was long since but one
gracious way out of this distemper, that was when your thumbs
were bigger than your brains, you should have put one upon
your head and turned it down, that you might pass out ere you
had entered in, otherwise you are like him who eats and who
does not void. Had you, however, done the thumb turn, men
might have been left a mystery, saying, 'Who was that who
knocked and who did not enter in?' For dignity requires that
either you pass unseen, or if seen, that you wave farewell,—'tis
only common courtesy."

The lad was by this time so disturbed and aching in mind
that he had upturned the pot, whereby the honey had all but
oozed away upon the earth. "What ho!" cried the doctor. "You
do not only write your own foolish epitaph, but illustrate it
as well, for you came by a pot of honey, and where is it now,
forsooth, but back into the earth from whence it came, and no
service rendered? You in like manner, my lad, will have pushed
out from the earth and back into it, an you do not change your
ways, without sweetening one tongue or leaving relish whatsoever, nor did I think," said he, "when I mentioned the tomb
not ten minutes since, that I had you at both ends, living and
dead, as neatly in one bag as a child in the womb, and that
is another point for my argument. One wrapping should not
cover all that is a man; the swaddling gown should not be the
shroud, for a man of parts should have two wrappings, the one
that shakes him out and the one that gathers him in.

"I know a man myself," continued the doctor, "who has a pity for this and not for that, and was much mixed, as men would say, of woman and man. He wept for a friend who said, 'I go to be queen of the carrier pigeons,' and with that flew out into the night, though he, poor dolt, was picked up garbage. And I think it a most charming nature, no less, that can be so touched with what, to a thicker nerve, would appear merely ridiculous."

"'Tis of a great ridiculousness indeed," said the boy. "I might as well claim, an I waded out into the sea, that I would be king of the bloaters."

"And why not, indeed?" said the doctor, seeing nothing to smile at.

"Why not?" said the boy. "Does regency follow whatever death one chooses, forsooth? Does one become prince of the hares an one goes head first into a rabbit hole? Or lady of the Lake an one sits in a pail of water?"

"Perhaps it might have something to do with it," said the doctor, not to be daunted or thrown from his first balance, "for whatever is in the heart of a person, somewhat of it hangs, not only about the mind and do make a smoke about the soul, but cannot an aroma be said to be with them wherever they go? So that dogs follow some for their dogginess, and lizards eat out of the hands of others, and yet a third has no trouble at all in reducing a lion to a purring accessory. Why, I know a woman myself who was so bitten by mysticism, come out of the Irish hills where she was born, and down from her mother's udder, possibly when she was nursing, that set her so away in the spirit world that holding word with her was like a good long pull at a vision itself.

"She had fairies in her drawers, I'll warrant me," went on the doctor, "for what people love most, that you'll find about

them, and if it's things of the spirit, there you will find a witch's
nest, and if it's things of this world, there you'll find things of
this world. Had you, to illustrate my point, turned the Celtic
dame upside down, you would have found a twig or two of the
supernatural, and if you had turned my mother, by the same
peradventure, upside down, you would have been somewhat
perturbed by tea-leaves, for she carried the herb in her bustle,
it was the thing nearest her heart. 'Tis why so many men carry
nothing at all about with them but that which they have, it
being their dear treasure, and women, likewise, the deep veneration for what they have not. So I should like to see about
you something but thy ill-gotten sweets, and would know what
is dearest to your heart, for that I am not a rummager of every
man whatsoever, merely to come upon his chiefest treasure,
still what a man eats that will he find when picking his teeth."

"Somehow," said the lad, "your wisdom sounds as if it were
ill-gotten, and when it is become matured, I would be the first
to fly from it, for it will be over-heady and burst its sides before
it comes to a priceless vintage. A man as young as you appear
should have a quieter ferment. Mine own, though it's but a
child's, lays a good foundation for what will be, in its sixtieth
year, something not so bad to set before a guest."

"Well put," said the doctor heartily, and kindly, laying a
hand upon the lad's knee. "I do take the rebuke as 'twas meant,
and there's something to what you say, but only because you
do not know what nature is mine, which will make all the difference in a moment, when I do better explain it to you. Then
understand that, though what you say has a truth, it's only true
for those who come slowly to a bouquet, which is the correct
way, I admit, for man to ripen, but I ripen otherwise, slow
vintage enough when bottled, but—came to my fermenting
overnight, and broke my bottle long ago. And what you see,"

said he, wiping away a bright tear that threatened to wend its way into his moustache, "is one of those creatures who have their bottom up instead of their head, and no proportion of wine and its fermenting could be correctly measured out for such a reversal of established order. It is a rare case, though not as rare as it was. Therefore, some day, if the matter continues to increase, as it threatens to, and comes to the eye of the mixer, he'll have the correct receipt, and then you will see nothing to complain of, for, lad, it's another mystery of man. So tell me where you think I stand."

"On the leg, one side," said the youth, "of an ox, and on the other, of a hare."

"'Tis bitterly put," said the doctor, "and I would resent it, if I were enough of either to take either's recompense, but should I run you down with the hoof of an ox, I should run away with the tail of a rabbit, so what's the good? Now that I know one to be an ox and the other a hare, I can lament as I run, slow on the one side, and fast on the other."

"I have let you run on to such length," said the lad, "for I saw that I should illustrate my point most fitly with you an I did not haste to interrupt you, for I am the son of this Ryder, and his plays at nothing have already produced naught, so where was the sense?"

The doctor clapped his hands to his side with a mighty roar, and the tears of mirth did trickle down into his moustache. "Most handsomely has that Wendell," said he, when he could get breath, "worked to his purpose, and where have you been, lad, all these years? For I myself must have brought you into the world, yet I do not remember to have seen you grow up into this."

"I," answered the boy, "am one of his plays with a kitchen slut in Shepherd's Bush, and much she has regretted me, for I

came forth a little fellow from under her heart, for the heart
seen from beneath is well enough, and it is so, that while it is
but a bottom, a child loves it well, but when one is old and
looks within at the top and sees what a moiling cauldron of
evil it is, then is it that lads leave home, and a mother's love
becomes a handful of aloes which she pitches into that brew to
simmer from then on forever. It is why parent and child are the
worst of friends, and why I, though but fifteen, have planned
it that no woman shall know that disappointment through
any offices of mine own, and why I am determined to go my
way, heedless and thoughtless and as uncrammed of learning
as a gooseberry. So it shall be, if I can get me to my end with
saddle as empty as it is possible for nothing to make it."

"This," said Doctor Matthew O'Connor, "changes the
whole aspect of the argument. To love thy fellowmen is also a
necessity." And with that he did gently put an arm about the
lad as, with the other hand, he turned the pot right side up,
to save what little there was left of a sweet matter.

Chapter 50

Whom Should He Disappoint Now?

In a high-backed chair, his feet scarcely reaching the floor, his hands clenched on the arms, Wendell sat, his face wet with unusual tears, looking with terror under his eyebrows at his mortal mother.

She was asleep in the dim circle of radiance cast by the oil lamp, a novel under her crossed hands. There was a faint odour of corruption in the room, for that which was to kill her was working within her—the worm in the wood—and of violet toilet water. Heavily, casting its soft weight against first one and then another of the walls, went a night-moth.

The logs in the open stove, creeping under their ash, glowed faintly, and the desk with its shadow ink-horn and plume rose up on the wall darker and higher.

She slept firmly and heavily, her little figure disturbing but half of the bed. The left hand, with its heavy bloodstone ring on the index finger, outstretched, touching the title "Adam Bede."

As he said "God!" she was dreaming of a white horse who looked down at her from a cliff with fear, saying, "Mother." Her breast shook, she repulsed the book in terror and awoke.

It rained gently against the window and she turned, with that look of the sleeper who, unaccustomed, accuses custom.

"It is I," he said, and she turned again. Sleep had unmothered her, but she remembered and said immediately, "Do not be frightened," in a frightened whisper. She heard him crying. Now she had never slept. "The women," she said suddenly, "where are they?"

Through his tears he said: "Conceiving apart"

She brought her hands together slowly, interlaced, powerful, aged. "We will talk," she said, looking straight ahead of her, her long upper lip firm from apprehension. There was a long silence.

"Do you love me?" she said presently.

"Yes," he said, "you are marvellous."

"And you," she said, "are marvellous. I have loved you often."

The rain continued untroubled, then: "What of the lamb?"

He moved his hands along the arm, pondering what lamb.

"What was it worth?" she continued.

And he understood his yesterday's bargain with a Polish peasant in which he had been ridiculous.

"Fifteen dollars," he said.

"What were you offered?"

"Five," he said again.

"What happened?"

"I gave him the lamb."

"You see," she said, "you do not know how to conquer. Only the great and the evil can conquer. You stood at fifteen, and you were cast down at five, and to regain your feet you gave it away. Do you not know," she continued, "that for your kind of strength there is no resistance, therefore you must fall?" She lay straight upon her back and went on, with a fierce pity.

"You are a lover of women, you commit them to children, you lust openly and sweetly like," she added firmly, "the beast of the field, because you are nature, all of you, all of you, and nature is terrible when law hunts it down. Your women too have been beasts of the field, for you have been fortunate in your women, as all men are fortunate in their women. A woman can be civilized beyond civilization and she can be beast beyond beast. A woman is what she loves. Downstairs you have two, and in the grave you have one, and the one in the grave rots as simply as she loved, and the two downstairs sleep as simply as they love."

"Yes," he said, "but what am I to do?"

"What have you done?"

"I have lied to the law, and the law does not believe me."

"Because you have lied beautifully. The people will accept anything but beauty. You must lie near the heart, and the heart of man is an insulting shape. That shape," she continued, "is an affront, there's something monstrous about it, obscene. It is a shape conceived outside of nature, and that is always terrible. Are you," she pursued, "prepared to fall?"

He sobbed silently, looking at her from under his brows.

"How am I to fall?"

"If you fall alone," she answered, "you will be as the beast; and your women will not be shocked, but stricken slowly, and entirely; but if you fall with help—"

"Yes," he said, "if I fall *with* help?"

"How many children have you?"

"Eight," he said.

"How many shall you keep?"

"I do not know."

"By Amelia you have five, by Kate three, you have your answer. In the end you will have either three or five."

"In the end," he said, "I shall have no children. I have unfa-
thered myself."

"That," she answered, "is what I want you to see. Listen,"
she continued, her whole manner changed, "have you spoken
to Kate?"

"Yes," he answered.

"And what did she say?"

"She was frightened at first, and got up and went about the
room putting her things together, drawing the curtains. Then
she took up her embroidery and began stitching on a rose,
and said, crying, 'You know well enough I can support myself,
there's a very good market for embroidery.' And then she said,
'I have borne four children, and one is dead, and one is a girl,
and the other two are boys; and the eldest was meant for trouble and the others will learn,' and then she got up and went
over and lay down upon the bed and began quoting dreadfully,
going through one of her old parts. It was pitiful and revolting at once, and I went to her and said, 'I will not leave you.'
And she said, trembling, 'Go away, you are nobody's father.'"

"And Amelia?"

"I have not spoken to Amelia."

"Bring her, speak to her. Wait! What hour is it?"

"It must be three in the morning," he said, and he began sobbing and striking his hands together, softly and without sound.

"To ask a woman to make a sacrifice, a great sacrifice, at
three in the morning, is brutality. Do you know that?" she
said. "At night a woman will do anything for the pitiful human
creature, for at night everyone, everywhere, is unprotected,
and she feels that, and for that she would do anything. It is an
advantage. Do you want to take it?" And she looked at her son.

"Yes," he said hurriedly, starting from his chair, "yes, by all
means let us call Amelia."

"It will be a hard memory," she said.

He turned at the door, though he did not stop. "What am I to do?" he said, and his face was convulsed.

"Never make the mistake of asking the other type of woman anything at night," she said.

"Kate?" he asked. "Yes," and he went out.

He came back presently, Amelia walking ahead in a heavy nightgown, her long black plaited hair over her shoulder.

"What is the matter?" she said, and did not listen. She went up to the fire, her hands crossed low in front of her, looking down, thinking of something, then putting a log on the embers, went and seated herself in the chair Wendell had left, looking about the room saying, "What is all this trouble now?" and still not waiting for them to answer, continued: "I can think of her by no other name. The history of Kate is Kate, why ask me to change it? Trouble has its name, and Kate is Kate's tragedy, and there's nothing that can be done about it."

"My son," said Sophia, "is keeping a tryst."

"Whose?"

"The vast and varying trysts of man," said Sophia.

"Vast?" repeated Amelia, and she looked perplexed and troubled. "My son suffers," remarked Sophia, as if she had suddenly, and only at that moment, thought of something quite definite.

"I awoke," she continued, as if she had to tell it to someone, and better someone who was compassionate, "and found him sitting there where you sit, weeping."

"Am I weeping?" inquired Amelia.

"True," said Sophia, "we are women, why should we cry?"

"What is all this about?" Wendell said abruptly, putting his hand to his breast and looking from one to the other in a puzzled way.

"What," said Amelia, turning round, "is it that you want of me?"

He looked absolutely astonished, like a child suddenly confronted by something definite, immediate and terrifying.

"Yes," he managed to say, "that's it, of course—if you will, why, there you are, and if you won't, why, there am I."

She smiled, and immediately he knew that she had not understood what he himself did not understand. He was perfectly still. He said, "I must kill myself." And saying it brought him down. "Oh, Amelia, Amelia," he said, "I am born, don't you understand, I am born and I must die, that is so, is it not? That is so of everyone, but I am born and I must face everything and I must die, and I cannot. You must not let me face this, don't you see! I saw you, and I fancied you, years ago, this body here in this chair, and now, away! away! Isn't that ridiculous, but isn't it true? Mother, explain! Oh, Amelia, go away from me, go away from me!" He put his face in her lap and shook her, "Why are you here?"

"Ryder," said Amelia, looking away from him, her hands held apart on the arms of the chair, "I have thought of you as great oftener than anything else. When you have lain with me, after lying with her, what do you think kept me from coming up from under you? It is twenty-six years that I have lain under you, knowing everything, and have not judged and have not forgiven. I said, 'He has a great sickness that is unknown to other men.' I said, 'He is nature in its other shape.' I said, 'He is a deed that must be committed.' Why, then, did you not once shift your weight if you were, in the end, to be bloody mortal, that I might have known?"

He put his hands in her lap, and said, "Yes, bloody, bloody mortal." Sophia got up out of bed hurriedly. "There is no money," she said, "but my brother will take care of you, he said he would, and you see it is necessary. You've never been

tender, but you have always been good," she looked around
nervously nodding, "always good and dependable in your way,
and if Kate goes, what will become of her and of him?"

"Yes, of course," said Amelia. She rose up from under
Wendell's hands and head, leaving him face down in the chair.
She seemed to feel something wrong. She looked about her,
saw the fire, pushed the door to a little.

Wendell was unable to control himself. "Well?" he said.

She went out then.

◆　◆　◆　◆　◆　◆　◆

In the wide field where the night was all among the grass
and about the animals, Wendell went, leaning far back and
yet stumbling.

The black calf breathed against his side, and the dark cows
breathed among themselves, and the horses, with no earth
beneath their feet, trembled, as they slept and lay.

And Wendell sat down among them and forbore to hide
his face. Whom should he disappoint now?

"Hee-haw!" said the ass beside him, and he put his hand
out and stroked the ass.

Whom should he disappoint now?

The horses whinnied as he touched their fetlocks, and the
kine were shaken with the bellows of their breath, and he
touched their new horns. The little mice of the fields fled about
him, and he gave them his unchanged position, and the night
birds murmured above and he moved not, and the creeping
things that he had not numbered or known, looked at him
from a million eyes, and his eyes were there also, and the things
in the trees made walking and running on the branches, and
he spoke not.

Whom should he disappoint now?

And everything and its shape became clear in the dark, by tens and tens they ranged, and lifted their lids and looked at him; in the air and in the trees and on the earth and from under the earth, and regarded him long, and he forbore to hide his face. They seemed close ranged, and now they seemed far ranged, and they moved now near, now far, as a wave comes and goes, and they lifted their lids and regarded him, and spoke not in their many tongues, and they went a far way, and there was a little rest, and they came close, and there was none. Closing in about him nearer, and swinging out wide and from him far, and came in near and near, and as a wave, closed over him, and he drowned, and arose while he yet might go.

And whom should he disappoint?

Afterword
"The Havoc of this Nicety"
Paul West

"Do people," asks Amelia's sister Ann in chapter 9 of *Ryder*, in which Amelia gets ready to quit London for America, "go to Timbuctoo every day in the calendar?" It depends on how you construe Timbuctoo, but one version might be that going to Timbuctoo is to write stylishly. In order to live up to Nashe and Carlyle, and the recently unearthed William Baldwin, author of *Beware the Cat* (1570), you go to America. One of the fascinating things about Barnes's antic novel is to watch her partly Anglo mind whisk across the Atlantic only to hustle back to the States; she was never a proper or a decorous author, but rather one who kept on declaring her own literary independence, much more inclined to favor the country that favored innovation and imprudence, not the one that doted on things traditional.

It was clear that, if the author of this kaleidoscopic, only desultorily narrative novel, published in New York in 1928, went on as she had begun, she would end up doing much more than *épater* the bourgeois. She wanted to *undo* all readers, to deflower them in one way or another, to stop them from expecting fiction to behave like some well-bred social organism. You have only to look at the pictures censored from *Ryder* (one of which shows a soprano wetting herself) to realize what she thought books were for. The female *Tom Jones* she called it, but I think it is more like *Sartor Resartus*, a book that looks forward to *Ulysses*.

Whatever impetus the American ethos gave the would-be scandalous author, *Ryder* got itself censored by the New York Post Office. Djuna Barnes and Charles Friede, an editor from Liveright, sat there in Paris removing passages having to do with body fluids. Furious, Barnes insisted that asterisks show where the passages had originally been, and she composed a sardonic foreword about expurgation, about the damage done to "sense, continuity, and beauty," and "the war, so blindly waged on the written word." Indeed, by the third paragraph of her four-paragraph foreword, she had carried the metaphor of outrage all the way from damage through war to mummification, speaking (or shrieking) of literature "murdered and so discreetly bound in linens." In those words, dated August 8, 1927, she was pleading for freedom of imagery, not so much for freedom of argument as for freedom accorded the mind's habit of free association, of unself-consciously chattering to itself. Perhaps, after all, she learned the virtues of eclecticism, restoring the woman who wet herself to the 1979 edition, but not the woman with feral dugs and equine legs, over which loomed a maned, winged ram with a serpent's tail (p. 145 in the present edition). In any case, the prose mass of *Ryder* needs no visual trimmings (as Breton's *Nadja* does) and indeed renders them superfluous; the offense, if there is one at all, is in the recitative that blots out whatever novel *Ryder* might have been.

To read *Ryder* is to remind oneself that most readers and critics tend not to think of fiction as a vehicle for wit or aphorism, for the concise or the lapidary. Barnes did; indeed, she thought more about prose than about plot or story, and her fascination with names—those in Dickens for instance— evinces her capacity for thinking about characters or people in a nonlinear way, as if the name were some achronic epitome, a badge of all the energy contained in such and such a personage, almost like the fieldpiece emblem of the Royal Artillery. She thought in this scrunched-up, infolded way, more of a wit than a witness, more of a dealer in synecdoches than a scrutineer of timelines. Of the novel as faintly consecutive sociology, aiming never to detain for too long with any one sentence or passage, she knew nothing at all. Writing fiction, she was a woman applying lipstick again and again to the same place, varying the hue or the emphasis, the shape and size, but larding it on thick whenever she got the chance. She belongs with someone such as Nathalie Sarraute who, as Sartre observed in his preface to *Portrait of a Man Unknown*, used the novel to destroy the novel. Barnes doesn't so much destroy it as geld it, chopping up the cantering horse into a series of equine tableaux, not a flick book, but more in the mode of Max Ernst's *The Hundred Headless Women*, a "novel" published the year after *Ryder*. What he draws, she writes; the effect on the reader is much the same. They both strain after the preposterous, intending with it to unlock something worthwhile in the spectator's own imagi- nation, purging the work of prudery, orthodoxy, and mono- filamental constraint.

I myself call it jittery literature. Wendell, setting forth from the earth with "stupendous great wings," an insect-bird, isn't far from Ernst's Loplop, Bird Superior, "transformed . . . into flesh without flesh," and his "thundering male parts hung like a terrible anvil" have something in common with the hand-shaped mask over Loplop's loins. Barnes thinks of sopranos wetting themselves and observes, through Amelia, that "To man is the vision, to his wife the droppings!" Ernst depicts two female nudes fallen embracing from a horse-drawn cab and captions it "Public garbage dump, or: all the pauses are equally worthwhile." *Epater la boue-boisie.*

One can only marvel at the literary taste of New York in 1928: *Ryder* was briefly a best-seller among those who could hardly have guessed they were reading a guyed, lurid version of Barnes's family history. They bought it for its prose, its dangerousness. There was even talk of suppressing the expurgated edition, and for several years there was no British edition at all. The point was that, to censor the book, you had to obliterate the whole thing as even its daintiest passages implied shocking things, much perhaps as Ryder is a *Wen* in a *dell*, a bloated boil in a variety of nests. For Barnes the human was ever a chemism, even as in Dreiser:

> For of the banquet doth the turdë tell,
> And rown in the belly's dark alway
> And secrets of the supper all bewray,
> For man hath at both endës got a door . . . .

She writes, also in this section entitled "The Occupations of Wendell," about the liver and the pylorus, intent always on the "dark alway" beneath the sophisticated frippery of well-bred life in barbarously behaving families. Beckett's people are born astride a grave, but hers are born astride a john. She lived long enough to have come across the phrase that turns up in British TV commercials—"body soil"—too euphemistic to be crude, yet too crude to be a true euphemism either. She might have relished its paradoxical demure bluntness, having in some ways always had the mental set of a nurse, putting on rubber boots to bear an ear in a box from England to America. To her, figs are laxatives, the belly is a "crying out," and "a man's member is like a mighty bloodhound, and a man's body, forsooth, nothing but the staple it tugs at." To be sure, she apportions her vision among different characters, but they are not different enough to distract us from the volcanic suasion of the prose, in which she goes about her phrase-building business, writing the novel as a *book*, treating her personages as windup images, relegating plot (and the little she knew of it) to the interstices, as in Ann's rebuking echo of Jane Austen: "'What I should like,' she said dreamily, 'would be some proper parson in a sweet old parsonage, who did a deal at sermons, and likes his tea on time.'"

Instead of plot, in whose absence she works like someone bereaved, nonetheless trying to distract herself and come up with ventriloquial recoveries of the beloved voice gone, she achieves something that few novelists writing in English have ever made much effort at. She does get her characters talking (Peacockian-Huxleian as they are), but more often she sublimes them into something else that hovers between Sarraute's sub-conversation and Beckett's inane oratorio. She divines from the very air, the white paper, around her speakers the things they never say, the things being said "off," the things said before, the things to be said in the future, and what counts for her is not so much the word as the tone, the tuning-in of an art of talk that reaches its consummation in the unquenchable Doctor of *Nightwood* (who is less baroque, more domineering than he in *Ryder*). I mean this kind of thing:

> 'Sblood's Death! Is it right, m'Lords? Ravished, and the
> Cream not risen in the Pantry! Ravished, and the Weather
> Fork not turned twice upon its Vane! Ravished, and no
> Star pricked upon its point! Can Hounds track her down

to Original Approval: the Law frame her Maidenly again;
the not-oft-occurring-particular-Popish dispensation
reset her Virginal?

Call it Elizabethan or Jacobean, it reads like a sample of ges-
ticulation, drawing attention to itself as an instance of *words
used*, as if to inform us: This is what it is like to word, this is
what it is like to *mouth*. To her it seems the generic human
noise—rant or rave—coming full spate from the raft of the
Medusa. It is her way of shouting: of using grammar, vocabulary's constabulary, to express something generic: not really
any given individual's views, but a racial cacophony meant to
widen the resonance of her dialogue. As in this:

To the Oblong Eye of the Deer, is not your Condition
lengthened? By the Owl, is there not purchased a Dreadful
Rotundity? To the Shallow Eye of the Fish, you are but a
little staled, but to the Bossy Eye of the Ox, you may ride as
High and Damned as Jezebel. And what of the Multitudinous
Insects, and the Infinitesimal Conclusions of the Ether? To
the Myriad Pupil of the Fly, what can it but manifold your
Grievance?

By novel's end, of course, the rhetoric has loosened up
somewhat, and the lapidary costiveness of this is something
the writer has visibly outgrown during *Ryder* itself. All the
same, we can see what she is after: a vision, almost a first
hearing, of the self-importance of language, as if she were
intent on producing La Brea tar pits of blather, just to get
us in a primitive mood, amazed that humans could come to
the Word. Call it human mooing. It is the symphonic, ora-
torical side of the woman who could also, when she chose,
write like this:

In the small British country seat of Tittencote (described in the last chapter) in the year 1869, John Johannes de Grier lay dying. A long horsewhip, his last partner in this world's work, lay out beside his bed. It had lain there twenty-four hours. . . .

Or this:

He greased his riding-boots every morning with super-superb yellow tallow, rubbed his horses down, and went flying over every hedge on the way to church, chasing the hag-ridden end of a rabbit. His wife said that he always came to the Lord, not as other men, but hanging on to the butt-end of a hare. Be that as it may, he liked the fields better than the prie-dieu, his furniture better than his wife. . . .

She can do it, you see, the bread-and-butter of narration, but she likes to get her arms up to the elbows in the custard and the trifle, raptly convinced that thin and taut omits too much of life, pleasing the lazy reader, of course, but subtracting too much. Like her own Sophia, she goes "to meet many destinies in little shoes," aware that life is a rapist, a plunderer, a destroyer, and not some dimity little counsellor with the human weal writ large on its hymnal-board of good intentions. What Falstaff called misrule—the ungovernable buzz of fecundity and death—she tries to heed in every sentence, adapting the sense of surprise into a metaphor for being taken aback or apart. Tiny maladjustments in the prose make the reader gasp and wonder:

Nay, but she must sit upright to achieve a trifle of heathenage, and would turn upon it with a killing gaze and a nocturnal farthing dip, to see if it were of the same mind.

Note the glaze and rumble in that, not the sound of lucid exposition at all, but more the tinnitus of zeal. She wants you off balance, prey to what's malleable. Consider "three tureens with melancholy lips" and "The paperweight with the falls thereunder" and "the shuck of the heart" and "Her house a pantry, with vigour's watermark bespattered" and "the puma, the duke of morning." Doctor O'Connor, that prototype, bursts into tears, explaining "It's always been my wish . . . to be called Hesper, first star of the evening." The style can make anything happen. The reader says, well if *that* can happen, so can anything else: I must stay loose, lithe, ready to leap after her who is so rollicking, so unsentimental, so addicted to impromptu emblems.

In the guise of the novel, Barnes narrates her temperament, using her characters as Edith Sitwell used megaphones: ample, ampler, amplified. Like O'Connor, whose soliloquy prefigures much of Barnes and wraps her literary past up for her in a neat, unleaking bundle, she bangs her head against "the scrofula and the tapeworm and the syphilis and the cancer and the pectoris and the mumps and the gleet and the pox of mankind." There are those who have called her *greasy*, and this is why. There is a Chaucer within her Baudelaire and he, like she, like Matthew O'Connor, is lost in his "bowels like a little child." Barnes wasn't squeamish, and she wasn't prudish either. Somehow it does not surprise us (much) that she let the painter Marsden Hartley bare his private parts before her and extol them in terms befitting an enraptured fishmonger or that, while dancing with her, Putzi Hanfstaengl—later to be Hitler's Fool—burst a blood vessel in his penis. Barnes knew she was made of meat and suet and words.

She was trapped between relish for the world and a sapping, stunning perfectionism. Contrast this

Felice had little hands, Alix had smaller; Felice had a tiny
waist and two breasts as delicate as the first setting of a blanc
mange.

with this:

Life is too long as it is, my dear sister, for does it not find time
in which to be unjust? Yet it is so short that we have no time
for anything *but* religion.

The first is in the style of Amelia telling a bedtime story, the
second in the style of Ann's increasingly proficient letters. And
see how *physical* the tender portrait of Oscar Wilde is. Wilde,
says Wendell, "was a man of beauty, who looked through a
privy-ring at the stars" and whose voice "had slid over every
woman's blandishments, from Oxford to Reading, like a
mighty cod on his way to the sea." On he goes:

"The scandal had burst, and though he was the core, the fragrant centre of a rousing stench, in a month he was a changed
man, not changing, sitting within his cell, weeping, writhing, plotting 'De Profundis,' his fingers outside his mouth,
shuddering in all his soft female body, direct suffering in his
breasts; a bull caught and captured, sentenced, hamstrung,
marauded, peered at, peeped upon, regarded and discovered
to be a gentle sobbing cow, giving self-suck at the fountain
of self. . . ."

Early, she discovered the principle of additiveness, meaning
that she could always add something to something else, not
because the first something was inadequate but because the
observing or defining mind required such elbowroom. Her
writing delineates, often with mordant accuracy, but she bloats

it too, just to tell us she is there, serving the cause of plenty. She is among those rare souls, the phrase-makers, to whom a phrase no one else could have dreamed up is more precious than whole sequences of action or talk. Her work is there to evince her own mind, and to overface ours. Sometimes you have to read her with tweezers, other times with a trowel and a scoop, especially when she has let someone loose in a soliloquy. I think she sometimes thought of the novel as the supremest form of soliloquy, which is to say the novel at its closest to poetry. She has a superb sense of rhythm, so much so that she hears the rhythm long before the words arrive and the rhythm brings the combinations into being. Her prose evokes Wendell's longing for "an extra large English pudding with whacking diamond-shaped goblets of suet shot through." Above all, she is the virtuoso of the sentence, the ability to make which kept her going to the age of ninety. She built with bricks when others trifled with straw. She remained intense. She attuned herself to the constant ambience of heroic voice. She was serious, critical, and terminal, like an illness.

The key to almost everything she wrote can be found in the last paragraph of her angry foreword to *Ryder*, in which she condemns "the havoc of this nicety," meaning that wrought by censorship. To rape and death, which were bad enough, she added mutilation, intent as she always was on the tyranny of power, on godlike violence aped, and the human refusal to be gentle. Thinking of the old Latin tag *homo homini lupus* (man a wolf to man), she may have cried wolf, but she cried havoc as well, with loud, purple, and pertinent voice.

Djuna Barnes (1892–1982) was born on Storm King Mountain in New York State. She worked as a journalist during World War I before leaving the United States to spend the inter-war years in Paris and London among the most celebrated writers and artists of the twentieth century. She returned to New York in 1941 and lived in Greenwich Village until her death. She published three novels as well as short fiction, nonfiction, poetry, skits, and a three-act play between 1914 and 1950.